Praise for Renee Collins's
UNTIL WE MEET AGAIN

"Moonlight, mystery, and murder make for a thrilling combination in this lush tale that bridges the present day with the Gatsby era on a time-crossed beach. *Until We Meet Again* is tragically beautiful with twists you won't see coming."

　　—Martina Boone, author of the Heirs of Watson Island series

"Just as epic and swoony as you'd hope, while still being able to feel poignant and realistic. The emotions feel so real and present, and the novel will put a spark into the darkening days."

　　　　　　　　　　　　　　　　　　　　—Bustle.com

"Mystery, romance, time-travel, and danger…this one has it all."

　　　　　　　　　　　　　　　　　　　—*Kirkus Reviews*

"A beach house, a mystery, and time-travel love make *Until We Meet Again* a romantic, engaging read."

　　　　—Deb Caletti, author of *The Last Forever* and National
　　　　　　　　Book Award Finalist for *Honey, Baby, Sweetheart*

"Time stood still as I read this breathtaking, beautiful story. I didn't want it to end."

　　　　　　　—Kasie West, author of *The Fill-In Boyfriend*
　　　　　　　　　　　　　　　　and *The Distance Between*

Also by Renee Collins

Until We Meet Again

REMEMBER ME ALWAYS

REMEMBER ME *always*

renee collins

sourcebooks
fire

Published by Sourcebooks Fire, an imprint of Sourcebooks, Inc.
P.O. Box 4410, Naperville, Illinois 60567-4410
(630) 961-3900
Fax: (630) 961-2168
www.sourcebooks.com

Library of Congress Cataloging-in-Publication data is on file with the publisher.

Printed and bound in the United States of America.
VP 10 9 8 7 6 5 4 3 2 1

For Mom and Dad, because I became a writer a little bit more every summer I spent in that motor home.

CHAPTER 1

They say you can't go home again. I always found that to be an odd statement. Of course, when you've lived your entire life in the same house on the same street in the same small town—a town where the biggest change in recent memory was the new coffee shop opening up on Pine Street ten years ago in 2006—there seems to be no danger of the familiar slipping from your grasp.

Driving back from Denver last night, however, I wondered if everything would feel different. Spending the entire summer away—for the first time in my life—will *surely* mean some things have changed. And I dread the thought. It seems ironic that I spent two months in therapy, trying to forget, trying to move on, and now I just want to remember.

I want to go home again. I *need* it.

Sitting here in my room, sprawled out across my queen-size bed, with Grace sitting cross-legged beside me, I have my first sense that all is as I left it. My room looks exactly like it did two months ago. The same pale cream walls covered in movie posters. My TV propped on my dresser, with stacks of DVDs piled on either side of it. The familiar smell of vanilla cookies—a candle whose wax I spilled on my floor forever ago, the scent somehow still permeating the wood. Even our snacks are the same. Two large Dr Peppers and two overflowing bowls of nachos from the gas station. Red licorice. Spicy beef jerky.

"I can't even tell you how much this summer sucked," Grace says for the fifth time tonight. With a tortilla chip, she scoops up some extra cheese from the bottom of her nacho bowl and pops it in her mouth. "I've probably gained forty-five pounds," she says between crunches.

I roll my eyes. "There you go, mistaking pounds for ounces again."

"I'm serious!" she insists. "My jeans barely zipped this morning. I'm going to be a whale on the first day of school."

Nothing has changed with Grace either. She has what I like to call Pretty Girl Syndrome. She's beautiful—long blond hair, sparkling hazel-green eyes, and a fantastic figure. But when you've been pretty all your life, you become dependent on the attention your good looks bring you. Grace seems to live in fear of losing even a drop of that perfection. And with a new school year—our supposedly triumphant senior year—less than a week away, her anxiety has only grown.

I tell myself that's one of the perks of being average looking. Low expectations means low stress. No one's watching the lanky drama girl with brown eyes and brown hair. Except when I'm onstage, of course. I certainly hope they're watching then.

"It's all your fault," Grace said, eating another nacho. "You shouldn't have left."

"It's not like I didn't have a good reason."

"I know," she sighs. "You needed to be there. But I can't handle being alone. You know that."

"Oh, trust me, I know."

Her smile fades a little. She scrapes her chip in the cheese. "I did something really stupid, Shelby."

An alarm goes off in my mind.

"Doing stupid stuff is usually my job," I say, trying to keep the conversation upbeat. But I know that look on her face. I know it all too well.

"I was so lonely," Grace says, her voice both defensive and distraught.

"Please don't tell me Mike called you."

Tears well up in her eyes. Grace has always been an easy crier, but this goes beyond that. I put my arm around her in a hug. "Come here."

She rests her head on my shoulder with a shuddering breath.

"Tell me what happened," I say softly.

"The same thing that always happens."

"A week or two of dating, and then you got restless and broke up with him. And then he made you feel like a horrible person."

Grace is quiet for a moment and then sighs. "Something like that."

"You swore him off, Grace."

"I know," she says, sitting up, looking mournful. "I know."

"When are you going to stop doing this to yourself?" She shakes her head, and I rub her back. "I hate seeing you like this. Look at what this get-back-together-break-up game does to you. I don't get why you can't stop."

"You hardly have room to lecture me about this," she scoffs. But the moment she speaks the words, she snaps her mouth closed.

"What's that supposed to mean?" I ask.

"Nothing," She shakes her head. "Never mind. I just meant that you…you don't understand."

"I don't," I say with a sigh. "And it hurts to see you like this." *For the hundredth time.* "You deserve better."

She nods, wiping her eyes. Deep down, I'm glad I don't understand what she's going through. If this is what love does to people, maybe I'm glad I've never been in love.

A shiver crawls down my spine, making my back straighten. I rub my arms, frowning a little.

"Besides," I say. "I'm pretty sure Mike can get arrested for dating a minor."

"He's only twenty-one."

"Well, that's *old*, Grace. He needs to move on from high school. He's not the basketball star dating the freshman on the pom squad anymore."

I say the words, but I know it's not quite true. As long as Mike Jasper stays in Orchardview, Colorado, he'll always be the basketball star. Even if some of us see him for what he really is: a two-bit mechanic at the Jiffy Lube who'll never fully let go of his high school glory days and never veers more than fifty miles away from home.

"You're right," Grace says. "I want to be rid of him for good."

"You have to stick with this. Remember how this feels the next time he comes around."

She closes her eyes, nodding with determination. "I have to. I can't forget. I *won't* forget. I'm not going to give him even one more day of my life."

"Exactly," I say, walking her through the conversation we've had many times before. "You've already given him too much."

"All those years," she says, her expression growing distant. "I can't get them back." She drops back on my bed and stares up at the ceiling "I wish I could erase all the crap from my life. You're lucky, Shelby."

Her words sting a little. "Lucky? To get in a car accident? Are you forgetting how bad the panic attacks got?"

"You know what I mean."

I do, but the casual way she talks about my therapy unsettles me. I can see Mama's wisdom in not telling many people about it. Most of our friends and neighbors think I spent the summer in Denver with a physical therapy specialist. Not at the neuroscience lab having my memory systematically altered. Orchardview folk either don't understand stuff like that, or they don't trust it. Probably both.

Grace sighs deeply. "To have a clean slate. Must be nice."

She sits up. "Maybe I'll ask my dad to take me to Denver this weekend. Could you get me in, Shelbs?"

I smile a little. "It's not that easy. There's, like, a two-year waiting list. It's still in trials." I pat her leg. "And besides, I'm pretty sure they wouldn't be willing to use their technology to erase a boyfriend."

Grace gives a sharp laugh. "This is so weird," she mutters, almost to herself.

"What's weird?"

She meets my gaze, her expression saying more. Words that she wants to say. I know that look.

"What is it?" I ask. "What's wrong?"

She gives a quick smile. "It was weird to have you gone this summer, that's all. And…I'm glad you're back."

"Me too." I try to act casual, but her behavior has put me on alert. Did two months of separation make things awkward between us?

Grace leans over the bed to her nightstand, where her large soda is gathering condensation. "Crap, my Dr Pepper's getting diluted." After taking a long sip, she shakes her cup at me accusingly. "Look at me guzzle this thing! This is what I'm talking about. I've fallen into all my bad habits with you gone."

My clenched insides relax a little. "Well, I'm here now, and everything can go back to normal," I say, hoping to convey sincerity in my voice as I attempt to keep the mood light. I grab my drink and take a sip as well. "And not a minute too soon.

The Dr Pepper in Denver tasted terrible. I almost switched to Mountain Dew."

Grace looks appalled. "How could you even think it?"

We both laugh, and the conversation shifts back to the local gossip I missed and plans to take the school by storm this year, but the unsettled feeling lingers deep down, even after I've dropped off Grace. Driving back to my house, I can't shake the growing pit in my stomach. Maybe things really are different. Maybe you can't go home again.

I scan the dark streets of Orchardview rolling past me. It's all exactly as I left it in May. Small brick homes built in Orchardview's heyday in the 1960s. Mature trees and dated hedgerows. Kids' bicycles laying on trimmed front lawns. Old cars parked in driveways, collecting rust until their owners eventually make it out to putter on them. A weathered, neon-pink flyer for the town BBQ stapled to a telephone pole. It's the perfect little American town. The only town I've ever known.

When did it start to feel foreign to me?

I tighten my grip on the steering wheel and shake my head firmly. No. I'm better now. Life is going to go back to normal. I'm going to go back to school in a week, a senior at last. I'm going to audition for the school play, *Romeo and Juliet*. Life will be exactly as it's always been.

But the words sound hollow. I scan the streets again with an intensity that clamps around my throat. These are the same streets. The same houses. The same street lamps and the same sidewalks. Everything is the same. So what's wrong with me?

Breathing hard, I jerk the wheel to the side and jam the car into park. I step out, slamming the door in the silence of the street. A pale-orange tabby rushes away, startled. I look around me in a slow circle, trying to calm my pulse.

Uneasiness washes over me, and it goes beyond Grace acting a little strange tonight. This feeling runs deeper. If I'm honest with myself, I've felt it since the morning I last sat in the sterile, white therapy room with Dr. Stevens, preparing to check out and head home. The thought has lingered with me in spite of my efforts to destroy it.

Something's not right.

A familiar feeling surfaces inside of me. A tightness in my throat. A pulse in my temples. The early twinges of a panic attack. I can't go through this again. Not now. I can't go back to the way things were before.

I need to forget again.

CHAPTER 2

I can't remember the accident. According to Dr. Stevens, that means his therapy is working as it should.

It's strange, losing a piece of your memory. Like staring at an unfinished puzzle. The pieces around the periphery are there, the color and scent and emotion. But then, searching for the actual moment—nothing.

I don't doubt that the accident happened. I have the scars to prove it. And oddly enough, I remember the panic attacks that followed. I remember the nights that I woke up screaming. Days when my hands wouldn't stop trembling. My heart seemed to constantly race in my chest. And hanging over it all like a dark, ripe cloud is the abiding sense that something terrible had happened.

Blake, also known as Stepdad Part Two, was the one to suggest neural restructuring. Two years ago, his war hero status had gotten him into early trials, and it did wonders for his PTSD. Mama used that status to press for my inclusion. My aunt Winonna was a nurse working on the trial, so she pulled some strings and tipped the scales. I was lucky to get in.

After that night with Grace, I spent five full days trying to convince myself that I was going to be okay, but the anxiety only grew. Different than before but undeniable. It curled around my insides like the roots of a dark tree. I could keep up the facade for only so long before Mama became aware. She always knows.

She's a contradiction, my Mama—seemingly indifferent to me most of the time yet always watching. Nothing slips past her. So when she found me in the bathroom one morning, struggling to get my breathing under control, it was back to Denver for an "emergency" checkup four days before school started.

Sitting in Dr. Stevens's office again is, ironically, the most familiar sensation I've felt in a while. The walls gleam whiter than white. Muted Mozart hums from a hidden speaker in the wall. Two tasteful paintings of the Rocky Mountains hang in perfect symmetry on either side of the wall. It smells like gauze and the slightest hint of lemon. Even Mama, flipping through a six-month-old *People* magazine on a chair beside me, completes the ambiance.

In the corner, the neural restructuring capsule sits, like a leftover set piece from the Borg commune in the *Star Trek* movies. It actually looks like an MRI machine. I've gotten into the capsule so many times before, I know what to expect. It doesn't hurt. Yet every time I lie down inside of it my pulse races.

A short, plump nurse in *Winnie-the-Pooh* scrubs breezes into the room. Aunt Winonna.

"Well, well. Look who's back," she says brightly.

Winonna is Mama's first cousin and the only one in the entire extended family to leave Orchardview for Denver. She still feels like Orchardview to me, though, with her big country bangs, pink lipstick, and the tattoo of her boyfriend's name around her ring finger.

"Good to see you again," Mama says, reaching out to give her a one-armed hug. "Didn't think it'd be so soon, but Shelby's… well, you know how she is."

I stare at my mother. So she's going to play the "Shelby is a drama queen" card instead of owning up to the fact that she pushed for me to come here? A flash of anger heats my throat.

"We want you to feel secure with your results," Aunt Winonna says, tactfully maneuvering around the comment. She pulls out her stethoscope. "But I'll leave that to Dr. Stevens. Let's take your vitals."

"Sounds good," I say, sitting up straighter as she sets the cool metal against my back. I'm relieved she doesn't make eye contact with me.

Winonna listens to my heart and lungs and scribbles some notes on her clipboard chart. She then sweeps out wordlessly.

Mama sighs and picks up her *People* magazine again.

My jaw sets. "Thanks for throwing me under the bus."

Mama's eyes flash. If there's one thing she doesn't tolerate, it's sarcasm. She calls it the gateway to liberalism.

"Don't you take that tone with me."

It takes all of my energy not to scoff. "I only came back because *you* made me."

"Well, if you had stayed relaxed, you wouldn't have needed to come back."

There are so many things wrong with what she's saying I don't even know where to begin. And I don't know if I feel more angry or hurt.

"Don't you think I'd *stay relaxed* if I could?"

Mama flips through her magazine, unfazed. "Look, I don't see what you're making such a fuss about. The treatments work. They worked for Blake. They work for you. We just can't take any chances on you remembering."

"Don't you mean we can't take any chances of the panic attacks coming back?"

Her hand stops for a beat in the middle of turning a page, and her gaze snaps up. Before she can respond, the exam room door swings open. Dr. Stevens breezes in with an economical smile.

"Good morning, ladies."

Mama sits up, setting her magazine on the side table. "Hello, Dr. Stevens."

I think my mother feels a little insecure around him. Dr. Stevens has gravitas and poise, with silvering temples and a calm voice. He looks, talks, and moves like money and education. Everything Mama isn't.

"Shelby," he says. "Nice to see you again. Though I understand you aren't feeling well?"

"I'm okay." The response is knee jerk. Dr. Stevens raises an eyebrow. Mama's eyes burn into me. I look down into my lap. "I mean…I feel fine now, but the panic attacks…they've started up again."

Dr. Stevens scribbles a few notes on the chart. "I see."

"It was a low-grade anxiety at first. But I can't shake it."

"And the memories of the accident?" Dr. Stevens asks. "Are they coming back as well?"

"No. That's all blank."

"Good," he says, nodding. "That's good."

He writes for what seems like forever and then finally looks up. He studies me, eyes narrowed slightly with contemplation. "Perhaps the anxiety has been caused by something else? You're still in a vulnerable place. Is there something going on in your life that might trigger stress and panic?"

"First day of school's on Monday," Mama chimes in. "I tried to tell her that's probably what it is."

"It's not," I say, firmly. I look to Dr. Stevens for a voice of reason. "I know what normal anxiety feels like, and this isn't it."

"What does it feel like to *you*, Shelby?"

I shrug, searching for the right words. "It's this sense that… something's not right. It's like something's…missing."

Dr. Stevens nods thoughtfully. "I think I understand what's happening here. Shelby, have you ever heard of phantom limb sensation?"

"Like what happens to soldiers who've lost a leg or an arm?"

"Precisely. Sometimes, when the body loses part of itself, the brain can trick it into feeling like that part is still there. Pain in a leg that's been amputated, for example. In your case, it's a piece of memory. We removed the negative memory, and your brain is trying to fill in what happened. It's rare, but we've had a few other patients complain of similar issues."

"So…this is normal?" I ask. "The PTSD isn't coming back? I won't start to remember the accident again?"

Dr. Stevens gives a half smile, the warmest his stiff, professional personality will allow. "The treatment works, Shelby. Those memories are gone forever. As is your PTSD. Consider this a quiet echo. An echo that will eventually go away."

Mama leans to be in Dr. Stevens's line of vision. "Should we not put her through one more time? Just to make sure?"

He glances down at his notes. "Yes, I suppose we can do that. If it will comfort both of you."

Mama sets a hand to her chest. "Thank you, Dr. Stevens."

Winonna motions me to the receiving table of the neural restructuring capsule. I draw a quick breath and stand. Maybe Mama's right. If this is what it takes for me to feel normal again, it's a small price to pay.

I know the drill. First, my arms are strapped to the table. This freaked me out the first time, but Winonna assured me it was only to keep me from flailing in my sleep and disrupting the therapy. I believe her, though I can't help but think this process would be a little less creepy without it.

Next, the electrode patches are applied to my temples and

forehead. Earphones cover my ears. A cool sterilizer preps the inside of my elbow. And then the IV pricks my vein. A "little bee sting," as Winonna calls it. I'm supposed to count down from ten while the anesthesia kicks in, but instead I chant a desperate plea to the machine in my head. *Please work. Please work. Please work.* The last thing I see is the inside of the white helmet closing around my face.

~

The therapy is always the same.

Images.

Scenes from my life, minus the accident.

The treatment is hypnosis combined with carefully coordinated brain stimulation. In the warm, watery place of semiconsciousness, I swim through one scene after the next. The images are always the same, in the same sequence. I'm in mostly familiar places. School, my old job at the movie theater, the lake. Sometimes there are people in my dream, and sometimes I'm alone.

My mind is reprocessing my daily life in a completely controlled, relaxed way without the "undesirable moments." That's what Dr. Stevens tells me. It makes sense. The images show my brain that everything is okay. And that's really all I want. I just want everything to feel okay again.

~

I'm walking through the halls of Orchardview High. Blurry faces on indistinct bodies pass by me, like a circular backdrop from silent movies that rotates to convey movement. I'm on my way to class. Not sure which one. It's a long walk. Soundless and boring.

Next will come the lake. It's one of my favorite images. I'll be sitting on the hood of my car on a blanket. Alone. Watching the stars pierce the darkening sky.

I'm loading textbooks into my locker. Shutting it slowly. And then, like the flip of a switch, I'm at the lake. Twilight. The buzz of insects fills the air. The swampy smell of the lake fills my nostrils. A warm evening wind ruffles my hair. I stare at the purple sky. It's a perfect summer night.

An impulse makes me turn to my left. The air beside me looks different. It's moving. Twisting. Like oil droplets on the surface of water. The swirling air suddenly comes together in a flash. A boy sits beside me on the hood of the car. He's reaching for my face, to brush a strand of hair from my lip. His dark, deep eyes are filled with intensity. His brow is thick. Long, disheveled black hair falls just past his ears.

The image of this boy lasts less than the time it takes me to gasp. As fast as he appeared, he's gone.

～

"Shelby?"

White, circular lights swim in my vision. I hear the muffled hum of voices, the sharper beep of my heart monitor. The deep haze of sleep still lies over me. I feel like I'm standing at the bottom of a swimming pool, looking up. But ice rushes through my veins.

Winonna's blurred, concerned face comes into view. "Shelby, honey, can you hear me?"

I blink once.

"I think she's coming to."

There's a chaos of movement around me. The coolness in my veins pulls me upward through the water. I kick and kick again, reaching for the surface.

Finally, the familiar therapy room comes into view around me. I can see Winonna and Mama, who both look worried. Dr. Stevens checks my vitals, his brow furrowed with wordless concern. I reach for my voice but only manage a rasp.

"What's wrong?"

"There was an abnormality during your treatment. We had to give you a dose of adrenaline to pull you out of anesthesia."

Abnormality. The boy. A flash of lightning in my brain reveals his face in the shadows. Dark, intense eyes. Tousled black hair. His hand reaching for my lips.

It's like a sparkler has been lit inside my chest. The sensation crackles over my skin, and I draw in a shaky breath. Winonna seems to notice.

"Did you sense anything different, honey? Anything out of the ordinary?"

"No." The lie falls from my tongue immediately, smooth as taffy. "The treatment seemed normal to me."

Winonna frowns but continues with her work.

Why did I lie? Why wouldn't I tell her about the boy? He hasn't been part of my treatment before. That's obviously what they're talking about. The machine must have malfunctioned and produced that new image in my mind as a result.

Dr. Stevens holds a pen-sized flashlight up to each of my eyes. I blink at the brightness. Can he tell that my pulse is racing? I hope he doesn't check it.

"It's probably nothing," he says, making a note on his chart. "This is still very new technology, and unfortunately, glitches happen. There's no need to worry, of course. You're perfectly safe."

"Should we run the treatment again, Doctor?" Mama asks.

"No," I blurt. I close my eyes. "I mean, I'm fine. I'm sure the machine was just acting weird."

Dr. Stevens considers this for a moment, makes a note on his clipboard, and then nods. "We should be fine to monitor her and see how things go. After all, you'll be coming back in six weeks for a checkup. In the meantime, let me know if you have any unusual symptoms. Headaches, trouble concentrating, vivid dreams, or hallucinations—anything that doesn't feel right."

The boy's face burns into my mind again, filling me with a strange, warm light. Almost like happiness. I should tell Dr. Stevens the truth. If I want to get better, I need to be completely honest.

But I can't make the words leave my throat. Something inside of me holds them back. It holds on to the image of that boy. It guards him. It keeps him close.

Everyone steps away and talks in hushed tones. I'm glad for the distance because I genuinely can't keep the smile from pulling at my lips, and I don't want them to see. The warmth sparkles in me like sunlight on water. I replay the image of him again, my skin tingling.

I don't know what my vision means, but I know that I have to find out.

CHAPTER 3

The first week of school at Orchardview High is always eventful. Assemblies. Pranks. Dances. It's tradition. Mama has told me stories from when she was in school. Nothing much has changed, and that's the way our town likes it.

Today is a doubleheader—pep rally during school and bonfire in the field outside the parking lot tonight.

After messing with my rusty old locker for about ten minutes, I finally get it open. At least I've been upgraded to a new awesome location. Seniors always get the best locker spots. I've been looking forward to this for three years. I remove a few carefully chosen items from my backpack. A little round mirror. A magnet with *The Godfather* logo. An original promo poster for *The Shawshank Redemption*. And finally, a Darth Vader bobblehead.

There. Home, sweet home.

I still can't believe I'm a senior. Feeling light with excitement, I remove my camcorder case from my backpack to do one quick inspection before the pep rally. Brushing a fleck of lint off the top off the camera, I pull it closer, with a frown. Is that a scratch?

"Hey, Shelbs. How's your baby?"

Grace leans her head against my locker with a smirk. I place the camera back in its case.

"This thing cost the school a fortune, you know. The least I can do is be careful with it."

"A fortune, huh? Nothing but the best for the class historian."

Grace likes to tease me about being involved in student government. It's not the coolest extracurricular in the world, but in my defense, I didn't really seek out the job. Brooklyn Belnap, student body president extraordinaire, heard from Mrs. Pavloski that I'm a big movie buff, and she practically forced me to run. I guess "movie fan" translates into "good with camera."

Grace checks her appearance in my locker mirror and smiles.

"Senior year, Shelbs. Senior freaking year."

"I almost can't believe it."

"Well, buckle up. This is going to be the best year ever. It's official." She taps Darth Vader, making his head wobble wildly. "Come on. I want to get a good seat."

We head through the crowded halls toward the gym. Brad Corbin and two other basketball players, clad in their uniforms for the assembly, stand in conversation in the middle of the hallway. Grace waves and murmurs a greeting as we maneuver around them. Brad gives her the cool-guy chin nod, and her cheeks flush.

"What was that all about?" I ask her when we've passed.

"What?" she asks innocently.

"Um, Grace, I'm *still* blinded from the sparks that were flying."

Grace laughs. "Hardly. We're friends. Our moms work together."

I point at her. "There's a story there, and I need to hear it."

"I'll tell you all the nonexistent details during the assembly," Grace says, rolling her eyes.

"I'll be filming, remember?"

"Right." She twists her lips to the side but then perks up. "Hey, I know! I'll be your assistant! I can help you…carry your bags and stuff."

The realization floods over me slowly. "And this wouldn't have anything to do with you being down on the gym floor with all the basketball players, would it?"

She gasps in mock offense. "Shelby Katherine Decatur. I have been your best friend since the third grade. I think I know where my priorities are."

"Yeah, I think I do too."

She tries to shove me, but I dodge, and she chases me to the gym.

I let her stand with me during the assembly. I'm a good friend like that. Besides, she could do worse than Brad Corbin. She *has* done worse. Though, I suppose it's not hard to beat Mike Jasper.

I focus on filming. I'd never admit how much I enjoy it, but maybe it *was* a good idea to pick a film buff for historian. Wes Anderson taught me how to fill a frame. Scorsese taught me how to change focus at the right moment. And Tarantino, well, he demonstrated how to give an audience what they want in a way they might not expect.

I'm taking just such a shot, zooming in on Principal Border at a brilliantly avant-garde angle, when the hairs on the back of my neck prickle. Like a whisper of eyes on me. I lower my camera and scan the audience.

The crowd is filled with hundreds of faces. Kids are watching the assembly with a broad palate of expressions. Some cheer wildly. Some talk with their friends, ignoring the proceedings completely. A few even look like they're asleep.

The same old crowd. The same people I've gone to school with for years. I don't see anyone watching me. So why are there goose bumps on my skin?

Mrs. Pavlovski sets her hand on my shoulder, and I startle. "Are you getting this?"

Vice Principal McMillan leads a piglet into the gym on a pink ribbon leash, much to the audience's delight. With a quick shake of my head, I lift my camera. Moving forward for a better angle, I try to ignore my feelings of uneasiness.

The rest of the day passes without event. In fact, I'm starting to feel like myself again. It's good to be back at school. This place is my home, quirks and all. It's made me who I am. So many firsts happened here. I remember being a wide-eyed freshman, huddled next to Grace, thinking the halls were so huge and the classes were so hard. I dated my first boyfriend here. Got my first kiss between the modulars during a football game. Went to my first prom. Had my first dramatic breakup at said prom.

So when Grace tells me we're going to the pep rally tonight, I don't fight it. Traditions make Orchardview what it is, and traditions demand to be upheld.

The bonfire is set up in the west parking lot. By the time Grace and I arrive, a huge crowd has already gathered. My stomach turns a nervous little flip. Somehow, after being gone all summer, I feel like an outsider. But Grace pulls me along without hesitation. We didn't spend the better part of an hour primping for nothing. We painted sparkly green OHs on our cheeks and curled our hair in high ponytails. While I painted my nails, she snipped and sewed our Orchardview High T-shirts until they were actually wearable and cute.

"I feel ridiculous," I say as we approach the jubilant crowd around the bonfire.

"You look fabulous," she scoffs. "Everyone's wearing stuff like this."

"I know, but…"

Grace gives me a swift glance. "Are you feeling…anxious again?"

"No, nothing like that. I'm fine." I wish we could drop the subject.

"Everyone missed you this summer," she says. "They'll be happy to see you."

"Yeah…"

A strong arm slaps around my shoulders. "Well, well, well. What have we here?"

Cam Haler. Possibly the last person I want to see right now.

"What's up, Seashell?"

Grace bites her lip, holding back a laugh.

"Speaking of happy to see you," she says, under her breath. Then she beams at Cam. "I'll let you two get caught up."

I give her a death glare. "That won't be necess—"

She waves coyly and slides away. "Have fun!"

Mental note: Grace is now and forever shunned.

"Heard you were in Denver all summer," Cam says. His curly blond hair has been carefully gelled, and he wears a cocky smile.

I lift his arm off me and drop it. "Yep."

"Cool. I'm probably going there next summer. Auditioning for *Hamlet.*"

He says this every year. He's off to Denver. Word of his talent has spread. Some swank theater company has reached out to him. I don't know why he lies about it. In reality, he's perfectly content to be the star of the Orchardview High theater program, perfectly thrilled to be the big fish in this tiny little pond.

"Best of luck," I say, moving away.

Cam steps in front of me. He tilts his head down to look me in the eye. "Hey. Can't we be friends? It's been, what, a year and a half since we broke up? Is your heart still shattered?"

I roll my eyes. "*Please.*"

He laughs. "Come here. I'll make it all better." He pulls me into a big bear hug.

"Hey!" I laugh in spite of myself as I fight him off.

"Hugs will heal the world," he sings, lifting me up. He puts me down, and I shove him away playfully.

"Don't be angry," he says. "I can't resist you. I'm madly in love with you."

I snort. "Now you're just mocking me."

"I'm serious!"

He's absolutely *not* serious. I give him a little salute and walk away. "Bye, Cam."

"You shouldn't run from your feelings," he calls out. "Accept your undying passion for me. It will be easier for everyone."

I shake my head even though I'm smiling. Cam can't sleep well at night unless he believes every girl is in love with him.

"Shelby!" he calls.

I glance over my shoulder, and he points at me. "You're going to audition for the fall play, right? Nothing's changed there, I hope?"

A cold shudder slides through my stomach. I manage a smile and a nod, but I'm thrown. I can't put my finger on what's wrong.

I shiver and rub my arms, trying to get rid of the feeling. "A natural reaction to the treatment," I say softly to myself. "Phantom limb sensation." Pushing away my nerves, I weave through the crowd to find Grace.

She's standing by Brad Corbin, laughing at what was probably a lame joke he made. When she spots me, she gives a little shriek and hides behind Brad with mock fear.

"Don't let her kill me!"

"Relax," I say. "I wouldn't do it in front of all these people. Too many witnesses. I'll wait until we're driving home. Alone on an empty country road. That way I'll also have a convenient place to stash your body."

The smile drops from Grace's lips. The color drains from her cheeks, but before I can say anything, Lila Thomas, a fellow senior in student government, runs up with an eager smile. I know what's about to happen. She's going to suggest a game of capture the flag in the empty school. Ah, tradition.

"Who's up for capture the flag?" Lila asks brightly. "The whole school is the boundary?"

As I mentally fist-bump myself, the crowd responds with enthusiasm. Maybe because they all know that this game is a thinly veiled excuse for people to get a little action in the dark corners of the school grounds.

"Two teams," Lila says. She motions with her hands to either side of the crowd. "This half is one team. This half is the other."

Nick Parsons rips off his football jersey. "This is our flag!"

"And your shirt will be ours," a junior in the back of the crowd shouts to Lila.

"In your dreams, Dameon."

Cam suddenly appears beside me.

"You're on the other team," I say, irritated. "I don't fraternize with the enemy."

"I've defected to your side," he says. "Better health care plan."

"Seriously, Cam. Get out of here."

Lila waves her arms to get the crowd's attention. "Game over in one hour, okay? Everyone meet back here at midnight."

The group starts to scatter into the shadows of the school grounds, laughing and shouting as they go.

Cam gives me a wink. "I'll see you out there." Before I can protest, he runs off.

I head in the opposite direction, to find Grace. She's gone, doubtless well on her way to keeping up tradition with Brad Corbin. Rolling my eyes, I make for the courtyard. It's an obvious place, and I'll probably get caught, but it's just as well. Better to sit in capture-the-flag prison than have my ex-boyfriend try to rekindle a long-dead relationship in the spirit of assuring his supreme hold on every girl in the theater program.

It's darker than normal in the courtyard. The single street lamp offers only a flickering yellow glow and obnoxious buzzing sound. I sit down on the worn metal picnic table closest to the cherry tree. The trunk of the poor old thing has been carved to splinters. Every young couple, sure of their eternal love, has at some point scratched their initials into the wood. I brush my fingertips over one that says *T.L. + S.V.*

I'm sure if I think hard enough, I'd know who they are. You grow up in a place like this, and you get to know pretty much everyone.

The shuffle of footsteps on concrete snaps me to attention. A tall male outline emerges from the shadows on the left. My muscles tense, but it's not Cam. He takes a hesitant step toward me. I squint into the darkness, trying to make out a face.

"If you're on Nick's team, you can call it," I say. "No need to tag me. I'll go to jail willingly."

The guy moves into the faint light. I don't recognize him. But then...

A hot charge cuts down my spine. I stand.

Those eyes. Dark and intense. Two thick slashes of eyebrows. Long, tousled hair that falls just past his ears.

It's the boy I saw during the glitch. The "abnormality" in my memory.

He comes toward me, staring at me with an unreadable expression. His lips part. His voice is deep and trembles as he utters a single word.

"Shelby."

CHAPTER 4

Everything around the boy blurs. My knees lock, but I feel as if I'm going to fall down. I stare at him, unsure if this is real.

Then Dr. Stevens's voice comes to my mind. *I need you to tell me if you have any unusual symptoms. Headaches, trouble concentrating, vivid dreams, or hallucinations...*

Is this a hallucination brought on by the abnormality in my anxiety treatment?

But...he's so real. So clear. His shoulders are moving with breath. His eyes scan my face. He looks a little stunned.

"You recognize me."

He speaks a statement, not a question, and it strikes me in the chest. "What?"

He moves toward me. If this is a hallucination, then it's incredibly long and realistic.

I've finally cracked.

I press my hand onto the table to balance myself. "Don't

come any closer," I say, and the boy freezes. My hand shakes. "Who are you?"

He starts to answer but pauses. "That's…hard to explain."

A low-pitched, exaggerated ghost sound echoes through the courtyard, making us both jump. And then Cam Haler comes galloping in, a dumb grin on his face.

"Found you!" He crows. "I'll be taking you to jail, little lady."

A wave of irritation passes over me. "We're on the same team, remember how you—"

As I'm speaking, I glance back toward the boy, only to discover that he's vanished.

My stomach drops. He's gone. Just like that. Just like…a hallucination.

"It was a trick," Cam says, triumphantly. "I'm a double agent. I was working for the other side all along." He gives an over-wrought evil laugh.

I stare back at the empty place where the dark-eyed boy had been. Am I losing it?

Cam grabs my arm, pulling me back into the moment. "You should never have trusted me. It's too hard to resist these baby blues and cherubic gold curls."

My head is spinning. I don't have a witty comeback.

"Shelby?" Cam's brow furrows with concern.

Nausea overtakes me. I feel like I'm swimming in a heavy, hot wave. "I think I'm going to throw up."

Cam leads me back to the bonfire to find help. One of the

adult chaperones gives me a blanket and makes me sit down. Cam crouches in front of me, his playful grin long gone.

"What's wrong? What happened?"

"I saw…"

He listens, expectantly, but I don't know how to finish the statement without sounding crazy.

"That guy," I say, edging around the topic.

"Who?"

The one in the courtyard who may or may not have been a manifestation of my mental breakdown. I squeeze the words down.

"Never mind. Would you find Grace for me, please? I need to get home."

Cam nods with forced cheerfulness that masks his obvious discomfort. As he walks away, I bend my head down between my knees, trying with every ounce of strength to fight off the wave of anxiety that's cresting in my body. I've never felt more desperate for someone to talk to about all of this, but I know there's no one. No one who could begin to understand.

~

We're home by midnight. The entire drive, I pressed my forehead against the cool window, but I didn't see a single thing. Instead, thoughts echoed back and forth in my mind, like two emotions playing tennis.

Fear. A cold, dark terror that I'm losing hold of my own

mind. But also a strange, tremulous excitement. Seeing that boy again. It has to mean something.

Yeah, it means you're going crazy.

Back and forth. Back and forth. I can't hold a thought long enough to know how I actually feel.

Grace pulls into my driveway and puts the car in park. "Okay. Are we going to talk about this?"

"I don't know what to say. I don't know what's happening."

"I thought you went back for another treatment. Didn't they fix these panic attacks?"

My throat tightens. "I thought so. I don't know. Maybe the therapy is messing with my brain."

"We need to tell your mom," Grace says. She shifts in her seat, looking as squeamish as Cam had earlier. "She knows how to deal with these attacks better than me."

"It's not an anxiety attack, Grace."

I want to tell her about my hallucination of the boy. But once again, something makes me hold back. Am I protecting him or simply too afraid to admit how screwed up I am?

"You're not going crazy." Grace clutches her key chain, keys still in the ignition even though the car is turned off. She's going to leave as soon as she's seen me safely inside. I can't blame her for being uncomfortable. I suppose I would be too.

"I'll be fine," I say, lowering my gaze. "I think I'm getting sick or something."

"You need sleep. You'll feel better in the morning."

I nod even though I know it's not true. Grace puts her arm

around my shoulder as she walks me in. Mama and Stepdad Part Two are watching their shows in their big armchairs. The house is dark except for the blue glow of the TV. The smell of meat lovers' pizza lingers in the air. Mama isn't much for cooking.

"You back already?" Mama asks without glancing up.

Grace takes a breath to tell her what happened, but I pull on her arm.

"Yep," I say, angling us toward my room.

"We have some leftover pizza," Blake says. "You girls are welcome to it."

"No thanks," I say. "I'm going to go to bed, I think."

Mama looks up now. She doesn't say anything, but she can tell something's off. Like I said, the woman has a sixth sense.

I head for my room. Only then am I able to take a deep breath. The familiarity relaxes my pulse. I flop on my bed, landing on an Eeyore stuffed animal from the time we went to Disneyland when I was seven—our one and only family vacation.

Grace lingers at the door.

"Are you taking off?" I ask, trying not to feel the sting at her obvious desire to get out of here ASAP.

"I probably should. You need to sleep."

I nod. Grace sets her hand on the doorknob and then glances back at me over her shoulder. "I'm here for you, Shelby. You know that, right?"

A lump hardens in my throat. "Yeah. See you tomorrow."

She offers me a tight smile and slips out of my room. I flop back on my bed, staring up at my white ceiling. After a moment, I put my ear to the door. There's a low rumble of voices. Grace is talking to Mama. Closing my eyes, I flatten my back to my door. I've never felt more alone.

A loud crack, like a bullet being fired, explodes through the room. I jump. Spinning around, I look for the source. It came from my window, I think...

I open the blinds, expecting to see a giant crack in the glass, but something even more unexpected waits for me outside. A small white square of folded paper sits on the brick ledge.

I look out to my darkened front yard. It and the street beyond are empty. Grace's car is parked in the driveway, so I know she's still talking with Mama.

I scan my yard again, squinting at every possible hiding place. But no one's there. I stare back down at the windowsill. The paper is lined, clumsily torn from a school notebook. Whispers of black ink peek through from the other side.

It's a note.

My heart skips at the thought. I know it wasn't here this morning. I unlatch and pull open my window. The bottom half of my screen easily comes off with the twist of a few screws. My hand trembles as I reach for the note. I hesitate, then slide my fingers over the cool, dry paper.

I don't read it immediately. First I put my screen back in place and close my window and blinds. Then, sitting on my bed, I set the note on my lap. Carefully, I unfold the small slip.

I'M SORRY IF I STARTLED YOU TONIGHT. BUT I NEED TO TALK TO YOU.

CALL ME IF YOU WANT ANSWERS. 555-8765

His face comes to me, like a hot iron pressed against my brain. The boy from the hallucination.

I drop the note as if it were on fire. My pulse throbs in my fingertips. The hastily scratched words seem to burn into the paper. My vision blurs and clears. I shake my head. It's impossible. This can't be a hallucination.

The note is real. Real words written in real ink on real paper. And that means the boy has to be real as well. He's as real as I am. This assurance makes my heart beat faster. I bite my bottom lip as the warm, light feeling returns. I lift the note and trace the letters that form words.

A knock rattles my bedroom door. "Shelby?"

Mama. I almost choke on my own breath as I jolt into action. There's just enough time to stuff the paper beneath my pillow and yank my comforter over me before Mama opens the door.

"You awake?" she whispers.

I don't dare answer for fear she'll hear my shortness of breath. Instead, I look over my shoulder, trying my best to seem groggy. Mama frowns and steps into my room. Beneath my pillow, my fingers tighten around the slip of paper.

"Gracie told me what happened tonight."

I swallow hard and look away. "I'm fine."

Mama sits on the edge of my bed with a sigh. "Oh, my Shelby girl."

She rubs my leg gently. The tenderness of the gesture almost makes me cry. I want to open up to her. I want her to know how afraid I am. There's a five-year-old girl inside of me who wants to crawl into Mama's arms and be rocked to sleep, into a safe and uncomplicated dream.

"Gracie said you had a short panic attack. I don't understand it."

"I don't either." I'm glad I don't have to meet her gaze as I speak the lie.

"What happened tonight?"

Maybe I should be honest with Mama. "I saw something that scared me, and—"

"Something that scared you?"

"Well…it's hard to explain."

Mama sighs again with an unmistakable note of exasperation. "I guess we need to take you back to Dr. Stevens *yet again*." The mixture of weariness and anger in her voice comes like a slap across the face. "Gosh, Shelby, how is this so complicated for you? You've got one of the best doctors in the country working on you in a groundbreaking therapy. Hundreds of people are on a waiting list—people who would happily trade places with you—and you can't seem to calm down enough to let the treatment work."

I turn to her, stung by the coldness of her words. "Mama, I'm trying—"

"Are you though? Doesn't seem like it to me."

A hot current of anger seeps into my heart, evaporating any

tenderness. "Maybe the therapy isn't working anymore. Maybe it's messing with my head."

"You know that's not true."

"It *is* true, Mama. You need to listen to me."

She stands, lifting her hands in frustration. "No. This is not the time to discuss this. You're all mixed up right now. You need to sleep, get your head screwed back on. We can talk in the morning."

Mama practically slams the door behind her as she leaves. Hot tears burn in my eyes. I glare at the ceiling, teeth clenched, breathing hard. I bring the note before my face. It's wrinkled from my clammy palms, but the words are still there. *Call me if you want answers.*

I *do* want answers.

Before I can second-guess myself, I grab my phone and punch in the numbers. I smash my thumb over the call button.

Connecting...

A single buzz. The first ring. All at once, it hits me that I'm actually calling a complete stranger and someone who may not exist. I hang up and flop back on my pillow with an exasperated laugh. I really am losing it.

My phone lights up. The ring chimes loudly. 555-8765 is calling me back. I stare at the number, not breathing.

One ring. Then two. Three rings...

A pulse of pure adrenaline rushes through my body, down my arm, and into my fingertips. That's the only way I can explain why I answer the phone.

CHAPTER 5

S helby?"

The voice on the phone sounds deeper than I remember from our earlier encounter. But maybe it's because he's talking quietly. Still, hearing him speak my name sends a strange shiver over my skin.

I don't know what to say. I still can't believe I answered. Am I allowing myself to fall farther down the rabbit hole?

"I know I'm probably freaking you out right now," the stranger/hallucination boy says. "I'm sorry."

"I'm not freaked out," I lie. "Just confused."

"I can only imagine what you're going through."

His empathy makes me uncomfortable, though I'm not sure why. "I can't talk long."

He's silent. Taken aback, probably. I look at his note in my hand. "You said you had answers. So start talking. Who are you? How do you know me?"

He takes a deep breath. "Okay. First, my name's Auden."

"Auden, like the Broncos running back?"

"No. Like the poet, W. H."

"Oh."

"My parents used to be hipsters."

We both laugh sheepishly, and I smile. "I see."

"Usually, I claim the football player namesake around here," he says. I can hear a smile in his voice as well. "Keeps things uncomplicated."

"So, you're new here. How long have you been in town?"

He's silent for a moment. "I'm not new. At least, not very new. I've lived here for almost two years."

I process his words, frowning. "Here in Orchardview?"

"Yes."

"Weird." I'm surprised I've never heard of him in all that time. New people in Orchardview are usually the topic of conversation for weeks, especially someone who looks like this guy.

Auden exhales, and there's a slight tremor to his breath. "Shelby…you *have* heard of me. We know each other. Very well."

The vision from therapy flashes in my head. Suddenly, the air seems thin.

"I'm not in the mood to be messed with, okay?" I say, my voice harder than I intended.

"I'm not—"

"I don't know you."

"Shelby. Just listen—"

"No. We don't know each other. I've never seen you before…"

His image comes again, him sitting beside me on the hood of the car, and the claim evaporates on my tongue.

"You need to trust me on this," he says. "I can explain everything."

The assurance in his voice only puts me on edge. It feels like someone is sitting on my chest.

"I have to go."

"Wait. Let me—"

I slam my thumb on the screen of my phone. In my blur of emotion, it takes me three tries to successfully end the call. Breathing hard, I jump up, pull out one of my dresser drawers, and slam my phone into a folded pile of shirts. I push the drawer closed hard and stand with both palms pressed against the dresser as I struggle to calm my racing heart.

~

I barely leave my room Saturday and Sunday, watching one movie after another, only coming out to get a plate of food, then locking the door behind me. I think everyone is relieved when Monday morning rolls around. I switch into autopilot as I head out of the house and off to school. Classes bleed into each other. The hallways are a haze of faces and noise. Even my interactions with Grace are robotic and carefully neutral.

But when I'm ready to go home to climb into bed and finish watching *Gone with the Wind* for the millionth time, Cam Haler corners me outside the lunchroom.

"Seashell!" he says, grinning. "How's the ocean?"

It's an old joke, one that was only funny when I thought he was hot. Still, you have to admire his dedication.

I smirk. "Getting warmer every year, or so they say."

"Science, schmience." Cam's expression softens. "Seriously though, are you feeling okay?"

"Much better," I say, with a bright (and forced) smile.

Cam is convinced. "Awesome. Glad to hear it. Let's walk to auditions together then."

"Auditions?"

"For the fall play. *Romeo and Juliet?*"

I blink. "They're today?"

"Uh, *yeah*. Try right now."

How did I not remember this? I normally spend days preparing for an audition. I'd have my monologue memorized, blocked, and polished. Now the thought of being in the school play sends a cold stab of dread through my stomach. I shift my backpack to the other shoulder. "I don't know, Cam. I wish I could, but—"

"Do *not* tell me you're backing out."

"I have a lot on my plate right now."

"Like what?" Cam's eyes are wide, incredulous. "What could possibly be more important? Shelby, you *picked* this play. Mr. Lyman only did a Shakespeare because you begged him."

I remember sitting on the edge of Mr. Lyman's desk, explaining how even though the play had been done a million times, our version would be special. Why did I think ours would be different? The memory is splotchy. It's as if there's a piece missing. I reach for it, but there's only emptiness, like thin, white smoke.

Cam shakes his head in exasperation. "I can't believe you're backing out. What is wrong with you?"

His words strike a harsh chord. This inward resistance is unsettling, even to me; I can only imagine how it must look to Cam. Not to mention everyone else. It's a serious crack in my carefully maintained facade that everything's fine with me. If I don't audition today, half of the drama club will be tracking me down, asking what's wrong.

"I'm not backing out," I say. "I'm going to audition."

"Damn right, you are," Cam says.

He grabs my hand and marches us forward. Stepping through the worn double doors of the auditorium brings an unexpected rush of comfort. That smell—a mix of wood and dust and stage paint. The sight of the red, padded chairs. The way the stage lights make the velvet curtains glow. The wide openness of the stage. This is exactly where I want to be.

~

Mr. Lyman likes to give his students what he calls "the real Broadway experience." I have no idea if he's ever actually been to New York, but to the small crowd of students who willingly bear the label "drama nerd," he's an expert, genius, and mentor all in one.

Part of the real Broadway experience is auditioning on the

empty stage. Mr. Lyman sits in the third row, in the dark, holding a clipboard. He's the only one who gets to watch, aside from the student stage manager, Ana Guerrero. The rest of us wait out in the hallway, running lines from the scene he gave us. I'm auditioning for Juliet. And Cam's going for Romeo. Of course.

I'm staring at my script when Ana breezes out of the auditorium.

"Shelby. You're up."

I follow Ana through the double doors and step onto the stage, blinking at the bright lights above me. I'm nervous, yet standing here sends a current of strength through my body. Strength I haven't felt in a long time.

"Good to have you back, my dear," Mr. Lyman says.

I dip in a low curtsy. "Happy to be here, oh Captain, my captain." Mr. Lyman and I share a love of *Dead Poets Society*.

"Excellent. So, you will be reading from act two, scene two. Famous balcony scene."

"Got it."

"Whenever you're ready."

"Um, don't we need a Romeo?" I glance around me. It's not like Cam not to miss a moment in the spotlight.

"Right," he says. "Let's give our new recruit a try."

I frown, squinting into the shadows offstage as a tall figure moves up the aisle from the audience. He obviously wasn't waiting out in the hall with the others. Since when does Mr. Lyman allow that?

And then he steps into the light and onto the stage with his dark, tousled hair and deep eyes.

Auden.

CHAPTER 6

He doesn't take his eyes off me as he steps into the center of the stage, staring in that same unreadable way he did the night of the pep rally. I'm so shocked I stare back until he's standing beside me. Then I turn toward the audience, unsure if I'm afraid or furious.

"What are you doing here?" I ask him, my voice low, but sharp.

"Auditioning." I glance at him with a raised eyebrow, and it's the first time I've seen him smile. It brightens his whole face, especially his eyes. My heartbeat skips a little.

"You guys ready?" Mr. Lyman calls out.

I open my mouth to respond, but no words come out. I'm utterly distracted, dazed.

"Should we start from Juliet's speech?" Auden asks. "At line thirty-three?"

Mr. Lyman gives a thumbs-up, and Auden points to the place on my script, his hand brushing mine. "That's you, Shelby." I blink at the script, trying to scrape together a semblance of composure. I won't let this guy, whoever he may claim to be, ruin my audition.

I draw in a slow breath, exhale, and hold up my script. Closing my eyes, I try to become Juliet. I've never known the kind of love she feels in the moment of this famous speech, but somehow, reaching inside me, there's inspiration. A shadow of passion. Of pain. Only fragments of an emotion I couldn't possibly know, but they are there just the same.

I open my eyes. "Romeo." My throat catches as I speak his name. "Romeo. Wherefore art thou Romeo?"

The rest of the speech flows from me, almost with a life of its own. Auden watches me the entire time, the flicker of a suppressed smile on his lips. I try not to let it distract me, but then my speech ends and it's his line. Out of nowhere, he drops his script and clasps my hands in his.

"I take thee at thy word. Call me but love, and I'll be new baptized; henceforth I never will be Romeo."

We run the entire scene. Auden has every line memorized. He's a perfect Romeo. Where did this guy come from? He holds nothing back, and while I know he's acting a part, my pulse reacts as he touches my face, kisses my hand. It's partly shock at his boldness. Surprise at his commitment to the character. And maybe it has something to do with his dark eyes fixed on me. It's almost more intensity than I can handle.

The scene ends, and Auden turns to the audience, giving me a moment of peace.

"That was fantastic," Mr. Lyman says, clapping. "I'm so glad you auditioned. It's not often we get fresh blood in this program. Especially someone from New York."

Auden shrugs and smiles.

"Okay. Thanks, you two," Mr. Lyman says. "Why don't you stick around in the hallway? I want to run another scene in a bit."

I nod absently and turn for the stairs. Casting a glance over my shoulder, I watch Auden rush to his backpack and jacket, which he left on one of the aisle seats. He looks up at me, as if to make sure I'm headed out as well. My stomach flips. I don't want to face him. I'm not ready to hear what he has to say.

The darkness of backstage looms before me like a safe haven. And in that instant, I have an exit strategy. Mr. Lyman is distracted, talking to Ana about who to call in next. Auden is all the way across the auditorium. Seizing the moment, I rush offstage.

I'm not sure if Auden will follow me. I don't want to risk it. Or am I really trying to find a place where we can talk alone? Am I actually hoping he'll follow me?

Scoffing at my own stupidity, I head into the maze of curtains and backdrops. It's dark here, with only faint red light to help me navigate. I inhale that familiar, dusty smell and try to calm my racing heart. I just need a moment to catch my breath and clear my head.

"Shelby?"

His voice comes from the other side of the curtain, and I

freeze. Footsteps shuffle to the left, then right. And then Auden's face peers into my hiding place.

"Can I come in?"

"No."

He smiles a little, stepping into my curtain cave. "Please."

But I'm not amused. "Don't come any closer or I'll scream."

He seems taken aback by my threat. "I'm not going to hurt you, Shelby."

"Why are you stalking me? What do you want?"

"I'm not stalking you. I just want to talk to you."

"You said plenty the other night."

He rakes a hand through his hair. "Look, I know I'm screwing this up, but you have to give me a chance to explain."

I swallow back my retort. Maybe I'm being unfair. It's entirely possible that I did know him before my treatment and have somehow forgotten. I wouldn't be freaking out so much if it weren't for that moment in therapy, the vision of him and me on the car hood. His fingers brushing the hair from my lips. Thinking about it now sends a shiver over my skin.

What does it mean? If he really can explain, I should let him.

"All right," I say, folding my arms, as if that would protect me from everything that's happening. "Talk, then."

His shoulders relax a little. "You're not going to run away from me again?"

"That depends."

He smiles, but then his expression turns unreadable. He shakes his head a little. "This is so weird."

The memory of Grace saying those exact words sends a shiver through me. Auden sighs and casts his eyes upward, as if searching for what to say somewhere in the dusty, reddish light.

"If I told you something that you wouldn't believe, never in a million years, would you give me the chance to prove it before deciding to ignore me forever?"

"What does that even mean?"

"Just answer the question."

I try to give it some thought. "I don't know. I guess so. It would depend."

He watches me for a moment, his intense gaze so deliberate I can almost feel it like physical touch. My heart pulses harder. He takes my hand in his. I almost pull away, but the warmth and strength of his grip stills me.

"You know me, Shelby. Better than anyone in the world. And I know you."

I can't look away from his burning, dark eyes.

"It's true," Auden says softly, his voice like kiss. "We're in love."

My words come out as a strained whisper. "That's ridiculous."

"You know it's true. You feel it." He encloses my hand in his two palms and brings it to his chest. "In your heart. You can feel this connection, even if you don't remember what it is."

A whir of dizziness threatens to take me, but I grab for my strength. "Don't touch me," I say, pulling away from him.

"I can see that you feel it," he says.

"*I* don't even know what I'm feeling, so how could you?"

He sighs. "I know this isn't easy for you."

"You keep saying that." My voice is sharp. "But you *don't* know me."

"I know where you were this summer. And I know what they were doing to you."

I stare at him. We only told our very closest friends about the therapy. Mama said it would be best not to draw too much attention to it. Simple country folk don't go to big cities for fancy new medical treatments.

"Selective memory erasure," Auden says. "Seems a little extreme for some panic attacks."

Heat flashes in my chest. "You have no idea what I was going through."

He gives an exasperated, mirthless laugh. "I do, actually."

I'm officially done with this conversation. Anger burns on my skin, and I step forward to push past him. But he moves into my path.

"Wait. Hear me out."

"I've heard all I care to."

"Shelby." His pleading holds me in place for a moment longer.

"Don't listen then," he says, his voice soft but urgent. "But look."

He reaches into his back pants pocket and pulls out a black wallet. His fingers draw a slim, rectangular piece of paper from the billfold. It's picture strip from a photo booth. Without a word, Auden holds it out for me.

I don't take it, but my eyes lock onto the three photos.

It's Auden. And me. We're cuddled together in each image. Throwing up fake gang signs and wearing sunglasses in the top photo. Cheek to cheek in the center image, smiling brightly. And in the bottom picture, our lips are pressed together. My eyes are closed. Auden's fingers curl around the back of my neck, interwoven through my hair.

"Do you want to know why you think we don't know each other?" Auden's words ring in my ears. "Do you want to know why, in spite of your mind saying that you know nothing about me, your body insists you do?"

He sighs.

"The accident wasn't the only thing erased from your memory this summer, Shelby. They also erased me. They erased *us*."

CHAPTER 7

One of the symptoms of a panic attack is disassociation from reality. A detachment. Almost like you're watching your life play out in a dream.

I feel that now, but I know I'm not having an episode. I'm very much here. In this moment. It doesn't make sense, but I'm oddly calm. Maybe because what he's saying is too ridiculous to get upset over.

Or does it make sense?

"I knew your mom hated me," Auden says, his eyes darkening. "But I never imagined she'd take it this far."

"How do you know about the therapy?" I ask. My voice sounds weak and small.

"How could I not?" His eyes slide closed for a moment. "This summer has been hell in more ways than I can explain. But living without you was the worst part of it. I had to find you. I had to find out what they were doing to you."

"They weren't *doing* anything to me. I wanted to be there. I needed the treatment."

"And you're sure you know exactly what was going on? If they can take one piece of your memory, doesn't it stand to reason they could take another while they're at it?"

For a split second, I can feel the cold electrode patches pressed to my temples. I can see the sterile helmet of the neural restructuring capsule gradually lowering over my face. The hairs on my arms and neck stand on end.

I'm suddenly aware that Auden is watching me intently. I take a step back. "It can't be true."

"I know it's hard to wrap your mind around, but you have to trust me."

He's so earnest I almost believe him. Once again, the image of Auden sitting beside me on the hood of that car shivers through me. It's too bizarre. It can't be real. My mind is arguably *not* a reliable source right now. Facts are the only things that matter.

I shake my head. "Mr. Lyman said you were from New York."

"I moved here with my dad two years ago."

My eyes narrow. "If you've lived here two years, why didn't Lyman know you?"

"Because I took classes online at first. I didn't want to be subjected to a small-town education." He smiles. "But then I had a reason to enroll here."

My cheeks heat, and I can't hold his gaze. His words seem convincing enough. But how could it be possible? Mama would never do something like that to me. Right…?

"I need proof."

Auden holds out the photo strip and shakes it. "What do you call this?"

"I don't know." I need fresh air. I need to sit down. I need to be by myself to think. "I don't remember that. It might as well be a picture of two complete strangers."

"Because they stole this memory from you" he says, fiercely, jabbing his finger at the picture of us kissing. "You have to feel that in your heart. Before you started your so-called therapy, you knew me—mind, body, and soul."

His words beat in my head, but still don't sink in. It's as if they're pounding on closed and barred windows. I try to grasp at them, try to make sense of it all, but there is a layer of thick glass between us. It makes me dizzy.

"I can't do this," I say, turning from him.

"Don't leave." There's so much pain in his voice it makes me stop for a moment. But I steel myself and keep going.

I only make it a few feet, however, before I nearly collide with Ana.

"There you are," she says, exasperated. "Didn't you hear us calling for you?"

"I…you were?"

"Uh, yeah. Lyman wants to see you run the balcony scene with Cam."

I blink at her. I feel as if I've been in an alternate universe for the last few minutes. Auditions and Cam and Mr. Lyman don't seem to belong in reality anymore. But they *are* reality. Auden and his…claims are what don't belong.

"Right," I say, struggling to appear composed. "Sorry. I was just…" My voice trails off, abandoning the lame excuse I might have concocted if I had the mental energy.

Ana rolls her eyes. "Whatever. Just hurry."

I grab a script and try to get my head screwed on right as I walk out onto the stage. Cam watches me approach with a frown.

"Are you okay?"

"Fine," I say with my well-used, false brightness, but it's barely a flicker.

Cam shoots a look offstage, then back at me. "I've been looking everywhere for you."

"Yeah… Sorry."

There's clearly more Cam wants to say, but he hesitates, and Mr. Lyman calls out for us to start. We run the scene, but it's nowhere near as good as it could be. Cam and I are the senior stars of the drama program. We're practically guaranteed the lead roles. But my game is off. Why did the chemistry come so naturally between Auden and me?

Mr. Lyman seems to sense it as well. "Shelby, why don't you stay, and we'll do a run with a different Romeo…" He flips through his notes and then looks up. "Act three. Scene five."

Cam stares at him for a beat. He glances at me before leaving the stage. It's a look of barely contained outrage only a jilted drama kid can conjure. A single laugh bubbles up in my throat, but I swallow it the moment Mr. Lyman tells Ana to find Auden.

He walks out onto the stage. The way he takes in every inch

of me in one look makes me feel like I'm inside out. I'm exposed before him, and it makes my skin burn.

"From the top," Mr. Lyman calls out. "Now remember, in this scene, Romeo has been banished. He and Juliet are saying goodbye, not knowing when they will be able to see each other again."

Chills prickle my skin. Of all the scenes, why did Mr. Lyman have to pick this one? One so eerily parallel to the story Auden just told me in the darkness backstage. I stare at the words on the page, struggling to stay in character. But Auden draws me out of thoughts and into the moment. I can't help but fall into the emotion of the scene. It's strange, but exhilarating.

In the back of my mind though, I know this scene includes a kiss. As Auden is reciting one of Romeo's lines, I scan down the page to the part. He wouldn't...would he? My stomach clenches, but I can't tell if it's with trepidation or anticipation.

Mr. Lyman reads the Nurse's lines from the darkened audience. "Your lady mother is coming to your chamber: The day is broke; be wary, look about."

My voice tremors slightly as I read Juliet's next line. "Then, window, let day in, and let life out."

Auden suddenly embraces me. My breath evaporates from my lungs as his arms surround me and my body presses to his.

"Farewell," Auden says, his gaze latched onto mine. "Farewell. One kiss, and I'll descend."

Then he gently draws my face to his.

CHAPTER 8

"An actual kiss will not be necessary, Mr. Keplar," Mr. Lyman calls, halting the moment. I can almost hear his smirk. "Though I applaud your commitment to the scene."

Ana coughs out a laugh from the darkness. Auden stops, but doesn't let me go. His gaze is on my lips. Breathless, I step back, out of his grip.

Mr. Lyman claps his hands once. "Actually, I think I've seen all I need to see. Thank you both. You were fantastic."

I take another step back. Auden still doesn't move.

"Well, that's a wrap," Mr. Lyman says. "Go ahead and let everyone know, Ms. Guerrero."

Ana sweeps out of the auditorium, and Mr. Lyman smiles up at us.

"Thanks again for coming out and auditioning. It was… surprising. I think we're going to do something really special with this."

I can feel Auden's eyes on me.

"I'll have a cast list posted soon," Mr. Lyman says. "Hopefully tomorrow."

I muster the best smile I can and move toward the steps. "Thanks, Mr. Lyman."

Grabbing my bag, I speed walk up the aisle of the auditorium and burst through the doors. *Just get out of here. Get to your car. Breathe.*

Out in the hallway, the rest of the actors gather up their bags, chatting with each other, no doubt agonizing over a line they flubbed or a moment when their voice cracked. We drama kids are pretty notorious for being overanalyzers. There's a reason the phrase "drama queen" exists.

I weave my way past them. I need to get out of school, and I'm sure it's only a matter of time before Auden turns up. I want to avoid Cam too. I don't need any more complications right now.

Outside, the crisp Colorado fall air fills my lungs, burning slightly in my nostrils. My eyes close involuntarily for a moment. I need answers, but I also long for peace of mind. It's been forever since I've felt that. I almost forget what it's like.

"I'm sorry." His low voice sounds behind me, sending a jolt of energy through my spine. The effect he has on me is very annoying. I walk for my car without turning back.

"You keep apologizing, yet you keep pulling stunts like whatever that was in there."

"What do you mean?" Auden asks.

I snap a glance over my shoulder. "The audition? Trying to kiss me?"

"It's in the script," he insists, coming up beside me. "I was in character."

There's a poorly hidden smile on his lips. I scoff and try to move faster, but he cuts me off, walking backwards in front of me.

"I promise I won't do it again. Until you want me to."

I roll my eyes. "Wow."

We've reached my car. I pull out my keys. "I should get home."

"Wait." Auden presses himself in front of my car door.

"Why do you keep blocking my path?"

"Why do you keep running away from me?"

"Like I have to explain? I don't know you—"

"But you—"

"I know. I *did*. Whatever. Even if that's true, I don't know you *now*. You're just some…really tall guy with intense eyes following me around and telling me that we used to date."

He pulls out the photo strip again. "I'm not only telling you, I'm showing you."

I snap the pictures from his hand and look at them again. "If this is true, why has no one mentioned you? I mean, even if most people don't know you because you weren't going to Orchardview High, surely some people would know who you are."

"They do. But they're respecting your mother's wishes to pretend I never existed."

"That's a little extreme."

"Shelby. Your mother has taken the extreme measure of literally erasing me from your brain. I think it's safe to say she isn't a fan."

"Why does she hate you so much?" I fold my arms. "What did you do?"

He gives a humorless laugh. "It's a long story."

"Try me."

"Think about it. I came here from the evil big city, and I'm a city boy in every way. I read Kerouac. I used to wear black clothes and hipster glasses. Do I look like the kind of person your mother wants you to be with?"

There's no doubt that Auden isn't the kind of guy that Mama would pick for me. I don't know much about him, but everything I've seen so far seems dissonant with the standard out here. Hearing that he's originally from New York fits perfectly. He has that kind of intellectual, cosmopolitan swagger about him. And intellectual, cosmopolitan swagger doesn't really fly in Orchardview, Colorado.

"Okay, but that's a big jump from disliking your personality to wanting you erased from my brain."

He sighs. "It's more than that. You mother values her control over you. I tried to set you free. Your mother wants you to wither away here in Orchardview, just like she has. I encouraged you to dream of bigger ambitions and new places."

His words make a knot form in my stomach. It's a truth so clear it hurts to look at. I change the subject instead.

"Well, what about Grace? She hasn't said anything about you. Does she hate you too?"

Auden's expression darkens. "I didn't think so. Guess I was wrong."

"I don't believe she'd lie to me."

"With how well known your stepfather is? Think about it, Shelby. If they'd asked your friends and the few people who'd know me in the community to play along with this deception, you know people would go along with it. Fact is, the people in this town are more loyal to those they've known their whole lives. It's certainly been no burden for them to play along and act like I never existed."

I study the three pictures of us. And once again, my mind fights to comprehend what Auden is telling me. It just doesn't make sense. It's impossible. It's like the best kind of horror movie. Realistic enough to be scary but in the end…still a movie. His is also a story invented for an audience.

When I look up, Auden's watching me. "What are you thinking?" he asks, quietly.

"I need more proof."

He presses his lips together. "All right. Can I show you something?"

"It depends. Does that *something* happen to be in the back of a windowless van?"

He gives a short laugh. "I see I've earned your trust." He shakes his head. "No, it's a place."

"Oh, so you *do* want me to get into your car. No thanks."

"We can take yours. You drive. It's not far. Give me fifteen minutes of your afternoon, and if you're still not convinced, I'll leave you alone. I promise."

I narrow my eyes, but I know it's partly an act. I don't really think he's dangerous, though I've seen enough movies to know you can't ever be sure. As much as I don't want to admit it, I'm curious. This guy is weirdly compelling.

Unpredictable.

That's the best word to describe him. And unpredictable people don't belong in Orchardview. Maybe that's why I'm drawn to him.

"All right," I say, with a shrug. I unlock my car and climb in the driver's seat. "I can't imagine what you could possibly show me here in town that would convince me."

He smiles as he slides in and pulls on the passenger-side seat belt.

The car starts with a sputter. Auden points forward. "Take a left out here. Head for Pine Street."

"Where are we going?"

"You'll see."

I grimace but follow his directions. Old Orchardview Main Street rolls by, and we pass the gently art deco stone bank from the 1920s. A cafe. A bike store. An older couple strolls the street, hand in hand. I steal a sidelong glance at Auden, and curiosity roils inside of me. What's going on behind those dark eyes of his? What's he planning? *Should* I be afraid?

"Make a left up there," he says.

I pull into a half-empty parking lot with a raised brow. "The movie theater?"

"Yes."

"Are we watching a matinee?"

"No, but what I want to show you is inside." He unbuckles his seat belt with a little smile. "See? Public place. You have nothing to worry about."

"Plus, I used to work here, so I'll be surrounded by people I know."

Auden stays silent, but he's still smiling.

We cross the parking lot in silence. The clouds have covered the sky, making the air cold and damp. The neon brightness of the theater's lobby provides a warm welcome. Immediately, the buttery smell of popcorn hits me, bringing back a wave of memories. I got my first job in this theater. Working here helped fuel my love of movies, my dreams of acting.

It's been a while since I stepped through these doors. I had to stop working when my course load got too heavy. Or was it because of the spring musical? Suddenly, I can't quite put my finger on the reason. It's like there's a fuzzy patch where the answer is stored in my mind. Like the information has been smudged out…

Or erased…

I snap a look to Auden, chills tingling my skin. Is this why he wanted to bring me here? He seems to read my thoughts, and his face brightens.

"Do you remember?"

"No—I mean, I remember working here. Of course. But…"

He motions toward the theaters, quickening his pace. "Over here. Hurry."

"First, explain what you're trying to prove."

But Auden doesn't stop. My old boss, Karen, stands at the entry podium with a scrawny new kid. From the looks of it, she's giving him a stern lecture on proper ticket-checking protocol. Karen's a short, boxy woman with outdated hair and a no-nonsense manner. She always took her job, and the tiny sliver of power that comes with it, *very* seriously.

As we approach, a rare smile brightens her face. "Shelby. Long time no see. How was Denver?"

"Great." I've spewed out the lie so many times it's almost convincing.

Karen nods and then nudges her head at Auden. "Your Mama okay with you two being here?"

"We're not watching a movie," Auden says, filling my silence. "I left my camera case in Theater Five. Is it okay if we duck in for a minute?"

Karen twists her lips to the side and checks her watch. "We've got one running in there right now."

"There're only two people in that theater," the scrawny new kid pipes in.

Auden gives Karen a charming smile, and she grins, shaking her head. "This guy." She smacks his arm in a chummy way that surprises me. "Go on, then."

Auden grins. "Thanks, K!" He turns to me and motions me on.

"*K?*" I ask under my breath as we walk. "How do you know her?"

"I know her because I worked here for two years." Auden

opens the door to Theater Five. The sound of violin music rushes out with a burst of air.

I open my mouth to contradict him, but the words evaporate on my lips.

Auden walks into the theater. I follow. At this point, I can't stop myself. Maybe this is how the moth feels when it catches sight of the bug zapper's blue glow.

A beautiful young woman weeps into a handkerchief on the huge screen. I remember seeing trailers for this film. It's a historical romance set in colonial India. It looked pretty good.

Auden sidesteps into the back row, and I follow him, running my hand along the tops of the red velvet seats. He comes to the center of the row and sits down. The light from the screen gleams on his eyes, making them sparkle. He watches me, his shoulders moving with tight breaths. Seeing him so nervous only makes my heart beat faster.

But I've come this far. I'm not turning back. Swallowing against the tightness in my throat, I sit down next to Auden.

"Okay," I whisper, staring forward to give the appearance of indifference. "So, what do you want to show me?"

"This. Right here."

"This movie?"

"This row. In this theater."

"You said you had answers. I don't feel like playing Twenty Questions," I say.

Auden puts a finger to his lips, reminding me that there are people trying to watch the movie. He leans forward—

uncomfortably close—and speaks in a low voice. "This is where we first met, Shelby. Right in these seats."

He searches my eyes as if he could find the memory behind them, lodged somewhere in my brain that I can't reach, and retrieve it. Make me see.

But I see nothing.

"There was a movie playing," he says. "Just like this. It was my first day working here. Karen sent me in to check the theater and make sure no one had snuck in. And as it turned out, someone had. One of her own employees. You. I think you were supposed to be cleaning the bathrooms or something, but you were in the back row. Right here. Watching."

My throat feels tight. "What movie was it?"

"You know, I can't even remember." His smile fades. "I only remember you. It was near the end of the movie, and you were crying. I remember your profile in the shadows, the way your hair rested against your shoulders. I remember the way the light from the screen made the tears on your cheek glisten."

He lifts his hand and traces his finger down my cheek. I forget to breathe. His hand curls away from my skin, but he remains close, barely a breath away from me.

"I sat by you and asked if you needed a tissue. You looked me up and down and said you actually needed a camera because hipster sightings were rare in these parts."

I can't help but laugh. "Well, that does sound like me."

"We talked about the scene, the excellent cinematography and emotionally manipulative music."

I smile a little. "Kind of like this?" I motion to the screen.

"Exactly like this." He brushes my hair from my face, allowing his hand to skim my shoulder. He looks back at me, his eyes begging me to remember.

I want to remember. Auden's words have painted the moment, almost like a scene in a film. I can see it. I want it to be my memory. But I know it's not.

He pulls back. "I'm sorry. I shouldn't touch you. I'm a stranger."

I look down into my lap, trying to muster some semblance of composure. We're both quiet. Then Auden leans his head back against the wall and exhales, frustrated.

"It's not right. No one should have the power to take away your own thoughts and memories."

I fold my arms around myself and think of the neural restructuring capsule, of Dr. Stevens, Aunt Winonna. Of Mama, sitting with her magazine as they place the electrode patches on my head and stick the anesthesia needle into my arm. Is my own mother really capable of such a thing? I can't say with complete confidence that she isn't.

Is that why she always avoids discussing my "therapy" treatments? Is that why she rushed me back for another session when I suggested I didn't feel right? The thoughts crowd my mind, and I press the heels of my hands to my forehead.

Auden turns to me again. "Shelby, listen to me. You don't have to try and remember anything right now. You probably can't, even if you wanted to. All I'm asking is that you entertain the notion that I might be telling you the truth. And give me the chance to prove it to you."

"How could you possibly prove it?"

"I'll tell you everything about us. If I have to, I'll re-create every date we ever went on, every moment we shared. I'll give you back every single memory they took from you."

If I'm honest, what little I know about Auden makes me want to know more. And of course, he's good-looking. Not in the conventional, Abercrombie model way. But in the dark, brooding, Heathcliff from *Wuthering Heights* way. A way that happens to be exactly my taste. I can see pretreatment me having a huge crush on this guy.

What do I have to lose by giving him a chance to prove it? If he's lying, it will come out sooner or later. You can't force memories that aren't really there.

But if he's right…it would seem I have a lot to gain.

"I'm willing to give you a chance," I say.

His entire presence brightens. "You are?"

"I'm not calling myself your girlfriend or anything like that. But I'm willing to explore the possibility there was an us. Because—and *only* because—something doesn't feel right, and no one is giving me any answers except you."

"I'll tell you everything," he says earnestly, but the moment he says it, a shadow crosses his face. His smile falters. Quick as it changed, he's bright again. "I'll do whatever you ask me to do."

"All I want is the truth," I say, firmly.

Auden nods. "And I'll help you find it again."

CHAPTER 9

The sharp ping of my alarm jars me from a heavy and dreamless sleep. I open my eyes slowly and stare at my cell phone. The numbers on the screen don't make sense. The room around me seems unfamiliar in the pale dawn light. For a single moment, I remember nothing.

And then it all comes rushing back to me. Auden. The audition. The three pictures of us. The movie theater.

If my memories of him had been erased, there are new ones now. And they strike me with an inexplicable force. I roll to my side, hugging my pillow to my chest. I can't decide if I'm terrified or excited to go back to school today. The idea of playing sick flits in my brain. It wouldn't be hard to convince Mama. Not that she cared much if I went to school anyway. Honestly, I always had the feeling that she'd rather I *not* do too well academically. It doesn't fit her image of who I should be and how I should end up.

Just as I'm starting to relax back into sleep, I remember that the cast list for *Romeo and Juliet* will be posted today. I exhale deeply. I hate to admit it, but that's reason enough to brave whatever strangeness awaits me at school.

Sitting up wearily, I reach for yesterday's jeans, which are in a clump on the floor. I hesitate. Instead, I wind up in the bathroom, cranking on the shower. I can lie to other people but not to myself. Standing there under the warm water, soaped up in pomegranate body wash, shaving my legs, I know exactly what I'm up to.

I stroll into the dimly lit kitchen, praying that Mama won't notice the extra effort. She's at the table, barely awake, nursing a steaming cup of coffee. But Stepdad Part Two looks up and smiles.

"Well, don't you look pretty today, Shelby. What a nice dress."

Mama's gaze flicks up and fixes on my wine-colored, peasant blouse dress. I can see the analysis starting behind her icy blue eyes. I rarely wear dresses. *Stupid.* I should have stuck with the usual. Now Mama is going to suspect something.

But her attention goes back to her coffee mug, and she is quiet.

"Thanks, Blake," I say, grabbing a banana. "I'd better go. Bye."

I rush out the door, hopefully before Mama can decide that something is amiss. *It's really not for him*, I tell myself. *I felt like wearing this dress.*

It's a nice dress. Pretty. Feminine. Kind of Juliet-ish… As I finger the soft fabric between my fingers, an image flashes in my mind. Me in an elaborate Italian gown. Auden wearing a doublet, climbing the vines that drape a marble balcony.

My stomach accordions, and I tell myself to shut up already. When I pull into the parking lot, I'm on high alert. My eyes scan the mob of passing faces. My heart beats faster than normal. I've never been more annoyed with myself, but I can't help it. What will happen when I see him again?

But I don't see Auden at all. History, math, and computer science pass without so much as a glimpse of him. Walking through the lunchroom offers nothing but the same old crowd. Going out into the commons area, I flop beside Grace on our normal bench, lunch tray in my lap.

She contemplates a crinkle fry, her brow furrowed. "I think I'm going to fail calculus."

I scan the commons. No dark, intense eyes. No Auden. "Turner won't fail you. Everybody passes his class."

"I think I might set a new record. The first student to get an F in Turner's calculus."

"Maybe you've got too many distractions. Large, Brad Corbin–sized distractions."

She laughs and then sets down her food with a sigh. "I think he's the one, Shelby."

I blink. "The one?"

"The one that's going to make me forget Mike for good."

"In that case, I wholeheartedly approve of the young man. You have my blessing to proceed with initiating a relationship."

"Oh thanks." She rolls her eyes, though she's smiling. Then she nudges me with her shoulders. "Speaking of the one, why don't you tell me what's going on?"

Tension zips up my spine, making me straighten. "What? What do you mean?"

Grace's blue eyes twinkle. "You and Cam seem to be awfully chummy again."

I laugh and relax a little. I shake my head. "No. Give me some credit, Grace. I'm not that desperate."

"You two are going to get married," she singsongs, taking a sip of her Dr Pepper. "Just watch. You're going to have two kids: Cam Jr. and Shelby Jr. And the two of you'll team teach Drama at Orchardview."

I force a laugh, but my stomach goes unexpectedly cold at the picture she paints. It's the life everyone wants for me. The life Mama wants for me. It sounds safe and comfortable, and I'm pretty sure I'd be happy in that life. Wouldn't I…?

I stare down at the burger on my tray. That familiar, dreaded itch tingles in my mind. It's as if everything is slightly wrong. Just a little…off.

Phantom limb. It's normal. I'm normal…

I carry the sensation with me the rest of the day. The only thing keeping me from going home early is the knowledge that Mr. Lyman will post the cast list for *Romeo and Juliet* immediately after school. The hours pass as slowly as drying concrete, but I push myself to make it through.

Walking through the halls at the end of the day, heading for the drama room, my spirit brightens. A rush of excitement swirls in me. For a few moments, I forget about everything except the play.

People rush past, eager to get home or at least get the heck out of the school, but a crowd has gathered around Mr. Lyman's door. The white sheet posted on it glows like a beacon through the blur of faces. It draws me forward. I have to stop myself from running.

As I approach, some of the freshmen girls gazing at the list turn and stare at me. One of them gives me a wistful smile. Holding my breath, I look at the list. The names on the paper blur for a second, then come into focus.

Juliet: Shelby Decatur

My heart jumps into my throat. And then:

Romeo: Cam Haler

I blink hard. But reading it three more times yields the same result. People crowd around congratulating me.

I smile. Thank them. Tell them how awesome they are going to be in their parts. Tell them how nervous I am to play such a huge role. All of the responses I'd planned in my head. As they trickle away, however, I turn back to the list and read it again.

I'm happy, of course. Thrilled. Playing Juliet has been a long-held dream. But I'm confused. *Cam* as Romeo? Not Auden? Is Mr. Lyman crazy?

Not that I want Auden to play Romeo. That would be too much…too much *something*. I scan the list for his name. Surely Mr. Lyman cast him as one of the other major roles. Tybalt, maybe. Or Mercutio?

But his name is completely absent from the page. He's not even an extra. I can't understand it. He's clearly a talented actor.

To not get any part at all? Am I the only one who saw how great he was?

I blink. He was at the audition, right? That all happened. There's no way a hallucination could go on that long…

I step back, glancing around me in mild panic. Is that why I didn't see him anywhere at school today?

Two arms hook around my waist from behind. My shriek is canceled out by Cam's exultant cheer. He lifts me up in the air.

"We are going to *rock*, Shelbs!"

I pull out of his grip and spin around to face him. "Stop doing that!" I say, more fiercely than I intended.

Cam holds out his hands. "I'm just excited! Aren't you? I mean, come on, Seashell. This is it! This is our break!"

It really is. It's the moment he and I had been dreaming of since we were freshmen: we are starring in the fall play. And not just any fall play—the most iconic of all Shakespeare's plays: *Romeo and Juliet*. This is my big chance to show what I can really do. Nothing should take away the significance of this moment. I force any thought of Auden from my head and smile.

"Of course, I'm excited. Are you kidding me?"

Cam crows, and we hug. Then he takes my hand and plants a firm kiss on it.

"It's going to be epic. They will be talking about our performance in the halls of Orchardview High for generations to come."

He's being dramatic, but it strikes me as sad that, even

when he's going for hyperbole, the best fame he can conjure stays contained to the narrow, pastoral confines of our small town.

"We'll be great. Especially now that your voice has changed," I tease.

There was an incident freshman year, involving a Shakespearean monologue, a school assembly, and Cam's voice cracking, not once, but four times.

"Yay puberty!" Cam says, grinning. "Come on. Let's go talk to Lyman."

"Maybe tomorrow," I say. "I have to get home."

"What?"

"Huge paper to write."

I'm not sure if Cam can tell I'm lying or not, but he seems too happy to care. I give him one last congratulatory hug and go. As I weave through the nearly empty halls toward the parking lot, I struggle to get a grip on my emotions.

I should be happy.

I am happy.

I should be happier.

With a frustrated laugh, I reach my car. As I click my seat belt across my lap, my phone buzzes in my pocket. Distracted, I barely glance at the number, but then I freeze. It's a text from an unknown number.

I'm not going to play Romeo. There's a reason for this.

Crazy how one stupid little text can have the same effect as if I'd stuck my finger in an electric socket. I bite my lip.

Are we still playing Twenty Questions? Or are you going to tell me why?

I watch my phone as the three dots scroll showing he's responding. I breathe out slowly. *Get a grip, Shelby.* I'm not going to get wrapped up in whatever game he's trying to play.

His answer comes. If I told you through text, I wouldn't have an excuse to meet up with you in person. Can't blame me for trying.

I bite back a smile. I don't like games.

You're right. I'm sorry. How's this: I'd love to see you this afternoon. Unless you're too busy?

I do a quick scan of the parking lot, which is mostly empty, and then look back down at my phone. My finger taps the screen, but I don't write a response. There's still a part of me that is nervous to meet him. I have this nagging feeling that I'm walking into a situation I shouldn't, that I'm stirring up something best left alone.

And yet, for the first time all day, I'm tired of telling myself how I *should* feel. For the first time today, I let myself acknowledge what I've been avoiding all day.

I *want* to see Auden. I want to know more about him. Even if I don't know if I believe him, I still want to hear what he has to say about us. I lift my phone and type.

Where do you want to meet?

CHAPTER 10

I half expected Auden to arrange to meet in some shadowy street alley, but he has me come to a coffee shop instead. Brewster's. It's not the one I usually go to. This one's on the edge of town, near the truck stop.

Auden waits for me at a corner table, his back to the door, bent over. As I move closer, I can see that he's concentrating on a notebook. He's writing furiously. But then he senses me and sits up with a jolt. His face brightens.

"You came."

"You didn't think I would?" I sit down across from him. My eyes fall to his notebook, but he smoothly closes it and slides it into his messenger bag on the ground by his chair.

"Yesterday, you thought I was trying to murder you," he says, smiling. "Now you're meeting me for coffee. I'd say we're making real progress."

At that moment, the waitress comes to take my order. But before she can speak, Auden points at me. "She likes your dark chocolate hot cocoa with one stick of cinnamon and extra whipped cream."

The waitress turns me to confirm. Startled, I nod before turning back to him. He has a satisfied little smile on his face. But I'm not going to be won that easily. So he knew my favorite drink? Anyone could have asked Grace and gotten the same answer.

"Nice party trick," I say, folding my arms.

Auden laughs a little. "Wow. You're a pretty tough audience, you know that?"

"I told you. I don't like games."

"I'm not playing games." His expression goes serious. "I'd never want you to think that."

His sincerity disarms me, so I change the subject. "So, why weren't you in school today? You don't look sick to me."

He slides his paper cup in a little half circle on the table. "That's because I'm not sick. Shelby…I don't go to Orchardview. I'm still taking online classes."

"Oh. But you said…" I shake my head. "I guess I was confused with you auditioning for the play and everything."

"I know. I should have been more up front with you. I'm sorry." He sighs. "Things are very complicated right now. I'm not sure I can fully explain."

"Try."

A smile flickers on his face, but then fades as he fixes his gaze on me. It's that same, intense look. Searching. Reaching.

"I wanted to be Romeo for you. I wanted it more than I can

express. And Mr. Lyman let me audition, and then he offered me the part."

This information electrifies me. "He did? What happened?"

"I turned it down."

"Why?"

"For the same reason I can't enroll at Orchardview."

He's being cryptic again. "And what reason is that?" I ask in frustration.

Auden starts to reply, but hesitates as the waitress approaches.

She sets my drink in front of me. The warm smell of cinnamon and chocolate tingles my nose. I can't resist taking a sip, even though it's piping hot. The flavor is even better than I remember. When was the last time I had one of these?

"Can I get you two anything else?" the waitress asks.

I smile up at her, wiping the whipped cream from my lip. "This is perfect. Thanks."

"Great. And let me know if you want a refill on that coffee, hon."

Auden barely acknowledges her. His attention remains fixed on me.

"I need to be up front with you," he says when she's gone.

I take another sip of my cocoa. "That'll be a refreshing change."

He spins his cup again in nervous semicircles. "If you and I are going to see each other, even as friends, it can't be…typical."

"Trust me, it's already *far* from typical."

"What I mean is…any time we meet, we have to do it in… secret." He cautiously glances up at me.

I raise an eyebrow. "In secret."

"Yes. Everything has to be kept secret. Phone calls. Texts. You can't tell anyone. Not even Grace. You can't tell anyone that you've met with me. Or spoken with me. You can't even say that you've seen me."

"Aren't you being a tad dramatic?" I ask.

Auden stares at his cup. Half turn. And another. His seriousness makes my smile fade.

"Your mother went to great lengths to have me erased from your life, Shelby. What do you think she'd do if she found out I was back? Back *and* trying to help you remember what they stole from you? Do you really think she'd let that happen?"

I stare at him for a moment, trying to process his words. "You're serious."

He sighs. With everything Auden has said, this shouldn't surprise me. But still…Who sneaks around like this? I press the bridge of my nose. It suddenly hurts to think.

"Wait. If we're supposed to be keeping us secret, why did you take me to the movie theater? What about the audition?"

"Karen and Mr. Lyman are exceptions," he says. "Believe it or not, there are a few people on my side. Very few. But they're there. Luckily, still being newish in town, most people don't know me. There are some popular places I can't go, like Jenny's or the grocery store. Too big of a chance I might see someone who recognizes me, but I can usually keep a pretty low profile."

My stomach goes cold. It's a chill that even the hot chocolate can't warm. "But why do you have to avoid people other than me? They didn't have their memories of you wiped."

Auden stops turning his cup. It's only a half second of hesitation, but it doesn't go unnoticed.

"It's hard to explain," he says, carefully.

"You said you'd tell me everything."

"I will. It's just…" Auden sighs. "I can't lose you again, Shelby. So for the time being, I'm asking you—I'm begging you—to go along with this. Pretend that you've never seen me. Pretend that you are exactly as you were when you came back from Denver. Pretend I don't exist. And it needs to stay that way. Or at least appear to."

The chill spreads. "You're kind of freaking me out."

"I know," he says, dropping his head miserably. "I'm trying hard not to, but it's impossible. Maybe that's the brilliance of using memory erasure. It makes *me* look like the crazy one."

I flinch, and his eyes widen.

"I'm not saying you're crazy," he says, swiftly. "I didn't mean it like that. I…" He scrapes both hands through his hair and exhales with frustration. "I'm really striking out here, aren't I?"

A heavy silences settles between us. Auden's pleading gaze returns to me. A part of me wants to get up and leave. I'm not sure if I can take much more of this.

Auden seems to sense my hesitation. "You probably don't want anything more to do with me."

"I'm not sure what I want," I say, quietly. I look down at my hot chocolate. Auden ordered it with such relaxed confidence.

He wasn't trying to show off or convince me. He knew, without missing a beat, what my favorite drink was.

"I'm not sure what to think of you yet," I say, stirring the cinnamon stick in the melting whipped cream. "You're a little intense. But…"

"But?"

I smirk a little, in spite of myself. "I've always had a thing for intense guys. Especially those who proclaim their love for me."

Auden smiles. "And that happens often?"

"Oh, shut up. This may the first time, but that doesn't mean I can't form a swift opinion on the matter."

The way he laughs at my joke makes my heart flutter. His eyes shine as if I were the most charming person in the world. I can't think of the last time someone looked at me like that.

"Are you still willing to give me a chance?" he asks. "In spite of the bizarre conditions?"

I drop the cinnamon stick into my drink and fold my hands on the table. "I think so. Yes."

He exhales with shaky relief. "Thank you. You won't regret it, I promise. I'll help you remember. I'll bring it all back."

"Don't make promises you can't keep," I say, softly. "Dr. Stevens said there's no chance of erased memories returning."

"He doesn't know everything."

"He's an expert in his field."

"Well, he doesn't know about *us*," Auden says, passionately. "About our love. You can't just blot out something like that. Not forever."

For the first time since I met him, I genuinely hope he's right.

Auden gives his cup another twirl, looking a little self-conscious. "I don't even know where to start," he admits.

"Start at the beginning."

He looks up with a glimmer in his eye. "Yes. That's perfect. I showed you where we first met. Now, I'll take you on our first date."

I shrug. "Can we do it in secret?"

"Absolutely. How about tonight?"

"It's a school night," I say.

"Friday, then. Do you think you can sneak away? Convince your mother that you're at a party or something?"

A nervous little thrill twists inside of me. "I think so."

"It's a date then."

CHAPTER 11

My whole life, through the highs and some pretty big lows, there's nothing a good movie couldn't fix. Or at least make me feel better for a while. I try to watch a new one every week, but I have my go-to picks for when I'm sad, mad, restless, depressed, bored, even happy—any mood can be improved.

Or so I thought.

I'm halfway through *The Great Gatsby*, the Robert Redford version, before I realize I've barely been watching. My eyes have been on the screen, but my thoughts are elsewhere. They're all over the place, in fact. Everywhere *except* the movie.

I press pause and sit up in bed. It's the scene where Gatsby shows Daisy the newspaper clippings of her that he's kept over the years. It sends a thought spinning above the others.

Proof.

I've already tried, unsuccessfully, to search for him online. I realized I don't even know his last name, so a Google search only turns up pages and pages about Mark Auden, the Broncos running back. And he doesn't appear to be on any social media. A fact that I find pretty weird. But then, Auden did say things wouldn't be typical.

Still, I'm determined to find some kind of clue. If I really *had* loved Auden, like he claims, surely there would be some kind of evidence in my room. Notes. Pictures. Dried roses. Teddy bears holding red satin hearts. I don't know…*something*.

Flipping on my light, I head for the overstuffed fortress of my closet. It would probably take the better part of a decade to sort through the boxes I have stuffed in there. I'm not a hoarder; I'm sentimental. At least that's what I keep telling myself.

The first box I pull out is filled with a bunch of stuff from the different plays I've been in. Programs. An outdated headshot. Old scripts, the pages filled with messages from other cast members on closing night, like a yearbook of sorts. With a smile, I flip through the script of *Our Town*, which we did last fall.

Cam drew an exaggerated caricature of me on nearly every page so that if flipped rapidly, there's a rough animation of me doing a side heel kick.

I laugh and shake my head. Scanning the other messages, however, I see little indication that I was in the throes of some great romance.

The next box is filled with old homework assignments and papers from sophomore year. Guess I can throw this one away. Or maybe it would make good kindling in case the zombie apocalypse forces us to shut ourselves in the house for a few months. I set it aside and dig for more.

After an hour of sifting through old art projects, abandoned journals from middle school, and half-finished attempts at screenplays, I fail to come across any convincing evidence I was ever in a relationship with Auden. After an hour, all I have is a knot in my stomach.

How could I not find a single shred of evidence? Surely I should have some keepsake. Mama once showed me an old stack of love letters she and Daddy wrote to each other in high school. Thinking of it now, I feel a pang of regret that we've abandoned note writing for texts and DMs. I've already looked through my phone and found nothing. That's the problem. A text is so easy to erase.

I sit back on my knees with a sigh. There's only one way to fix this situation. My tried-and-true solution for moments of spiritual darkness: eat food.

Standing in the coolness of the open fridge, I'm about to balance a can of Dr Pepper on top of my Pringles can when I hear the sound of the front door opening. My eyes dart to the hallway. Maybe I can make a run for it, before they notice me...

"You don't need another soda today, Shelby," Mama says.

I puff out a breath, eyes rolling up. "I'm not getting a soda," I lie.

I turn to greet Mama. She looks at the soda can, then at me, and her eyebrow raises.

"I have a big paper to write," I say, moving past her. "I need brain food."

"You were watching a movie, and we both know it."

Actually, right now I'm having an annoying conversation with you, I think.

"Can I go?" I ask, holding back the sarcasm that roils inside of me. Mama's chin notches up with wordless expectation. I swallow a sigh. "Can I go, *ma'am*?"

"Not yet. I need to talk to you."

"Okay. About what?" I ask, impatient.

"Let me put my stuff down and get settled first," she says, with irritation. "I've been out all day."

Grinding my teeth, I silently go to the couch beside her armchair. Those are our usual spots for her lectures. Mama takes her time, hanging up her purse and fishing out a beer from the fridge. She sits down in her chair with a sigh and twists open her beer. I have to tap my foot to keep from snapping at her.

Finally, she turns her attention to me. "I was talking to Meredith Lloyd today." She takes a slow sip of her beer.

"Okay. And?"

"And she says you're doing another school play this fall. Says you got a big part in it?"

"Oh. Yeah, I am," I'm a little surprised that she cares and sheepish that I was being such a brat. "I got the lead, actually. Juliet."

Mama's face instantly corrects my assumption. She's not pleased or proud. Her eyebrows bunch together in a scowl of disapproval.

"I don't like it, Shelby."

"What do you mean?"

"I don't like you doing all of these plays. It's a waste of time."

Heat crawls up my throat. "And what else should I be doing? Focusing on my studies? We both know you don't really care about them."

Mama shakes her head. "I don't think you should be giving all of your free time to that crowd."

"*That crowd?*"

"You know what I mean."

I stare at her. "No, actually, I don't."

"Most of those theater kids are weird," Mama says, definitively. "And I don't like you spending time around them. It makes you act differently."

My face is burning. "I don't act differently around my friends. I act like myself. You may not like it, but this is who I am."

"Oh please," Mama scoffs. "Once you're done with high school, you'll never think of acting again."

"That's not true," I say, anger bringing me to my feet. "Maybe I'm going to make it a career."

"In Hollywood?" Mama asks, with a wry, mocking smile.

"Maybe. Why not?"

"Don't be irrational, Shelbs. You wouldn't last five minutes in that hellhole. You don't belong there. That's not who you really are."

My throat clenches. "And you know who I am?"

"Of course I do. You're an Orchardview girl, born and raised. Your family's here. Your whole life is here. What more could you want?"

I stare at Mama, fighting back the burning threat of tears.

I've heard her say this all before. It's nothing new. And nothing I say will make a difference. For some reason, tonight, her words sting more than usual. It makes me weary. Just talking to her drains me.

"Are you going to let me be in the play or what?" I ask, too resigned to sound sharp.

Mama sighs deeply. "I shouldn't. It's my job as your mother to do what's best for you. Trouble is, I'm too damn soft."

I wait for her to finish her rant. I refuse to provoke her any further. *Just wait her out and get out of here.*

"I suppose I can't really stop you. You're so stubborn that you'll do it anyway." She shakes her head. "Go ahead. Waste your time if you want."

I set my jaw. "Thank you."

Mama points at me. "But this is the end of acting. It's a high school hobby, you understand?"

"I understand." Then I add, with venom, "*Ma'am.*"

⁓

Friday approaches like a rain cloud in the summer, with an electric anticipation. It's not good or bad. There's just the tingling sense that something's coming.

Gathering my books at my locker at the end of the day, my gaze darts around, looking for knowing glances. Intellectually, I understand that no one could possibly know I'm meeting Auden tonight, but I can't help feeling that people suspect anyhow.

A clank beside me startles me to the point of nearly throwing my books. Grace leans against the locker beside me with a dreamy sigh.

I can't help smiling. "Let me guess. Brad Corbin?"

She sighs again, dramatically flinging a hand to her forehead.

"You look like a lovestruck princess in a Disney movie," I say. "Next thing you know, an anthropomorphized sparrow is going to land on your finger."

"I *am* like a princess in a Disney movie. Because after tonight, I'm going to live happily ever after."

"What's happening tonight? Brad's going to kill the evil sorcerer who has held you captive in the Castle of Stone Sorrows?"

Grace giggles and then grips my arm. "He asked me out, Shelbs. On a for-real date. Just me and him. Our first date!"

My face lights up. I'm about to tell her that I'm going on a first date too, but then I catch myself.

Secret. I'm not used to keeping those from Grace. It makes me a little sad, actually, that we can't both be giddy about our dates. At least I can be giddy for her.

"About time," I say brightly. "That was probably the most drawn-out buildup to a date in the history of high school romance."

"Right?" Her dreamy smile returns. "He's going to kiss me tonight. And it's going to be amazing."

"Is that so?"

"When it's right, it's right, Shelbs. You can feel it."

I give a tight laugh at the irony of her statement given my situation. "If only it were that easy," I say, under my breath.

Grace doesn't notice. She has a distant look on her face, no doubt envisioning the amazing future kiss.

"Have fun tonight."

"Oh, I will," she says, with a sly grin. She shoulders her bag. "I better go. I only have three hours to get ready!"

I wave and watch her go. But nerves quickly bleed into my amusement. I only have three hours too. Not to primp and pick the perfect outfit, but to prepare myself for the truth. If that's even possible.

~

Driving up to our designated meeting spot, I'm suddenly not sure if I can go through with our date. I glance around the dark, empty parking lot. He told me to come to the old foot-hills trails. Maybe this is a huge mistake…

But there Auden is, walking toward my car with a nervous smile. His hair has been carefully gelled into cooperation, and he's dressed in a sleek, dark blue button-down shirt and black slacks. He looks like a waiter at a fancy restaurant. As he comes to open my car door for me, I feel the blood rush to my face.

"You look lovely," he says, holding out a hand to help me out of the car.

I manage a weak smile. His palms are clammy. For some reason, his nervousness makes this whole situation even more awkward.

"This way," Auden says. "I hope you don't mind an outdoor dinner. It's a nice night. I checked the weather."

"It's okay with me."

Auden leads out on Creekside, the shortest of the trails. Try as I might, I can't come up with a single conversation starter, so I just follow. We're quiet for two full minutes. The only sound is the gentle flowing of the creek, water running over rocks and past cattails. I press my lips together. Not sure how much more of this awkward silence I can take.

Just as I'm about to speak, a new sound glides past me on the breeze. Violin music. My brow furrows. Auden glances over his shoulder with a sheepish smile.

"Right this way."

The trail curves around a huge cottonwood tree. As we pass it, the glow of candlelight immediately comes into view. The trees form a natural circular clearing under the stars. There's a table set up on the grass, covered in a thin, shimmery white table cloth. A bouquet of lilacs, my favorite flower, blooms from a vase in the center. A second table holds two covered plates and the little portable speaker, currently playing Vivaldi. Dozens of white candles in hurricane vases surround the scene, flickering through the evening darkness. Lilac branches have been scattered everywhere, their perfume filling the air.

Auden gives me a hopeful look. "Do you like it?"

"It's...very romantic," I say. Too romantic? I knew Auden was intense, but I wasn't prepared for a spread like this.

He laughs and then motions to the table. "Would you like to sit down?"

It's an invitation, not an earnest inquiry, yet I consider for a moment. I'm not sure why my feet resist, but I sit down despite my nerves.

Auden senses my hesitation and busies himself with serving the food. Plates of lasagna and french fries, my two favorite foods. A glass of chilled Dr Pepper on ice. He sets out the meal, then sits across from me.

"I hope you like it," he says again.

"It's a really fancy first date." I touch the lilacs lightly.

"It was summer," Auden says. "Our actual first date. July seventh. You'd just gotten back from a Fourth of July lake trip with your family. You still had a little bit of a sunburn on your cheeks."

I remember that lake trip. Blake rented a boat, hoping we could water ski or that it could pull us around on a tube. But Mama doesn't like water. She stayed on the shore the entire time, sipping beer and gossiping with Aunt Nancy and Uncle Jim.

I don't remember a romantic candlelit date three days later, of course. I examine a french fry and drop it back onto my plate. My stomach churns. I don't think I could eat if I wanted to.

"How did you know I like all of this stuff? We weren't dating yet."

In the candlelight, Auden's eyes look darker than ever. Almost black.

"I knew it because I wanted to know it. I wanted to know everything about you from the first time we met."

The violin music soars along in a romantic cadenza. Auden watches me. I shift under the intensity of his gaze.

"So…on our first date, we ate and stuff?"

"We can dance if you'd like."

My brow furrows. "We danced?"

"Well, not exactly, but…"

"I don't want to dance," I say cautiously.

Auden nods. "That's fine." He looks down at his plate for a minute, and then his gaze shifts. He stands and grabs a small cardboard box from under the serving table. "I have something I want to show you."

Reaching into the box, he pulls out a little stack of pictures. Some folded sheets of paper. Old greeting cards. Some artwork—crayon stick figure drawings, from the looks of it, and a pencil sketch of a face. My face.

My throat tightens.

"You wanted proof," Auden says. "I have lots of it. I kept everything. Pictures. Gifts you gave me." He sets a hand on the folded sheets of papers. "Every valentine and love note we wrote to each other."

I reach out and slowly take the top picture from the stack. Closing night of *Our Town*. I recognize it immediately. Auden's sitting on the kitchen table set piece. He's talking to someone outside the frame of the picture, his eyes bright. I'm sitting in his lap, dressed in my costume and stage makeup, gazing at him with untempered adoration.

Everything about the picture is familiar except him. And that look on my face.

My pulse beats in my throat. I nudge the photos, fanning out the stack. Two pictures display sequential kissing selfies. We're laughing through the kiss in the first one and lost in passion in the second. The sight of it almost makes me push out of my chair.

It reminds me of that scene in *Harry Potter and the Prisoner of Azkaban* when Harry is borrowing the Time-Turner from Hermione and she warns him not to let his past self see his future self. I cover the pictures and lean back, struggling to calm myself.

"This is one of the first letters you wrote to me," Auden says, lifting one of the folded papers. "You should read it."

The smell of lilac seems to choke me. The violin music sounds loud and shrill. The sight of the lasagna makes me queasy.

"I don't want to look at all of this stuff," I say.

Auden's brow lowers with concern. "I didn't mean to upset you. I just wanted you to see I'm not making this up." He unfolds the letter. My handwriting glares back at me. "I *couldn't* make this up, Shelby."

"I know." I press a hand to my temple.

"I just wanted you to remember how much you loved me," Auden says. He points to the letter. "Look. *Auden,*" he reads. "*I'm not going to fight it anymore. I love you. You have made a mark on me. A mark that won't wash out. I don't think it ever will. I love you, and I want you to be in my life forever.*"

"Stop," I say, scooting back my chair. I feel dizzy.

"Shelby—"

"No." Words come with difficulty through the tightness in my throat. "I'm sorry, but I can't do this."

"But…"

"It's too much, okay?"

Auden shakes his head. "What do you mean, too much? This is reality. This was *your* reality before it was taken away from you."

The truth behind his words doesn't calm me.

"Well, maybe I'm not ready for reality yet." My legs shake as I stand.

Auden rises from his seat, as if he's been slapped across the face. He stares at me, probably trying to find the words to make me stay. But I just shake my head.

"I'm sorry. I can't."

He calls out my name, but I'm already running toward the darkness of the trail.

CHAPTER 12

Climbing into my car, I slam the door shut. A stab of shame passes through me. Why am I freaking out like this? Yes, it's beyond bizarre to see pictures of moments from my life that bring absolutely no recognition. But nothing has been normal in a long time. So far, the "answers" have only added more questions spinning around in my head.

Still, Auden's only trying to help. I shouldn't have left him like that...

I bite my bottom lip, my keys hovering at the ignition. I exhale and start the engine. I'm not ready to deal with all of that. I only want to escape.

Back at home, I go to my usual distractions: snacks and a classic movie. But I glance at my phone every few minutes. He hasn't called. Hasn't texted. I probably hurt him pretty bad. The thought makes my chest heavy. But I can't muster the guts to call him. Not yet. Maybe tomorrow after my brain has a night to process all of this.

Near the end of *The Godfather Part II,* right as Michael Corleone is orchestrating the deaths of Hyman Roth and Fredo, my phone lights up with a call. It's like I've put my finger in an electric socket. I sit up with a start and grab for the phone.

But it's not Auden calling. It's Grace. I stare at the phone for a moment and then answer.

"Calling me in the middle of your magical first date?" I tease.

"Where are you right now, Shelby?"

The tension in her voice is clear. I frown, turning to sit on the edge of my bed. "Are you okay?"

"Can you pick me up? Me and Brad, I mean?"

"What's wrong?"

"It's Mike. I know it."

Alarm zips through me. I grab my shoes. "Where are you? I'm leaving right now."

As I make the turn off to the lake, my thoughts race. I'm worried about Grace—and I'm trying my best not to remember that image from my last treatment. The lake is where Auden sat beside me on the hood of the car. It's even more disorienting now that my mind has a tangible impression of Auden. It knows who he is, but that moment still seems like a dream, not an actual memory.

Pulling up to the empty parking lot, my headlights illuminate Grace. She's wearing Brad's letterman jacket, hugging it to her firmly, her face pale. She stands by Brad's silver Corolla. It's up on cinder blocks, the tires removed.

I park beside them and rush to Grace. She looks stoic, but I know better. I know that tone in her voice. She trembles as I put my arms around her in a wordless hug.

"It'll be okay," I whisper, rubbing her back.

"I can't get away from him, Shelby."

"Yes, you can. You already are."

She pulls back, shaking her head. "Then what do you call that?" She points at the car.

I glance at Brad, who looks beyond pissed. He's taking pictures of his car from several different angles.

"Did you look around for the tires?" I ask.

He snaps me an irritated look. "Of course we did."

"You should call the police."

"Grace asked me to wait until you came and got her." Brad jabs his phone screen, taking another picture.

Grace watches him with a brokenhearted expression. I can't blame her. It's not exactly a great way to end a date. Or to start a relationship, for that matter.

I gently grab her arm. "Let's get out of here, okay?"

She nods and lets me guide her to my car. Neither of us speak as I pull the car into reverse. Searching for the right words, I come up blank. I knew Mike had issues, but I never imagined him to take his vindictiveness quite this far. He had to have been watching her to know she was going out with Brad. And he obviously planned this prank in advance. I doubt he had four cinder blocks sitting in his car.

"You didn't contact him, did you?" I ask, gripping the steering wheel.

"No," she says, fiercely.

"I'm not suggesting it's your fault, Grace. I'm just trying to piece together what happened."

A heavy silence falls. She doesn't need to spell it out. He must be stalking her.

"You need to file a police report," I say. "And get a restraining order against him."

She stares out the windshield. "I already have one."

"What?"

"I already have a restraining order against him."

"Since when?"

"It was a while ago. Your mama helped me get it."

I turn her, startled, almost swerving the car into the curb. I right the wheel quickly, but I'm still blinking back my surprise. "When did this all happen? How come you never told me?"

Grace sighs, rubbing her face wearily. "It doesn't matter, does it?"

"No...I'm just surprised that you wouldn't share something like that with your supposed best friend."

Her voice is quiet. "You had your own problems to deal with."

I feel like I've been hit in the stomach. Problems or not, how could I have not realized what she was going through? How could I have not been there for her?

"I'm sorry," I finally say.

"Don't apologize, okay?" Grace rests her forehead on the passenger side window.

We don't speak for the rest of the drive.

CHAPTER 13

There seems to be an unspoken agreement between Grace and me not to discuss the awfulness of the weekend. Back at school, we both do our best impressions of our former, cheerful selves. All week we chat about class and the upcoming football game and who's going to be homecoming queen. I find out from Mama, who always seems to know the latest town gossip, that the police couldn't find any fingerprints on Brad's car, therefore they couldn't file any charges against Mike. Not yet, anyway.

I keep trying to think of what to do to help Grace, but I'm useless. Maybe she'd be better off without me. I've been so absorbed in my own issues that I missed my best friend's distress.

The worst part is, my mind keeps trying to find some truth deeply embedded in the parallels of our two respective dates. Two first dates, both ending badly in empty parking lots outside of town limits, mine in the foothills and hers by the lake. Of course, I was the one who destroyed my date.

I don't want to admit how often I've checked my phone. It's

been a week. No messages. I definitely pissed off Auden. Or hurt him. Either way, the fact that he hasn't tried to contact me in five days is definitely a bad sign.

The *Romeo and Juliet* rehearsals remain a bright spot in my days. I'm determined to enjoy myself in the biggest role of my high school career. I'll have fun with Cam. If Auden had been cast as Romeo, it would've been complicated. And for once, it's nice to escape the drama in drama.

We meet three times a week for an intense eight weeks of rehearsal leading up to our performance. It's the end of week one, and Mr. Lyman always has something new and different to get us into the zone for rehearsal. Today, soft Renaissance-era music plays over the speakers. I smile as I take off my backpack.

We sit in a circle, sizing each other up as we wait for rehearsal to start. Every one of us wants to stand out, to make this more than a run-of-the-mill performance. And each of us probably secretly thinks that we will be the one to make this performance special. I'm glad of that. This way we actually stand a chance of putting on a truly great show.

"Okay," Mr. Lyman says, standing in the middle of our circle, arms folded. "Today we're blocking Act Two. I want each of you to find your spot on the stage and start getting into character. I need my Mercutio and Benvolio center stage. Romeo, stage left. The rest of you backstage, please."

There's a murmur of conversation as people shuffle to their places. I stand, dusting off my pants, and Mr. Lyman gives me a funny little smile.

"And Juliet, you're up in the balcony, of course."

He motions to the two-story balcony set piece, and I smile, dipping in a low curtsy. "As you command, my captain."

I put myself in Juliet's mind. It isn't too hard. I know this play better than any of Shakespeare's other plays, and I've seen every movie adaptation. (I favor the Baz Luhrmann version, though Zeffirelli's is a close second.)

Climbing the steps, I smell the lilac before I see it. The scent makes my skin tingle. My brow furrows. Parting the curtains and stepping out onto the small balcony, my eyes go to the fragile, purple blooms tucked beneath the railing. A pulse beats in my throat. I look toward Mr. Lyman, but he's already coaching Mercutio and Benvolio for the first scene.

I glance back down at the flowers. A piece of paper peeks out from beneath the blossoms. I scan the shadowed audience for Auden's tall outline. But he's nowhere to be seen.

Biting my lip, I grab for the note and flowers. I bring the lilac sprig to my nose and inhale the sweet, clean scent. No one's watching me up here. The note is cool and dry in my palm. My breath trembles as I unfold the page.

SHELBY,

FORGIVE ME FOR FRIDAY NIGHT. IT WAS TOO MUCH TOO FAST. THOUGH CAN YOU BLAME ME FOR FIGHTING FOR A GIRL LIKE YOU? NOW I SEE THAT I CAN'T FORCE YOUR MIND TO REMEMBER. SO I PROMISE I WON'T PUSH ANYMORE. I WON'T TRY TO MAKE YOU REMEMBER. BUT

I BEG YOU FOR ONE MORE CHANCE. A CHANCE TO SPEND THE EVENING WITH YOU.

I WON'T TRY TO CONTACT YOU AGAIN. I WILL WAIT UNTIL YOU ARE READY TO CONTACT ME, HOWEVER LONG THAT MIGHT TAKE. I WILL WAIT FOREVER IF I HAVE TO, SHELBY.

YOURS,
AUDEN

I call him as soon as practice is over. Of course I call him. How could I not after a letter like that? We agree to meet for a do-over date. I'm stuck going to my aunt and uncle's this weekend, so when Auden suggests meeting on a school night, I don't object.

This time the location is much more my speed: the local Taco Town. It's a slow Tuesday night, so the only other people eating in the restaurant are an elderly couple and a trucker who's probably just passing through.

Auden is there when I arrive, sitting tucked away at a table in the corner. When he sees me, he jumps to his feet. He looks nervous but genuinely happy. The guy has quite the smile. I'll give him that.

"I've spent all day planning the perfect hello for when I saw you," he says, sheepishly. "But that's me trying too hard again, isn't it?"

"Maybe a little," I say, playfully. I motion to the gleaming menu board hanging overhead. "Should we get something to eat?"

"Absolutely."

We approach the front counter, and a short girl with a bored grimace and a faded blue stripe in her hair resentfully takes our order.

"Welcome to Taco Town, where Delicioso is mayor."

"Well, I like the sound of that," Auden says. He turns to me. "Let's move to Taco Town. What do you say, dearest?"

He says it in the perfect corny way a 1950s sitcom husband would, and I can't help laughing. Bored, Blue-Haired Girl, however, is unamused.

Auden clears his throat. "Sorry. I'll take a number five with a side of chips and salsa, and she'll have—" He winces. "Crap. Sorry. I said I wouldn't do that anymore."

"It's okay. You don't need to pay for me either."

"Um, yes, I do."

I give him my best stern look. "Auden." But he offers only a resolute smile. Bored, Blue-Haired Girl clears her throat. She is nearing the end of her rope. And it was a pretty short rope to start with.

"Fine," I say. "I'll have a number seven, extra guacamole."

"I knew you were going to say that," Auden says, under his breath. I roll my eyes and elbow him, and we both gratefully accept the soda cups the girl hands us.

"Sorry we're so annoying, Julie," Auden says, reading her name tag. "First date."

Julie remains expressionless. Auden swallows down any more

cuteness and pulls out his credit card. As he pays, I grab the cups. "Coke? Dr Pepper?"

He pauses for a beat, then smiles. "Mountain Dew."

"Are you serious?" I shake my head. "This might be a deal breaker, Auden."

From the expression on his face, he expected that response. The thought makes me lose a little of my sass. "We've had this conversation before, haven't we?"

Auden's eyes flicker with a rush of hope. "You remember?"

"N—no. I could tell from your expression."

"Oh." He nods. "Well, yes. It's a rare point of incompatibility for us."

"I suppose we are starting fresh, so I'll try to be understanding of your strange and troubling drink preference."

"Generous of you."

I smile to myself as I fill the cups. It's kind of amazing how much more relaxed I feel. I'm actually enjoying myself. Not bad for a Tuesday night.

I take our drinks to the corner table, and Auden joins me a minute later with the tray of our food.

"I don't think Julie's a big fan of me."

"Unfathomable," I say, shaking my head with overly dramatic shock.

He laughs, and we both start unwrapping our tasty, greasy, mass-produced Mexican food. After a few moments of eating, Auden puts down his burrito and looks at me with a twinge of embarrassment.

"I have a confession to make."

"Okay…"

"This was the actual location of our first date."

My eyebrows raise. "Really?"

He sighs. "I'm afraid so. I figured I owed you an authentic re-creation."

I glance around me. Taco Town is a little different from the moonlit clearing in the foothills. We've traded Vivaldi for soft '90s hits. And the dated, neon décor and sun-faded pastel flowers on the table are a far cry from lilacs and white candles in hurricane vases.

"This works for me."

"It's cheesy and pedestrian," Auden says, rushing to apologize. "I should have taken you somewhere special."

I bite back a smile. "So you decided to make a few tweaks? Revisionist history?"

He shrugs. "It was stupid, but you'd actually agreed to see me in spite of the situation and the terms I required." He looks down at his tray. "I guess I tried a little too hard to impress you."

"A *little* too hard?"

He meets my eyes, and I can't help my laugh from escaping. Auden blinks with surprise.

"What? What's so funny?"

This only makes me laugh more. "The comparison," I say, between giggles. "I just…I can't."

A smile brightens his face, and he shrugs again, sheepishly. And then we're both laughing. Full, free laughs. I toss my head back, and a snort escapes. I cup my hand over my mouth in embarrassment, but that only makes us laugh harder.

"I'll just die now," I say, trying to catch my breath while still covering my face.

He pulls my arm away. "No. Don't stop. I love your laugh, Shelby."

The comment calms me a little. Auden lets go of my arm and sits back in his chair. His gaze is like a warm beam of sunlight. You don't have to see it to know it's touching you.

I take a bite of my food, feeling a little self-conscious.

"It's too bad we couldn't have our first date in New York," Auden says, dipping a chip into a little cup of processed nacho cheese. "If you like tacos, there's a place in Chelsea that would make you weep with joy."

"There's Mexican food in New York?"

Auden laughs. "Shelby, there's *everything* in New York. Any kind of food you can imagine. Because there are people from every country in the world there."

"Sounds like an exciting place to be."

"You have no idea." He smiles around his straw as he takes a drink. "There was a bit of culture shock moving here. I never knew a place could be as white as Orchardview."

I can't help feeling embarrassed. If the uniformity of this town bothers *me*, I can only imagine how it must look to a person of color or someone like Auden, who's been surrounded by other races and cultures his whole life.

"It's pretty bad," I agree.

"Well, it's no New York City, but this place has its charms. Some of the local girls are pretty amazing. Well, one in particular."

I smile down at my food, shaking my head.

"So," Auden says. "Tell me about practice. Do you think Cam will cut it as Romeo?"

We roll into an easy conversation about theater. I keep starting to explain people to Auden, only to realize that he knows them all well. Apparently, he spent a lot of time at drama practices and the theater group's social events. It actually makes the conversation much more fun.

We sit in the corner booth, talking about theater and plays and drama kids until long after our food is gone. Even Julie eventually gives up and returns to the back room. But neither of us wants to leave. However, right in the middle of talking about the time he and his friend ditched school to catch a show on Broadway, Auden stops talking. Midsentence. His gaze stretches out the window. He squints, and then his eyes widen.

"What is it?" I ask, turning to see what he's looking at.

The answer jumps out at me. An all-too-familiar car has parked in Taco Town's parking lot. And Blake and Mama are on their way in.

CHAPTER 14

R un!" Auden shouts, grabbing my hand. He pulls me to
my feet and starts to cut across the small dining room.

"Run where?" I say. "There's only one set of doors."

His eyes flash to the front counter, and he gets a mischievous
grin on his face. "But there's always an employee door."

"We can't just—"

"Jump!"

Like an Olympic hurdler, Auden clears the front counter, and
I have no choice but to follow. My legs aren't quite as long as
his, so my jump is more of a flail. But we both make it over the
counter without cracking our skulls. Auden scans the kitchen
area swiftly and then points with triumph.

"There!"

The door chime fills the air. Mama and Blake are in Taco Town.

"Hurry!"

Still holding my hand, Auden bounds forward—only to be
intercepted by an incredulous Julie.

"Hey!"

"My apologies," Auden says, swerving and pulling me past her. "Tell Mayor Delicioso the food was excellent!"

"Stop!" Julie says, furious.

But we're already out the door, laughing so hard we can't breathe.

We don't stop laughing until we've driven far from Taco Town. Auden's driving my car. I look over at him and shake my head.

"You are trouble," I say, hitting his arm playfully. "I've managed to go seventeen years without seeing the inside of the police station, and I plan to keep it that way."

"Oh, we're fine. No damage done. And besides, now Julie will have a fabulous story to tell her coworkers."

Thinking of the outraged look on her face almost makes me crack up again. Can't say I blame her, to be honest. But I guess Auden was right. We couldn't let Mama see us.

"Hey," I say, sitting up. "What about your car? Won't Mama recognize it in the parking lot?"

"I walked. My house is close by."

"Do you live in the Vista Valley subdivision?"

He nods. "The very same."

"New money," I scoff.

"Hardly," Auden says, with a grin. "Though I'd gladly be poor if it meant I got to spend time with my dad."

"What does he do?"

"He works in oil and gas. Some kind of management job. I don't know. We don't really talk."

I scratch at the fading leather upholstery beneath the door window. "I'm sorry."

"Ah, it's okay. We haven't really gotten along so well since he divorced my mom."

"And you couldn't live with her?"

"I wanted to. Believe me. But her job has her traveling all over, and she thought I needed stability." There's a touch of pain in his voice. He drives quietly for a moment, his eyes distant. Then he turns a little smile. "Still, it all worked out. If I hadn't moved in with my dad, I wouldn't have met you. And you're…" He hesitates.

"I'm what?"

"It's nothing."

"Tell me then."

He draws in a breath. "You're the best thing to ever happen to me, Shelby."

A warmth prickles over my skin, settling deep inside me. On one hand, I don't know how to react. He seems to feel so strongly for me, and I barely know him. But how can I not melt a little when he talks like that? It's as if he's a character out of one of my favorite romantic movies. Dropped right here. In boring, boxed-in Orchardview. And he happens to be in love with me.

"So," I say, avoiding his gaze and still picking at the chipping faux leather. "How did our first date end? I imagine we didn't escape through the back room of the Taco Town and drive away like Bonnie and Clyde."

Auden laughs. "Nope. Not quite. Though I think this is an improvement."

"More revisionist history?"

He grins and then tilts his head a little. "Actually, we ended with a doorstep scene. A pretty good one, if I recall."

"No way did I kiss you," I say, folding my arms. "You're making that up."

"I didn't say we kissed."

"Well, what happened then?"

He turns on his blinker and makes a swift U-Turn. "Shall I walk you through it? For memory-recovery purposes, of course."

"Oh, of course."

Auden pulls up to my house and parks the car. "I think we're safe since we know your parents aren't home."

I raise an eyebrow. "What exactly did this doorstep scene entail?"

I've started to open my door, but Auden touches my arm. "Wait here, please."

I comply, and he circles around to open my door for me.

"What a gentleman," I say. "Are you sure we didn't kiss?"

Auden laughs. "Alas, no. It was all very chaste and polite. I opened the door for you and held out my hand like this."

He helps me out of the car, not unlike the prince does in *Cinderella*. This guy is climbing the charts by the second. When I'm out, he takes my arm and tucks it in his.

"Okay, so then what happened?"

"We walked up to your doorstep. I think you were telling me that you could already sense signs of Taco Town revenge."

"Glad to hear I kept it classy," I say, rolling my eyes.

"It was charming. *You* were charming."

We arrive at my doorstep. Turning to face him, physically close for the first time tonight, a little flutter passes through my heart. He's uncomfortably good looking, with his brooding eyes and careless dark hair. I almost can't believe we dated for that reason alone. He's definitely out of my league.

"Pleasant and witty banter ensued at the front door," Auden says.

"Let me guess. I told you I had a lot of fun."

"Naturally. And I said the same. I brought up a movie that was coming out the following week in a thinly veiled attempt to procure a second date with you."

"Did I take the bait?"

"You did. And I gave myself a mental high five."

"And then what happened?"

"Well," Auden grimaces. "I'm afraid to tell you what I said next."

"No revisionist history. You promised."

He sighs. "Okay. I said, 'I'm passing out free hugs. Want one?'"

I burst out laughing. "No. You didn't."

"I did," he says, hanging his head in shame.

"Please tell me I laughed in your face."

There's a glint in his eye. "Sorry, doll, but you were all over it."

I shake my head. "I must have been having a *really* good time."

"We both were."

A charged silence falls between us. Suddenly, I find myself unable to meet Auden's eyes. And yet…I want him to keep talking.

"So, we hugged," I say, in a small voice.

"Yes."

Another pause. I finally look up at him. The way he watches me sends goose bumps over my skin. He starts to put out his arms but hesitates, fists curled. And then, slowly and gently, as if he were embracing delicate crystal, he draws me into his arms.

He's warm. And so tall. His hug envelops me completely. Every inch of my body tingles with pleasure at the exquisite sensation of being held in Auden's arms. I sink against his chest and breathe in the cool, clean scent of his cologne.

A flicker of thought shoots through my mind, like a shooting star. Not so much a thought, but a feeling. A familiarity.

Familiarity. *Almost as if I remember…*

My eyes snap open. I draw in another breath of the cologne. The sensation is there again, though faded. I press my face to his shoulder and inhale. Fast as it had come, the memory is gone.

Auden releases his grip and looks down at me. "Are you smelling my armpits? I don't stink, do I?"

I laugh, embarrassed. "Not at all. You smell great. Actually…" For some reason, I don't tell him. I'm not sure if it really was a flicker of memory or just a random feeling of déjà vu. No need to tamper with an otherwise lovely moment.

"You're wearing my favorite cologne," I say. "That's Acqua Di Gio, right?"

Auden turns his face to the sky with a mixture of amusement and frustration.

"What?" And then I close my eyes. "I bought it for you, didn't I?"

He nods. His smile shifts to an expression of longing, wistfulness. For a long, shimmering moment, Auden and I just gaze at each other.

Auden is the first to look away. "Thank you for giving me another chance."

"I'm glad I did."

"Can I see you again? Sometime soon?"

I tuck my hair behind my ear, glancing out at my dark, empty street. "I'm not sure how often I can get away on school nights. You know how Mama is."

"I understand."

"But yes," I say, putting my hand on his arm. "I want to see you again."

His eyes shine. "Call me. Any hour, day or night."

The impulse to kiss his cheek runs through me, which startles me a little. I don't follow through, but the vision of doing so quickens my heartbeat. I bite back a smile.

"Good night, Auden."

He takes my hand. My breath catches as he slowly brings it to his lips and presses a soft kiss to my skin. "Good night, Shelby."

I watch him walk away. Halfway down the front walk, he looks over his shoulder at me. Even in the dark cover of night, I can see his smile. I wave a little and go into my house. Closing the front door, I lean my back against it. I bring my hand, the one he kissed, to my chest and close my other hand over it. Fireflies dance inside of me, shimmering, bright and hot. Closing my eyes, I savor this delicious feeling.

CHAPTER 15

The problem with having the same best friend since third grade is that you know each other too well. Of course, that's only a problem when you're trying to keep a huge, heart-fluttery secret. Which happens to be exactly what I'm faced with.

I've seen Auden again this week and made plans for another time. I can't help it. I tell myself that I'm still trying to figure out if his claims of our relationship are true, but when we're together, I hardly think about it. I just like being with him.

On Wednesday afternoon, Auden picked me up after *Romeo and Juliet* rehearsals, and we went for a drive up the canyon. In the cooler high elevations, the fall colors were in full bloom. Driving past the kaleidoscope of burning reds, oranges, and bright yellows, the conversation flowed effortlessly. Each new detail I learn about him makes him stand out more and more from the Orchardview crowd. And that makes it more and more convincing that he's the kind of guy Mama would want me to have *nothing* to do with.

Grace, however, is a different story. Parked in the drive-thru restaurant Friday night, waiting for our fries and milkshakes, I pretend to listen to her story about the latest drama on the pom squad, but I'm analyzing her instead. She's the one person holding me back from fully embracing Auden's claim. We've been best friends for basically our entire lives. How could she keep a secret like this from me?

"Hello? Are you even listening?"

I blink. "What? I mean, yes. Of course I am."

Grace rolls her eyes. "Lost in Shelbyville again."

"I'm sorry," I say, shaking my head. "I'll listen now."

"You've been distracted all week."

"It's the play. Trying to memorize my lines." The lie falls easily enough from my lips, but not without a pang of guilt.

Thankfully, the worker arrives at my car window with our food. We pay her and separate our various late night snacks. A grasshopper shake with spicy fries for me and a strawberry shake with onion rings for Grace. Same order since we were thirteen.

I watch Grace joyfully crunch into an onion ring, and I'm filled with affection for her. I want to share everything with her.

This isn't the first time I've had the urge to ask her outright about Auden. Something always holds me back though. A pulling on the base on my gut. It's the same feeling that kept me from telling Dr. Stevens what happened during that last therapy session. I need to keep Auden to myself, at least for now.

Nothing's stopping me from fishing for clues though...

"So," I say, dipping a french fry into my shake. "Mama thinks I should maybe do one last therapy session in Denver in a few weeks. I'm doing much better though. I'm not sure why she's so determined."

Grace pauses for a split second; then she takes another bite of her onion ring and shrugs, trying to appear casual.

I set down my shake. "It seems weird, doesn't it? After an entire summer in therapy. I mean, I know the panic attacks were bad, but…I've almost done as much therapy as Blake did. And he was in a war."

"So?"

"So, I'm starting to wonder if there isn't more to the story."

Grace drops her half-eaten onion ring back in the paper carton. She has yet to meet my eyes. "You're overthinking this."

I lean forward, forcing her to look at me. "Am I?"

There's a flicker of panic behind her expression, though she's trying her best to hide it. "It was a bad accident, Shelby."

"I know. But my memory therapy has lasted twice as long as the physical therapy. Why?"

Grace releases a sharp, incredulous laugh. "You're so casual about it. Are you forgetting what a wreck you were? I've never seen you so bad. I mean, you barely had time to recover physically before the trial—" Her eyes flash, and she clamps her mouth shut.

I turn to her sharply. "Trial?"

Grace presses a hand to her temple. "I…" She swears under her breath.

A needle of ice cuts through my stomach. "What do you mean trial, Grace? Tell me."

She shakes her head. "It wasn't a big deal. It was about the accident. Insurance stuff… I don't even really know. But it was super stressful for you, okay? They probably erased that memory too."

The words seem difficult for her to say. I frown, straining to remember anything about a trial.

"Forget I even said it, okay? After all the therapy you've been through, your mama would be royally pissed if she found out I was bringing up old stuff."

I stare at Grace, hoping for more of an explanation. But she's closed up completely. I won't get another scrap of information. We sit in silence, our milkshakes melting.

"Let's go," Grace finally says.

I wordlessly start the car. Her expression brightens. "Want to binge-watch season three of *Celebrity Date Wars?*"

This makes me smile in spite of myself. "Do you even need to ask?"

~

Auden told me that our next date would re-create a "very important first." To say I'm jittery as I get ready would be an understatement. My stomach won't unknot, and my mind flies to a million places at once.

Standing in my bathroom, I give my reflection a stern look

in the mirror. *You aren't going to kiss him. It doesn't matter if you used to be boyfriend and girlfriend. He hasn't earned kissing yet.*

I grab my dark red lipstick and apply it. Cam said once that guys don't like kissing girls with lipstick on because they don't want to get any on them. Maybe Auden will get the message? I still don't know what I need to know about him. Not even close, and I can't let myself get carried away.

We've arranged to meet in the school parking lot again. It's a Saturday night, and Auden's worried that most other places will be too crowded. Too many chances that we'll be seen together.

Pulling into the lot, I draw in a slow breath and park next to him. Auden jumps out to open my car door for me and escort me to the passenger side of his.

"You look great," he says, with a confident smile. He's not nervous around me anymore. Maybe I should be worried about that.

"Thanks."

"I like your lipstick. I guess you're hoping I won't try to kiss you."

My gaze snaps to his, but he's smiling. I raise my chin defiantly. "That's right. So don't try anything."

Auden closes the passenger door with a chuckle and comes around to the driver's side. "Don't worry," he says, starting his car. "I'm saving the re-creation of our first kiss for a special occasion."

Butterflies in my stomach. I could smack him for the effect he has on me.

We drive in the direction of town and then veer off into one of the newer, nicer housing developments called Vista Valley.

"Are you taking me to your house?" I ask, my guard coming up fast.

Auden gives me a sidelong smile. "Not exactly."

He pulls into a cul-de-sac, up to a pretty two-story house. I search my memory, but there isn't the slightest flicker of recognition.

"This is your house," I say accusingly, folding my arms. "And from the looks of the dark windows, your dad's not home."

"Yes, but we're not going inside. I promise not to try and lure you into my bedroom...yet."

I roll my eyes.

He gets the door for me again, but after helping me out, he doesn't let go of my hand right away. Dual urges prick at me. One says pull away, but the other keeps my hand in his warm grip.

He leads me to the side of the house, through the tall, white vinyl fence, and into the backyard.

The landscape is more simple than I imagined. No elaborate flower beds or faux Tuscan decor or whatever I assumed rich people put in their yards. Just grass and an empty wooden deck. I suppose a single father and teenage son wouldn't spend much time out here sipping iced tea in patio chairs or grilling up steaks.

That said, Auden has done the best he can for tonight. A love seat sits in the middle of the grass. It faces a large white screen, which hangs on the fence. A projector sits on a bar stool on the other end of the yard, humming softly in the darkness.

"We're watching a movie?" I ask.

"Yes," he says, escorting me to the love seat. "The very first movie we watched together. We watched it right here. Just like this."

I sink into the comfy, worn couch. A large blue quilt is folded beside me.

"It was summer when this originally took place," Auden explains. "I've made a few minor but necessary adjustments."

"There's only one blanket." I say, raising an eyebrow. He's broadcasting his hopes to snuggle pretty clearly.

"Well, better get this started," he says ignoring my question and cheerfully busying himself with the projector.

I smirk as I toss the quilt open over my lap.

Blue light illuminates the screen. The projector whirrs to a start, and the backyard goes dark. And then a black-and-white Warner Brothers logo flashes, heralded with old-school trumpets. My brow furrows with surprise as the image of an old map of Africa appears, along with the names Humphrey Bogart and Ingrid Bergman.

"*Casablanca?*" I ask as Auden comes over.

He's nods, beaming. My heart squeezes a little. I keep forgetting that he knows me. *Better than anyone.*

But I don't want him getting too confident about how much he's hitting it out of the park. Trying not to let him see my smile, I pull aside a corner of the blanket, opening a space next to me. Auden sinks to my side. The warmth of his body beside me sends a wave of heat over my skin.

"I think this is revisionist history," I say as the opening credits roll.

"What do you mean?"

"The first movie we watched together happens to be the most romantic movie ever made?"

He gives me a sly look. "I knew what I was doing then, and I know what I'm doing now."

I nudge him with my shoulder. "You know, your cockiness is going to get on my nerves one of these days."

"Yes. Yes, it will."

We both laugh as the music shifts and the movie begins.

Casablanca isn't only one of the most romantic movies ever made, it's also one of the best movies ever made. When I was twelve, my love of movies started to shift into a passion for film. Mama had started dating again after her marriage with Stepdad Part One fell apart, and she seemed to be gone all the time. I turned to the company of good movies. I knew that if I wanted to be an actress, I'd need to study the greats, so I decided to watch all one hundred movies on the American Film Institute's "100 Years…100 Movies" list.

I admit I didn't quite swoon with admiration over *Citizen Kane* like I was supposed to, but then I got to number two on the list: *Casablanca*. Watching the movie then, during that tumultuous time in my life, something changed inside of me. As Ilsa tearfully tells Rick how much she still loves him, a crack opened in my heart that I knew could only be filled with a love as true as that.

That scene, which I know so well now, plays again, and my heart beats furiously in my chest. So much so that I'm worried Auden will somehow feel it. The crack in my heart is still there. Or is it?

I must be squirming nervously because Auden glances over. I force a weak smile and turn back to the movie. I can't meet his intense eyes right now. Not feeling as vulnerable as I do. Instead, I lean back into couch and try to still my pounding heart.

On the screen, Ilsa and Rick fall into the kiss they've been waiting so long for, and I momentarily forget to breathe.

At that moment, a hand closes around mine beneath the blanket, lacing our fingers together. I look up at Auden. His eyes aren't intense but warm and filled with love.

Breathing doesn't get any easier.

Our eyes stay locked for a long moment. I finally turn back to the screen, but I can feel his gaze linger on me, and we keep our fingers interlocked for the rest of the film. We don't break the grip until the closing, when Auden wordlessly pulls a pack of tissues from his pants pocket and hands me one. I laugh a little but take it.

"I'm guessing you've seen me cry at a lot of movies," I say, dabbing my eyes.

"I have."

I sniff. "Grace thinks it's weird."

"Well, I think it's sweet."

"You're probably the only one."

He scoffs lightly at the comment and shakes his head. "Maybe here in Orchardview. Outside of this one-stoplight town, there are plenty of people who watch movies for art, not explosions."

His words make my pulse jump again. "You're a film buff too?" I ask, tracing a circle on the quilt over our laps.

"Much more than that, Shelby." He sits up. "Can I show you something inside? I promise that is *not* a terrible pickup line."

I can't help but smile. "All right."

I follow him into the dark house. "Sorry about the mess," Auden says.

It's cluttered inside but mostly ordinary. A pair of jeans hang on the stair railing. Soda cans sit in the sink. An empty pizza box is perched on the coffee table in front of the couch. This is definitely a man cave. Auden kicks aside a pair of sneakers, and we head up the stairs. He pauses at his door.

"I was going to wait to show you my room. A. Because it's not the cleanest right now, and B. Because I think it might trigger some memories if I present it right. We spent…a lot of time in here."

My face burns with blood. "Oh."

"Not like that…necessarily." Even in the dim hallway, I can see Auden blushing too. "I just mean that we hung out here a lot."

"Well, there's no need for formality and grand setups, remember? It's fine how it is."

He nods. "You're right. Of course you're right." He opens his door, and my breath catches at what I see.

If I didn't know better, I would think that I'd decorated this room myself. Movie posters hang on the walls. There's a large TV and a bookcase filled with DVDs. There's even a mock Oscar statue by the laptop on his desk. I step in and circle, taking in every detail.

"This looks like a messier, boy version of my room."

Auden folds his arms, amused. "That's almost exactly what you said the first time you saw it."

I sink onto his unmade bed. "Either you and I have an awful lot in common, or you are pulling off an CIA-level scheme to make me think so."

"Trust me, if this were all an elaborate ruse, I'd have made sure my room was clean." With his foot, he scoots a plate with dried-on food under the bed.

"What is it you wanted to show me?" I ask, still taking in the posters on his walls. He's got some great ones. *Star Wars*, of course. *Inception. Amadeus. Gladiator.*

He goes to a waist-high cabinet beside his bed. Brushing a crumpled T-shirt off the top, he opens the doors to reveal a stash of digital tapes, two external hard drives, and the most beautiful camera I've ever seen. The camera makes the one I use as school historian look like a toy bought with five hundred tickets at Chuck E. Cheese's.

Auden takes the camera of the cabinet with the care of an OB delivering a newborn. He brings it over and sits beside me on the bed.

"It's a Canon C300," he says with pride.

"That thing probably cost a fortune," I whisper.

Auden shrugs. "One of the few perks of living with my dad."

"That's quite a perk." I dare to brush my finger along the sleek, black body of the camera. "So, you want to be a filmmaker, then?"

"*Going* to be," he corrects. "The minute I graduate, I'm headed to film school. Either back to Manhattan at NYU or California for USC." He pauses. "It depends."

"Depends on what?"

His focus is on his camera, but I can read his silence. My throat constricts. "It depends on me?"

Auden sighs. "We don't have to talk about this. It's too soon. I don't want you to feel weird."

"Did we…talk about going to Hollywood together?"

His voice is soft. "All the time."

A weight presses against my lungs. "And I was going to do it? I was really going to leave Orchardview?"

"You were close," Auden admitted. "It's never been an easy decision for you to think about."

Words fail me. All I can do is stare at Auden's camera. All I can think about is Mama's disapproving frown. Puzzle pieces click together in my mind. The truth feels very close to the surface.

"Let's change the subject," Auden says.

I want to know more about our Hollywood plans. I need to know more. But I don't fight his suggestion.

He stands abruptly. "Come on. Let's get out of here. We'll go for a drive or something. Unless you want to go home…"

Telling myself to live in the moment, I tap my chin, con-spiratorially. "The night is rather young."

"Exactly! As are we. I say we seize the day. Carpe diem!"

Back in his car, I pull on my seat belt with a smirk. "So, what are your grand plans for seizing what remains of this day? Because I was thinking something along the lines of a drive to the gas station to buy some snacks and a Dr Pepper."

"I like the way you think, Ms. Decatur. I really do."

We drive to the Go Station because it's closer, though I would argue that the 7-Eleven has a superior syrup-to-water ratio in their fountain drinks and therefore a tastier Dr Pepper. But we all have to make sacrifices sometimes.

After getting our drinks and various treats, Auden remembers that he is almost completely out of gas. I lean against his car, watching him fill the tank under the harsh white flood lights.

A broad white Buick pulls up next to us. Recognition glimmers in me, and I lift on my toes to see. Sure enough, it's Karen, my old boss from the movie theater.

"Hey," I call out, waving.

Karen's resting scowl warms to a smile as she gets out of the car. "Well, well, well. This is an interesting sight."

Auden, who's been tending to the gas pump, startles. I notice his cheeks color as he gives a somewhat forced grin. "Hi there, K."

She eyes our drinks and nachos. "Looks like a party night."

"Something like that," Auden says with a laugh that's undeniably tinged with nervousness.

I'm a little surprised at his reaction, and then it occurs to me. "Did you call in sick on a busy Saturday night so you could take me out on a date?"

I expect Karen to exchange a knowing smile of exasperation with me, but her brow furrows.

"Auden doesn't work at the theater anymore."

I blink, and Auden offers another tight chuckle. "Yeah, not anymore."

Kay folds her arms. "Not since last fall, when…well, when everything went crazy."

The color drains from Auden's face, but he forces another laugh, so false it makes me cringe.

"All full," he says, returning the gas nozzle to the pump. A quick glance to the meter shows that he's only put in about five gallons. "Nice to see you, K."

"Nice to see you too. Don't get too wild," she says, with a wink.

"Hey, no promises," he replies, again his cheerful tone ringing false. He gets into his car quickly, and I follow.

"Good call on the nachos," he says, as we pull away. "Pretty sure I read an article once that said nachos are the only true superfood."

"Is that so?"

Auden is clearly trying to refocus our conversation, so I don't push for him to explain what Karen meant. But the exchange settles in the corner of my mind. Maybe it doesn't mean anything. But it's another reminder that there are still pieces of my story that I don't have.

CHAPTER 16

Mama has always called herself a "good Christian woman." Whatever that means. For her, it doesn't seem to include going to church on Sundays. So when she strolls into the kitchen in her old floral skirt, I assume she has simply been taken by the urge to dress a little fancier than normal.

"You'll have to fend for yourself until dinner," she says, sitting down in her chair to adjust her heels. "Blake and I are heading to Sunday services."

I'm loading the breakfast dishes into the washer. "Church?"

"Of course." Mama sniffs at my surprise.

I stack some cups on the top shelf of the washer, my mind spinning. They'll be gone until dinner. That means I have all afternoon to myself. My heart skips a little. My phone burns in my pocket, practically screaming to text Auden and let him know. I have to tell him before he makes any plans. My fingers itch, but I don't dare do it until Mama's safely gone.

Blake comes out of their bedroom, holding the ends of his

tie, which is draped around his shoulders. "LouAnn, would you help me with this?"

"I'm fixing my shoes."

"Here," I say, wiping my hands on my jeans. "I've got it."

"Thanks, dear," Blake says with a warm smile. As I loop his tie in a classic knot, I can feel his admiration.

"You ought to come with us to church," he says.

"I'd love to," I lie. "But I've got a huge paper to write."

Mama's expression shows a mix of disapproval and irritation. "You sure have a lot of homework lately. Maybe all that time at play practice is getting in the way of your studies."

Rather than comment, I move back to the sink to finish the dishes. The last thing I need right now is a huge fight. Nothing can compromise this windfall of a free afternoon.

I dip my hands into the warm water and grab another plate. Mama finally fixes the buckle on her shoe. She stands, smooths her skirt, and orders Blake to help her find her keys. She's always losing those things. Sooner rather than later, she's going to need to wear them on a chain around her neck.

Blake reaches a hand into Mama's purse, which she's carrying on one shoulder, and pulls out the keys. They both laugh. I can't help but smile. Seeing the easy affection between them brings a mixture of longing for a love of my own and a tingling sense of hope that it is closer than ever before.

"We're off then," Mama says, pulling me in for a quick, one arm hug. "See that you get your chores done before you start on that homework."

"Yes, ma'am."

I watch them leave, hand in hand. Mama and I may have our differences, but she's not a bad person. That's why I struggle to reconcile that knowledge with Auden's claim.

How could Mama erase not just events, but *people*, from my memory without my permission? And why? Because she sensed her control over me slipping? Because she didn't want me to make my life different from hers? It seems unbelievable. Unreal. Like something a villain would do in a movie.

As angry as I could and should feel about it, another thought always needles in the back of my mind: maybe there's more to the story.

I shake away the questions and grab my phone.

Hey, I text. What do you have going on this afternoon? Mama's going to be gone until dinnertime.

He responds almost immediately. Seriously? Best news ever! I was planning to go on a hike. Care to join me?

That sounds great.

I do a giddy little spin-squeal combination, grateful for texting because he can't see how ridiculous I look right now.

We drive back to the foothills under a sparkling sun and clear, blue skies. Auden claims to know a secret trail to an abandoned gold mine. It sounds like a concocted excuse to get a girl alone in the mountains if ever I heard one, but it's fine, seeing as I'm mainly in this for the flirting, not the sights.

It's unseasonably warm today, and the trees have just started to melt into reds and oranges. The air smells of rich, wet soil and pine. We walk side by side along the shady trail, talking about movies and acting and Hollywood. Occasionally our arms touch as we walk the uneven terrain. When there's a rock or felled tree in our path, Auden takes my hand to help me over. He does it without even thinking.

Being together feels completely natural, and I'm filled with a sense of well-being. Of belonging. I keep stealing glances at Auden as we walk. He's wearing a red baseball shirt and khaki pants. More casual than I've seen him dressed, but even still he looks like the cover boy of *Hot Artistic Guys* magazine.

As he helps me down a particularly steep dip in the trail, his hand rests on the small of my back. When I come to even ground, we're face-to-face. And close. We don't move.

"Can I say something that's probably too much?"

My pulse quickens. "Sure. I think."

"Spending time with you like this makes me happier than I've been in a long time."

My heart blossoms. "I'm happy too. I like being with you, Auden. It feels…right."

"Because it is right."

Being up on that hillside with Auden passes like a dream. We talk for hours, sitting side by side, with the wind in our hair and the valley stretching out before us. Life, truth, beauty, love—it's so easy to move past mundane conversation with him. I'm still tingling from it all. Somehow I feel closer to him now than I have with any other person.

The sun hangs low in the sky by the time we get back to

Auden's car. The thick golden light sharpens every color and splashes orange and red on the clouds. I text Mama that I'm at Grace's and will be until later. I put my phone away before her reply comes. It doesn't really matter what she thinks. I'm going to spend more time with Auden. As much time as I can.

"Okay," he says. "Where to next?"

I stretch my arms and sink into my seat. "I don't even care. Just drive until we run out of gas. Until we get to California. We'll swim in the ocean as the sun rises."

My words seem to both delight and touch Auden's heart. He says nothing, only smiles and drives.

"Of course, we could always just get some food," I say. "That'd be a little less complicated."

He laughs. "That's the Shelby I know."

"Hey," I pout, folding my arms. "I can be spontaneous and dramatic. But I happen to enjoy food as well."

"Food is a beautiful thing, and your commitment to it is admirable."

I grimace. "It won't be so admirable when it makes me fat."

Auden shakes his head. "Oh *please*. Like you have anything to worry about. Don't be that girl, Shelby."

"I'm not *that girl*," I say, defensively. "Though, I'll have you know that the teenage years are a treacherous time for self-confidence. Or so my health teacher says."

He sighs. "If only you could see yourself how I see you."

I scoff, and he says, "I mean it, Shelby. You are beautiful." I start to refuse the compliment, but he continues with determination. "Radiantly, elegantly beautiful. And I'm not just saying that because I'm in love with you."

He says the phrase so casually, but the words fall over me like sparks. In every movie, there's that moment when the main characters dramatically confess their love to each other. I've always watched these scenes with an ache of longing in my chest, wondering what it would feel like. And here I am, in my own moment. And it feels like I'm flying. I stare down into my lap, a smile pulling at my lips.

Auden stiffens, seeming to realize what he's said. But he doesn't make light of it or backtrack. His turns to look at me, and I meet his gaze. I feel exposed and safe and desired all at once. He doesn't need to dramatically confess his love. Those eyes say everything.

Red flickers in my peripheral vision. My brain processes this from a deep, hidden place. Brake lights.

Brake lights.

I whip my head to face forward. The back of a Chevy pickup flies toward us. I grip Auden's arm.

"Look out!"

All at once, I'm flung forward. The seat belt tightens sharply across my shoulder and my arms fly up to cover my face.

But instead of an explosion of glass shards and the bone-chilling crunch of car meeting car, we jolt to a stop, and I slam back against my seat.

I'm numb. In shock. Not even breathing. Auden's nervous laugh pulls me into focus.

We haven't hit the truck. Not even close. I press my hand over my racing heart and breathe in sharply.

"Are you okay?" Auden asks.

No words can escape the iron clamp around my throat. I nod, and his brow furrows deeply.

"What…" Comprehension settles over his face. "Oh Shelby. I'm so sorry."

He hastily pulls the car to the side of the road. "I'm so, so sorry," he says again.

I still can't speak, but my breath no longer feels like it's coming through a narrow straw. Auden watches me, his face ashen. If he can recite my regular gas station snack order, he definitely recognizes what my panic attacks look like.

"I'll be okay," I say in a gasp. "It just…took me to a bad place for a second."

"I'm so sorry."

"It's okay, Auden."

"It's *not* okay." He grips the steering wheel and stares through the windshield, looking like he's killed me rather than scared me. For a long moment, the only sound is the tick of his hazards.

I focus on breathing, slow, deliberate pulls of air. I calm my mind, and soon enough, my pulse follows. *We're fine. I'm fine. I'm safe.*

I put a hand on Auden's arm. "Nothing happened. I just freaked out a little."

"I know, but…I didn't mean to…I would never—"

"I know you'd never hurt me," I say, softly. "Stop beating yourself up. I'm fine, okay? I'm not some delicate, broken person."

He pinches the bridge of his nose hard.

"I know that. It's just..." He sighs, frustrated. "I'm trying so hard to do everything right. I can't afford any mistakes."

"What are you talking about?"

His gaze is distant, stormy. "I want you to remember me, Shelby. More than anything. But at the same time, I would *never* want your bad memories to come back. Maybe it's too dangerous to try and draw out one and not the other."

"It's worth the risk," I say, softly.

He shakes his head. "I'm not so sure. Maybe I should let it be. Maybe I should back off."

"Are you kidding me? If spending time with you today was even part of what we were like together, then I want our relationship back." I press my hand hard over his. "I want to remember you. I want to remember *us*."

He takes my hand and presses it over his heart. His eyes close, and he sighs as if my words are sweet relief. He releases my hand and turns sideways in his seat to face me. I do the same.

"Okay," he says, finally. "So what do we do now?"

He means in general, but my mind has gone other places. It's traveling along the angular lines of his face and through the dark softness of his hair.

"I can think of a few ideas," I say, and I bite my lip.

His eyebrows raise, but then he turns away with a frustrated sigh. "I've been so good, Shelby."

"What do you mean?"

"I've been so good at resisting the urge to kiss you. It's not easy, you know. But I keep having to remind myself that we aren't that couple anymore. Not to you, anyway. To you, we're just two people getting to know each other."

I lean the side of my head on the seat. "I'd say we've moved beyond that stage, haven't we? I think we're easily at the 'waiting for the first kiss' stage."

His gaze slides to on my lips, then my eyes, and back to my lips. "Is that so?"

I nod.

"I've never wanted to kiss you more than I do right now."

"If you did, I'd gladly let it happen," I say quietly.

He exhales. "You're not going to make it easy for me, are you?"

"Actually, I'm trying to make it *very* easy."

He slowly cups my face. His touch sends a current of fire all the way to my toes. He draws closer. My eyes slide shut, and I tremble with anticipation.

His forehead presses to mine. "I have to wait."

"Why?"

He sits back. His breath shakes as he exhales. "A kiss is powerful. We should save it."

The sharpness of rejection makes me sit back a little. "What do you mean?"

"I keep thinking that these re-creations are going to work, but they don't seem to bringing any of your memories back."

"But I'm getting to know you. Doesn't that count?"

He jumps to clarify. "Of course it is! Shelby…these moments with you are everything to me. You have no idea. I waited months just to see your face. Spending time with you is beyond amazing. What I mean is, maybe re-creating our dates isn't enough. Maybe we need something more powerful in order to draw those memories back."

"Powerful like a kiss?"

He nods slowly. Warmth blooms in my cheeks.

My heartbeat quickens, but I'm suddenly more sure of this than anything I've ever felt. "Then kiss me, Auden."

CHAPTER 17

Auden gives a nervous little laugh. "The time of day is actually very close to when we had our first kiss."

"Were we in this car?"

"Not for the first one." A sly grin tugs at his lips. "Though we did spend many an hour making out in this car."

"One step at a time, champ."

He presses his lips together in thought, then starts his car. "You're right. I'll take you to where it happened."

He doesn't head into town. Instead, he stays on the outskirts. And when we turn off on Jackson Road, it's as if the world around me blurs.

The lake.

All at once, I see it. The glitch during my last therapy session. It's twilight. The buzz of insects and swampy smell of water and reeds fill the air. The warm evening wind. The purple sky. The boy beside me on the hood of the car. He reaches for my face, brushes a strand of hair from my lip. His dark, deep eyes are filled with intensity.

I gasp.

The anomaly. Was it the flicker of a memory? A memory of our first kiss?

The sun has set, taking with it the fires on the clouds, leaving only cool purples and blues in its wake. The surface of the water is like a silver coin. Auden pulls up as close to the water as he can. After parking, he turns to me, and his expression immediately bends with concern.

"Shelby?"

"Where were we when we kissed? Were we…were we sitting on the hood of the car?"

Without waiting for him to collect his thoughts, I get out of the car and stand in front of it. The hood is warm beneath my touch. Auden scrambles to join me.

"Do you remember it?"

"I—I don't know. I…"

He gestures that I should climb onto the hood. My feet are iron weights, but I slide up onto the warm metal. Auden takes a tentative place beside me.

I scan the scene around me. "It was a summer night. It was warmer. Perfect."

Auden's voice is a hoarse whisper. "Yes."

Everything about this moment mirrors that flash I saw during the last treatment. Goose bumps tingle on my arms. I turn to

Auden. The same intense stare. Same dark curls, rustled gently by the wind.

"You tucked my hair behind my ear," I say, barely able to form the words.

He does so slowly. Exactly like that moment.

My mouth has gone dry. "And then…"

"And then," he whispers.

And then, his lips are on mine.

Soft and warm, this single, sweet kiss stirs something unexpected in me. A memory.

I remember.

I can finally see that moment clearly. I remember how I felt. How his lips tasted. How my heart raced. I remember the smell of the lake, the warmth of the night, and the sound of distant birds singing across the trees to each other.

I remember.

Auden breaks from our kiss with his eyes closed. He exhales, shakily, and then looks at me. The shock must be written all over my face. Auden's eyes widen. "Do you…?"

I can only nod. Tears prick my eyes.

"You really remember? Are you sure?"

"Yes." Emotion chokes my throat, though I feel like I'm soaring from the sudden happiness. "I remember just a few seconds, but it's there."

Auden cradles my face in his hands. "You remember."

"I remember."

"Maybe I should kiss you one more time to make sure."

"I think that's a good idea. Just to be safe."

He pulls me into another kiss, this one longer and more passionate. His hand hooks around the back of my neck. I melt into the intensity of it.

After a moment, we both sit back, breathing a little harder. "Wow. That was a great second first kiss."

I'm dizzy, though I can't tell if it's from the kiss or the revelation. "Actually, I think I might be in shock."

The pieces click together fast and hard. "It's true." I whisper, "Everything you've said. We really did date. And…that means Mama really did let them erase you from my memory."

Like a slow-moving fire, anger overcomes the pleasure of our kiss and the thrill of remembering.

"How could she?"

Auden shakes his head, his brow furrowed.

"And why would she?" I demand.

"You know why, Shelby. I threatened her control over you. You were going to step away from the future she planned for you, and that terrified and infuriated her."

I press a hand to my temple. "But to take such a step all to take you out of my life? I can't believe it."

"It doesn't matter," Auden says, setting his hands on my shoulders. "We'll get it all back. If this worked once, it will work again. We'll get back all the memories they've taken from you."

Had he spoken the words even an hour ago, I wouldn't have believed him. But now I feel hope like I never have before.

CHAPTER 18

I move through the halls at school as if I'm carrying my secret in my arms, and the slightest bump from a passerby will spill the content for all to see. It's a delicious feeling, holding all of this beauty and intrigue and keeping it to myself. I feel like a different person from the girl who started the school year.

My stomach flip-flops every time I think about our kiss. Both kisses. The memory and the re-creation. I've turned a page that can't be unturned. Everything he said about our relationship is true. I loved Auden once. I can feel that in the very roots of my soul. And he loved me—loves me still.

After school, I drive straight to the Taco Town parking lot, my new designated spot to hide my car. I've built an alibi with Mama that I like to study there. Auden meets me there and drives me to his house.

"What do you have planned for today?" I ask, glancing around his living room, trying not to show my nervous anticipation at the prospect of being alone here with him. "Are we going to try and relive a memory?"

There's a mischievous glint to his smile. "Yes. All of them."

I raise an eyebrow, and he holds out his hand. My stomach flutters, but I let him lead me up the stairs to his bedroom.

"I can tell you're nervous," he says, glancing over his shoulder. "Don't be. My intentions are strictly honorable."

"Isn't that what the bad guy in *Pirates of the Caribbean* says?"

Auden gives a look of mock confusion and then winks as he swings his door open. His room has been cleaned. As best as a teenage boy can clean, that is.

"As I mentioned, we spent a lot of time in this room. For obvious reasons, your house wasn't our prime hangout."

"This works," I say, admiring his movie posters again. "Where was our usual spot? You sat on the bed, and I sat on this chair?"

Auden grins sheepishly and props his pillows against the backboard of his bed. He sits down and pats a spot beside him. "Actually, we both sat right here."

I fold my arms. "And now you're going to tell me I always wore my bra and underwear?"

"Another recovered memory!" Auden's eyes widen in mock surprise.

I grab a shoe from the ground and playfully smack him. He holds up his hands to block the attack. "I'm kidding!"

When I strike again, he grabs my wrists and pulls me on top of him. I squeal, and he locks his arm around my waist, pinning me close.

"Rule number one of combat: know your enemy's strength."

We're both laughing. I struggle to free myself. He is surprisingly strong, which is quite sexy, but he relents, rolling me to his side.

"Okay," he says. "Believe it or not, I didn't bring you here to wrestle on my bed."

"Sure you didn't," I say with a smirk.

Auden bends over and fishes something out from under his bed. I recognize the box he sets on his lap immediately. It was the memory box he pulled out on our disastrous, fake first date.

"Now I know this didn't go over well last time," Auden says, preemptively. "But I think it's important that you see some of it."

I touch his arm. "I *want* to see it now, Auden. I want to see everything."

He smiles and gives me a quick kiss on the cheek.

"We'll go slow. One piece at a time. I'll tell you the story behind each one, and we'll see if we can't trigger more memories."

"Do you really think we'll be able to? I mean…how do you bring back memories that have been erased?" I ask.

Auden considers this for a moment. "Maybe they're not actually erased," he says. "Maybe they're just hidden. Maybe you just need the right trigger to help them break free?"

The thought warms my whole body with a sense of hope. "It's worth a try."

"Indeed." He fishes out a small USB drive. "We'll start with this."

He places the drive in his computer, and his TV lights up.

Crackly old music plays as a black and white title screen appears. *Another classic?* The title scrolls with a swell of violins.

Muse: A Modern Love Story in the French Style
Starring: Shelby Decatur
Directed by: Auden Keplar

I look to Auden in surprise, but he just smiles.

As promised, the film is told in the style of 1930s French cinema—artistic, melancholy, mostly free of dialogue. It's all about me. In one shot, I'm sitting on my bed watching a movie. The screen zooms in on my face, slowly and tenderly capturing my awe as I watch. Another scene shows me running across an empty parking lot toward the camera.

The care that Auden took with each frame is a little overwhelming. The glowing light, the intimate yet artistic angles. The way the camera lingers on my face, adoring and celebrating me all at once. It's like a love poem told in film. I couldn't ask for a more beautiful gift.

Auden is with me in the final scene. We're kissing on a blanket in a tall, grassy field. I've seen the pictures of us kissing, but this is something else. The sight of us entangled in one another's arms makes my heart pound. In the final moments, we break apart and look at each other. The love we share crackles on the screen.

Auden holds out his pinkie finger, and I hook mine with his. Smiling, Auden brings it to his chest. Then the screen goes dark.

Fin.

Auden uses his remote to turn off the TV.

"Well?" He finally asks. "Did you like it?"

I nod. "What was the pinky swear?"

"It's a little thing you and I used to do. A silent promise."

"A promise to what?"

Auden links his pinkie with mine and holds it to his chest. "I bet you have a pretty good idea."

I swallow hard.

He slowly runs his fingers through my hair, resting his hand on the back of my head. I close my eyes, awaiting the feel of his lips. He doesn't disappoint.

Later, as we stand by my car in the Taco Town parking lot, I ask when we can see each other again. He doesn't even hesitate.

"Tomorrow."

"Tomorrow? I have rehearsal."

"After that, then. I can't go a day without seeing you." He sets his thumb on my bottom lip. "Or without kissing this gorgeous mouth."

I struggle to inhale, and he makes it worse by replacing his thumb with his lips. My eyes sink closed. The warmth of his kiss engulfs me.

When we break apart, I'm drunk on the feeling of it. "Tomorrow," I say.

~

Sure enough, we see each other every afternoon. We sort through the memory box. Auden paints the story of our past, and I'm a captive audience. We talk about life. Sometimes we talk about the future. We run lines together from *Romeo and Juliet*. Especially the kissing scenes. I find myself falling for him more and more. It's like gravity. I can't fight it. I don't even want to try.

Friday at school, I can't stop checking the time on my phone. It feels silly to count down the minutes to the end of the day. But I can't think of anything else. Only three more hours until I see him. After school. Right after play practice. I'll drive straight to the Taco Town parking lot to meet him. Three more hours until we can try again to bring back more memories.

Grace isn't at lunch, so I have no one to distract me. I'm pretty sure she's off with Brad Corbin. Guess he didn't let the little incident with Mike deter him. I'm glad. She needs this.

As I load up my backpack at the end of the day, my phone buzzes with a text from her. Don't hate me for ditching out at lunch! I was with Brad. Sorry to be MIA lately!

The truth is that her budding relationship with Brad has worked out quite nicely for me. She's so distracted and busy with him that she hasn't noticed how distracted and busy I am with Auden.

Don't stress. I type. I'm happy for you. Have fun!

Thanks, girl. Love you!

Love you too.

Smiling, I put my phone away and head to rehearsal. Most of the cast has already gathered on the stage, sitting in small groups, talking through the dramas of their day. Cam spots me and motions for me to sit by him. As I walk up to the stage, he examines me.

"Don't you look fancy today?" he says.

I glance down at my outfit with a twinge of embarrassment. "I do not."

In truth, I'd spent a fair amount of time putting together my outfit last night: A deep red peasant blouse with shimmering jewel beads woven in around the collar and skinny jeans. I pulled out my old jewelry box to find the chandelier earrings that matched perfectly.

Cam grins. "You dressed up for me, didn't you?"

I sit down and shove him. "Always."

He leans back on his palms. "Hey, what are you doing this weekend?"

I pause, probably too long, before answering. "I think Mama has some family thing planned."

"A 'family thing?'"

I can hear the air quotes in his voice as he asks it. I shrug and rummage through my backpack to try and look distracted. "You know how she is."

"Too bad. There's a group of us getting together."

As if this is anything new? It's been this way since middle school. The same group getting together to hang out at the same houses to do the same stuff they've always done. Compared to the prospect of an evening with Auden, I almost laugh out loud. Thankfully, I find my script in my bag and pull it out.

"So," I say, in an attempt to move the conversation along. "What scene are we running today?"

Cam's gaze lingers on me for a moment, but then he flips open his script as well. "Party scene, I think. And you know what that means?"

"What?" I ask, not really paying attention as I turn to the scene.

"First kiss."

My hand freezes midturn of the script page. Cam waggles his eyebrows. "I hope you have minty gum on you because I had garlic bread pizza for lunch."

As it happens, I made sure to have a full supply of mint gum in my bag. But it's not for him.

"Looks like I'm in for an amazing experience," I say, faking a gag. I stare at my script, a small knot forming in my stomach. It feels wrong to be kissing Cam after what I've shared with Auden, even if it is acting. I wish we were running any other scene.

Cam taps his script. "I need to take tips from this Romeo dude."

"What do you mean?"

"One look and the chick is in love with him. Then they make out after exactly three minutes. And the next day, they are married and gettin' it on. The guy has skills."

I scoff. "Way to bring one of the most timeless love stories in the history of theater to your juvenile level."

"Oh come on," he laughs. "You don't fall for this stuff, do you?"

"Maybe I do. You don't think people can fall in love quickly?"

"No way. In fact, the thought of teenagers being in 'love' is a joke to begin with. It's all hormones at this age. I read an article about it for health class. It said the undeveloped teenage brain isn't capable of the maturity and depth required for real love."

Blood rushes to my face. "You're so full of it, Cam."

He laughs. "*Romeo and Juliet* is hardly a timeless love story. It's about two horny fourteen-year-olds who want to hump and then kill themselves when their parents say no."

I'm gripped with the sudden urge to punch his smug face. "If you think the play is so stupid, then why did you audition for the lead?"

"How else would I get the chance to make out with you again?" He grins. "It's all hormones, Seashell."

Thankfully, Mr. Lyman breezes in before I can smack him.

"All right, people. Act one, scene five. Get in your places. Those of you not in this scene—backstage. And keep your chatter to a dull roar, please. Last week's rehearsal was unacceptable. Why can't you all be more like Jake and Amy and quietly make out when you're not onstage?"

Amy's face goes bright red.

Cam elbows me. "Hormones," he whispers triumphantly.

~

I've never been more relieved for practice to be over. In a twist of luck, Mr. Lyman didn't require Cam and me to actually kiss.

We only touched foreheads, though even that felt too close. Normally it wouldn't bother me, but our conversation left a sour taste in my mouth. It's still there now.

As I push out the double doors to the auditorium, the crisp, wet fall air pushes against me. It's rained, and silver clouds hang low in the sky, trapping the chill. The puddles mirror the gray sky above.

A tall figure steps out from the side wall of the school, and I spin with a startled gasp.

"Auden!" My surprise immediately flips into concern. I look around the parking lot. "People are still leaving rehearsal. They'll see you."

"Maybe I don't care," he says, taking my hand.

"Well, you should."

He laces his fingers in mine. I give him an exasperated smile and pull him toward my car, which sits alone on the far corner. "It's risky."

"I couldn't wait," he says. "I've been sitting out here for the last hour. Waiting to see you."

"You're too bold," I say, though it sends a thrill through me to know that he's been thinking about me as much as I've been thinking about him. "We can't do anything here."

"Can't we?"

He's close. So close. He brushes hair from my face, tucking it behind my ear. My hand tightens around the key fob. He brings his fingers beneath my chin. I straighten, guided by his touch. His dark, warm eyes burn into me as he puts his hands on my shoulders, then runs them down my arms. My skin tingles, and my mouth has gone dry.

I lift my face, longing to feel his lips on mine, when a car pulls into the empty space next to us. Auden's arms tighten, pulling me against him.

It's Grace.

CHAPTER 19

Grace slams her car into park and gets out, the engine still running. I've never seen that look on her face before. Not only shock but fury. And pain.

"What in the *hell*, Auden?"

"Grace. Let me explain." The sharpness of desperation rings in his voice.

"No. *No*. I don't want to hear it." Her fierceness shocks me. "What are you doing here?"

"What are *you* doing here?" I ask, bristling at her tone.

She laughs, incredulous. "I came to pick you up after practice. To spend some time with you. I was feeling guilty. But I guess I didn't need to since you were busy sneaking around behind my back anyway."

I stare at her. The knee-jerk guilt of being caught has melted into anger. "I don't have to explain myself to you. I'm not doing anything wrong."

She scoffs, and I double down. "*You* are the one that should be explaining."

"What are you talking about?" she snaps.

My jaw tightens. "How do you know Auden?"

Grace tenses, and that tells me everything I need to know.

"You know what happened. What *really* happened when I was in therapy. You've always known. And you've gone right along with it."

"You don't understand—"

"You're right. I don't. I don't understand how you could let my mother erase a part of my freaking *brain* without my permission."

Grace looks as if she's going to reply, but bites back her words. "You don't know what you're talking about, okay?"

"Why didn't you tell me I had a boyfriend?" I demand. "How could you let her do this?"

"There's a lot to this story that you don't know. And I'm sure Auden hasn't told you either."

Rage burns in my chest. "He's the only one telling me anything! The doctor didn't just stop my panic attacks, he took away part of my mind, Grace. Part of my *life*. *Good* parts. And you're pretending it never happened."

"No," she says, shaking her head. "This is not about me. I'm not going to let this become about me. *He's* the one who's been hiding the whole story." She points furiously at Auden. "Ask him, Shelby. Ask him to tell you to *real* truth."

"I'm not hiding anything from her," Auden snaps. "But I have the right to tell her in my own time."

She laughs bitterly. "Whatever that means. Come on, Shelby. I'm taking you home right now."

I back away. "Not until you tell me what's going on."

Grace comes toward me with determination. "I'm not leaving you with him."

"She's allowed to stay if she wants," Auden says, moving between us.

Setting her jaw, Grace pulls out her phone. "Fine. Then I'm calling LouAnne."

Auden's eyes flash at Mama's name, and we both cry out at the same time. "No!"

Grace scrolls to Mama's number with a determined grit of her teeth. "If you don't want her to know, I suggest you get out of here right now."

"Don't you dare bring Mama into this," I say.

Auden grabs her arm. "Please don't do this."

Grace pulls herself free and, rage flashing in her eyes, jabs her phone. The call screen appears, and the soft sound of the first ring cuts through the air.

Auden pleads with her. "Grace, I was going to call you when the moment was right."

The phone rings a second time.

"If I could talk with you," Auden says, struggling to keep his voice calm. "I need you to understand—"

"I understand better than you know."

A third ring.

"You don't. I promise you don't."

"I'm not falling for it," she says, her eyes welling up with tears. The sight of it shocks me. Suddenly, the ground feels unsteady beneath my feet.

"Tell me what's going on right now," I demand.

Mama's voice comes through the speaker. "Hello?"

Auden's whisper is choked with emotion. "*Please.*"

"Grace?" Mama's voice buzzes. "Are you there?"

"I'll go with you," I say, in a sharp whisper. "Leave Mama out of this, and I'll go with you."

Grace wipes the tears from her eyes and lifts the phone to her ear. "Hey LouAnne. Sorry. I think I called you on accident."

I can't hear Mama's reply. Grace forces a weak laugh and says goodbye. She hangs up and stares at the blank screen for a moment. Auden exhales a shaky breath.

Grace doesn't look at him. "Let's go, Shelby. Right now."

I meet Auden's eyes. He looks cornered. Hopeless. "I'll call you in a little while," I say, but it doesn't seem to comfort him.

"Trust what you know," he says softly.

He watches me as I get into Grace's car, then jogs to catch up with Grace as she walks to her side of the car. He speaks in a low, urgent voice. I can only hear the murmur of sound. As Grace listens, her tense body seems to relax a bit. She gives a single nod. Then she gets into the driver's seat and slams the door.

I watch Auden recede in the side mirror as we pull out of the parking lot. Grace and I drive in churning silence. My arms are folded tightly across my chest. I can't pin down a solid emotion in my mind. I'm not sure if I'm furious, sad, confused, or afraid. All of them, I guess.

But when I look over at Grace, tears are sliding down her cheeks.

"Grace. What is going on? If you care about me at all, you'll tell me everything."

She wipes her face. "I know this must be so confusing to you, Shelbs. I can only imagine. I wanted to tell you about Auden so many times, but your mom begged me to keep it secret."

"Can't you see how wrong that sounds?"

"You need to hear the full story, okay? All you've heard is Auden's side. And I'm sure he's filled your head with stories about how great life was until your mean mom came along and erased your memory."

A knot tightens in my stomach. "And that's not true?"

"It's not the full story. It wasn't all roses between you two, okay?"

"What relationship is?"

She shakes her head. "No. It was different. It was too intense."

"What does that mean?"

"There was always so much drama. Huge fights. You'd break up, then get back together again. When you were dating him, I saw you cry more times than you ever had before you met him." She lets that sink in for a minute. "You didn't seem all that happy to me."

We park in front of my house.

"Your mama was really worried about you," Grace goes on. "We both were. She had serious concerns."

"I know all about her concerns. She thought he was trying to take me away from her precious Orchardview way of life."

"She *thought* he was emotionally abusive," Grace spits back.

"Oh please. I may have just met Auden—again—but that's ridiculous."

"So, because he's charming and good looking, he can't have a dark side?"

"I didn't say that. I said it's ridiculous to accuse him of being abusive because we broke up a few times."

Grace's eyes flash. "It's more than that, Shelby. The warning signs were there."

"Warning signs? What, are you an expert now on emotionally abusive relationships?"

"As a matter of fact, I know quite a lot. More than I want to know."

"What's that supposed to mean?"

She presses her head back against the headrest. "Did you honestly never realize that Mike was?"

"*Mike?*"

"Yes. Mike. All those years, all the crap I went through. It wasn't because I loved him. It's because I was afraid not to." Her eyes glisten with tears. "He had…maybe still has…control over me. At first it was subtle. Like, if I didn't text him back right away, he'd accuse me of not loving him and be mad for days. He'd call and wake me up me in the middle of the night to tell me he loved me. And if I didn't act like I thought it was romantic, he'd get upset. Once he thought I was flirting with the waiter at a restaurant, and he said he was going to kill himself. Every day, I lived in fear of his love."

I always knew Mike had issues, but I never saw this side of him. I, her best friend in the world, never knew all that happened. Grace's words from earlier ring in my ears now. *You had your own problems to deal with.*

I open my mouth to speak, but words fail me. Grace squeezes her eyes shut and takes a shaky breath.

"It doesn't matter, okay? I'm moving past that now." She wipes away more tears. "Your mom helped me a lot with that."

"Mama?" I ask, dazed.

Grace nods. "She'd been through it before. With your first stepdad. She was there for me when no one else understood. They all said, *Mike's so sweet. He loves you so much.* They didn't understand the way he used that love to control me. But your mom did. She was the one who gave me courage to break up with him. And when I had moments of weakness and went back to him because I was afraid, she didn't judge me. She supported me."

A sudden headache pulls at my temples. This is too much to take in all at once.

"I'm so sorry, Grace." My voice cracks as I whisper the words.

"It's okay. You couldn't have known."

My house, the street beyond it, the inside of Grace's car—it all seems to have changed shape and color with this new revelation. I scoffed at Grace saying she wished she could have her memory erased, like me. But suddenly it doesn't seem so silly.

You'd certainly want to forget pain like that. The thought chills me like a slow winter wind.

"And you think Auden was this way…? Abusive?"

"Kind of…maybe. I don't know, okay? I saw you cry a lot. Your mom said that's what he was."

"Well, did you think he was like Mike or didn't you?"

She shakes her head. "It's not that simple."

"You can't tell me he was abusive because Mama said so. She'd probably say anything to get you on her side."

She's holding back. I can tell. "Please, Grace."

"I agreed to let him tell you in his own way."

"No, I'm sick of everyone withholding my own life from me!"

"Fine," she says. "You want the truth? Buckle up because it's not pretty. While you were in Denver getting your therapy, your knight in shining armor spent the summer in prison."

I roll my eyes. "Prison? Seriously? For what?"

Grace doesn't react. Silence fills the car like water. And in that moment, I know it's true.

CHAPTER 20

I stare at Grace, stricken silent by her revelation. A dozen different questions fly around in my mind, but only one makes its way out in a feeble whisper.

"Why?"

"That's for Auden to tell you, okay? I don't want to talk about it. I've cried enough."

"Grace—"

"I'm going home. Talk to Auden if you want to know more."

"But—"

"I'll call you later."

She refuses to look at me. When Grace digs in her heels, there's very little that can change her mind. I wordlessly get out of her car. She drives off as soon as the passenger door shuts.

I turn to my house, numb. A gust of cold wind brushes past me. The pathway to the front door glistens from the rain. The memory of Auden re-creating our first doorstep scene glows through the haze of my mind, then vanishes. I swallow hard.

Shouldering my bag, I walk slowly inside. I bypass Mama and Blake and go straight into my room.

I sit on my bed, tense in every joint. Almost instinctively, I pull out my phone. There are four missed calls and six frantic texts from Auden.

We need to talk. Please call me.

I need to explain what Grace told you.

Call me as soon as you can.

And on and on. I turn off the screen and toss my phone to the side. I have a headache, and even though my stomach is empty, I feel like I'm going to throw up. I press my hands to my face and lie back on my bed. *Focus on breathing.* Repeating the words from therapy should help. *Slow, deep, complete breaths.*

But it's not relaxing. I'm jumpy. Tense. I don't want to sit. I need to move. If I were sportier, I'd probably go on a run to clear my head. I glance at my tennis shoes on the floor and grimace. A walk will have to do.

Outside, the cool air fills my lungs in a bracing but pleasant way. The slight smell of burning firewood mixed with wet ground tingles my nose. I draw in a long breath. It does feel better to be outside and moving. I need to think. I need to make something of this chaos.

A buzzing in my pocket robs me of any hope for clarity. Out of habit, I pocketed my phone on my way out the door, and I'm wishing I hadn't. I know who it is before I check. Staring at his glowing number on the screen, I almost turn off the phone. But emotion rises up in me, above the confusion and shock.

Anger.

I answer.

"Shelby?"

"I wasn't going to answer," I say.

"I'm glad you did." His voice sounds different than usual. Or maybe I simply don't know what usual is anymore.

"Where are you right now?" he asks. "Can I come to you?"

"We can talk over the phone."

"But I want to see you. I want to be at your side."

I stop. An image drifts into my mind of Auden at my side, wrapping his arms around me, his lips brushing against my throat. The fantasy takes my breath for a moment, but I start walking again.

"I'm not ready to see you yet."

"Shelby. Talk to me. Tell me what Grace said. I can explain everything."

"I'm sure you can." The venom of my words startles me. Auden has been the voice of truth in recent weeks, the only one I really trusted. But now I feel like I'm free-falling again.

"Don't do this," he pleads. "Don't shut me out. Remember that night by the lake."

"That was one memory. How many others are there that I don't know about? Obviously, there are plenty of not-so-great ones if they were taken by the therapy."

"I wasn't planning on hiding anything. But did you honestly expect me to start with the bad memories?"

"I don't know what I expected. It's not like I've been in this situation before."

Auden sighs. "This is a mess." He sounds so despondent. It softens me a little. My pace slows. There's an empty bench ahead under a large cottonwood. It's a bus stop with only a morning and night pickup. I wipe the water droplets from the metal and sit down.

"Grace didn't tell me much." I say. "She was upset. She told me…she said…that you spent the summer in prison."

A long silence follows.

"Is it true?" I ask, hugging my knees to my chest.

More silence.

"Auden. Tell me."

I can barely hear his voice when he speaks. "It's true."

Even though I believed Grace, having Auden confirm it brings a burning sense of betrayal in my chest. A betrayal of the image I had built of who Auden is.

My voice becomes stronger. "Why?"

"It's…difficult to explain."

I laugh bitterly. "Somehow I knew you'd say that. Does everyone think I'm stupid? Do you guys think I can't handle whatever happened?"

"It's not that straightforward."

"I'm willing to bet it is," I say, teeth clenched.

Auden exhales with frustration. "It's not like I murdered a cop or robbed a convenience store at gunpoint, Shelby." He pauses. "Sometimes good people make bad choices, and the results are worse than anyone expected."

I don't have a response to that. Auden continues. "You have

no memories of me. Which is why I wanted to wait to tell you. How else can I rebuild the events and circumstances so that you have the full context like you did then?"

"Oh, so I was fine with you going to prison?"

"Of course not. But you understood why. You understood because you had lived all that led up to it. And because you understood me."

I strain to think of a possible scenario that would make sense with the Auden I have come to know and come up blank.

Blank. *Erased.*

My throat tightens. "Well, I want to understand right now. I need to."

Auden is deathly quiet. I don't even hear him breathing.

"You need to tell me," I press. "Or I'm going to start imagining the worst. You said I understood once. Well, I'm still the same person. I'll understand again."

"Okay," he says, finally. "I'll tell you how I got in trouble." He releases a shaky breath. "It's really complicated, and I'll spare you all the unimportant details. But basically, I tried to run away. I wanted to go to California. My dad was against it, but I left anyway. And…I might have taken his credit card. Anyway, I told you that he and I don't have the best relationship."

"He pressed charges against you?" I ask, surprised but also filled with a rush of empathy for him.

"Something like that."

"I'm sorry."

"It's okay. I survived. Got out early on good behavior,

actually. Truth is, I shouldn't have gotten jail time in the first place. It was an overzealous judge. He wanted to make an example of me."

I think of how I let Grace down when she needed me, and my heart jumps into my throat. "I probably wasn't there for you through all of this, was I? Too caught up with my own problems."

He's quiet for a moment. "It was a complicated time for both of us."

I can't decide which is worse, the fact that I wasn't there for the people I cared about most when they needed me most or that I now can't remember any of it at all. The thought makes me want to cry. Suddenly I feel like curling up in a ball on my bed and sobbing my eyes out. A good, long cry to drown out this aching emptiness in my own memory.

"I want it back," I say. "I want my old life back."

"I'd do anything in the world to give it to you."

I turn my eyes upward to keep the tears from spilling out.

"Shelby. Please let me come to you. Leave your house. Meet me at the usual spot."

"I'm not at my house. I'm just not ready to see you yet." The words feel sharp coming out of my mouth, but I can't hold them back. "I care about you, Auden. I was actually starting to care for you a lot. But that doesn't change the fact that you're a stranger to me."

"I'm not. You know me, Shelby. You've felt that what we have is special."

"I don't know what I feel," I say, shakily. "I need time to sort this all out."

"How much time?"

"I don't know."

"I'll wait," he says, a broken sadness in his voice.

～

I dream of darkness. Not the soft, indigo of night. I dream of the kind of darkness of being trapped in a windowless room. Of a thick, suffocating void. And around me, I see the color blue.

I'm crying. Hard. Though I don't know why.

Then, beside me, a light appears in the blackness. The light is round and too small. It moves gently up and down in a strange, rolling way. For some reason, I know it's higher than it should be.

The moving light draws closer. Closer still. Except it shouldn't be here.

A terrible sense of foreboding engulfs me. Despair, terrible and complete. I'm drowning in it. It's all wrong. So wrong. The light disappears, and I scream at the top of my lungs.

My eyes snap open with a deep, guttural sob. Darkness still surrounds me. It feels like someone is standing on my chest. The despair and panic linger from my dream.

I rub my face and try to catch my breath. *It's not real*, I repeat to myself over and over, though I'm not sure I can pinpoint what I'm so afraid of. I rip off my blanket and stumble through the dark hallway to my bathroom.

Clicking on the light and shutting the door, I slap my hands down on the countertop, squinting at the sudden brightness. I'm shaking, breathing raggedly. My cheeks are red and splotchy from the tears. I splash some cold water on my face and try to calm down.

The clock on the wall reads three thirty. I'm not going back to bed. I won't risk another dream. Still breathing with effort, I stumble into the living room. A beam of pale yellow from the streetlight outside drapes across Mama's big armchair in the corner. I suddenly feel six again. Grabbing the blanket from the couch, I wrap myself in the softness of Mama's chair. It's warm, and I'm small in the big leather folds. I breathe in the familiar smell of our house, and for a brief flicker, I feel safe. Or at least a little safer.

A hand on my shoulder wakes me. I blink back the sleep and sunshine in my eyes and Mama's frown of concern comes into view.

"Are you okay?"

My dream surges back. I sit up, rubbing my face. "Um… yeah. I'm fine."

"Did you sleep out here?" Her concerned expression shifts to alarm. "Was it a nightmare?"

Mama remembers the nights my panic attacks woke me, screaming and sobbing. I breathe a sigh of relief that I kept myself mostly under control last night.

"No. Just a little insomnia." The lie comes easily.

Mama searches my face, and then straightens. "Well, it's time to get ready for school. You'll be late."

"Yes, ma'am."

I watch her as she goes to make the morning pot of coffee. Grace said Mama helped her through her breakup with Mike when I couldn't. I ponder this as I fold the blanket and drape it back over the couch.

"Oh by the way," Mama says, stepping out to meet me as I head to get changed. "You should put your phone on silence. It's been ringing all morning."

I freeze. She's holding my phone in her hand.

"Who's calling you at this hour on a Monday morning?"

Panic grabs me. I didn't hear from Auden all weekend, but there's no doubt it's him. My mind has gone blank as to how I saved his contact information in my phone. Surely I wouldn't have been so stupid…

In slow motion, Mama raises the screen to show me the number.

CHAPTER 21

'll turn it off," I say, reaching for the phone.

But it's too late. Mama presses the button and the screen illuminates. Her brow furrows. My breath stops in my chest.

"Are you getting calls from telemarketers again?" she asks, handing it to me. "I told you to get online and fix that."

I snatch my phone from her. "Yeah, I need to," I say, my heart pounding.

I wisely hadn't saved Auden's information in my phone at all. It's a random number with an unfamiliar area code. My shoulders sink with relief. Pocketing my phone, I head to my room to get dressed and try not to meet Mama's eye as she watches me go.

On my way to school, I spot a familiar car in my rearview mirror.

"What in the…"

He pulls directly behind me, and my phone starts to ring.

"So, you're stalking me now?"

"I need to talk to you." His voice sounds strained, exhausted—like he didn't get much sleep last night.

"I have to go to school."

"Please, Shelby."

There's a park nearby with lots of trees. We could probably find a hidden place to talk there without worry of getting turned in for truancy, which is a real possibility when your stepdad is drinking buddies with half of Orchardview's small-town police force. I exhale.

"Holmgren Pond. I can't stay long, though."

We park side by side in the empty lot. Seeing Auden again sends a strange surge of emotion through me. There are dark circles under his eyes, and he looks paler than normal. I'm gripped with the urge to hug him.

He comes right beside me. His arms open to take me into an embrace, but I pull back.

"You look beautiful," he says.

It's a ridiculous statement. I basically threw on jeans, pulled my unwashed hair into a ponytail, and zipped a gray hoodie over my tank top.

"Why were you calling me so much this morning?" I ask, pushing past the small talk and niceties. "Mama almost found out."

He scruffs a hand through his hair. "I'm sorry. I just needed to talk."

I glance to the street as a car speeds by and then grab his sleeve. "You're reckless. You know that?"

We walk to a little bench beside the pond, partially hidden from the street by a pair of maple trees. It's quiet except for the sound of morning birds singing in the branches above. The water on the dark green pond ripples softly. It's a peaceful spot, yet my stomach is in knots.

Truth is, inside, I'm ready to forgive Auden for withholding the story of his arrest from me. I'm sure I wouldn't want to lead with that either if I were trying to help someone build a picture of me. And besides, in a way, it actually fits with the impulsive, intense Auden I have come to know.

But I can't help feeling uneasy still. I'm in a vulnerable place. Anyone can tell me anything they want, and I would have no reason not to believe them. I hate the blind, helpless place these gaps in my memories leave me. And feeling this way makes me want to close up behind my wall. It makes me want to push Auden away, resentful of the knowledge he has that is rightfully mine, but it also makes me want to cling to him, as he is my strongest link to that information.

He sits down beside me and leans forward, elbows on his knees, hands clenched together. I picture myself stroking his disheveled hair, and I hate my weakness for wanting to do it.

"Okay, you wanted to talk to me. So talk."

"For starters, I'm sorry. I should have anticipated that we'd be discovered sooner or later. I should have prepared you for that. But I swear to you, I just didn't know how to do that, otherwise I would have. Don't you think I wanted you to hear my dark past from me? Do you think I wanted it to come out this way?"

Auden rubs his face. "I wanted you to really know me first. Before what came next."

"I don't judge you for having gone to prison," I say, my voice tight. "But the truth is, I *don't* really know you."

"I'm an open book," he says.

"Grace said we fought a lot."

His eyes flash. "What?"

"She said she'd never seen me cry more than when I was dating you."

"That's not true," he insists. "She has no idea what she's talking about."

"She's my best friend. I think she'd know."

"She doesn't…" Auden presses a fist to his forehead, his jaw tense. "She only saw pieces of what we were, Shelby. Surely you can understand that. Everyone who saw us—Grace, your mother—they didn't see half of what we really were. And what little they did see, they colored with their own perceptions."

I think about Mike Jasper, about the years Grace quietly suffered in that relationship. It makes sense that she'd probably see most guys as potential abusers after that. I hold my jacket tight around me against a sudden chill.

"Why should I trust you?"

Auden lowers his face to meet my eye. "Haven't you felt that what we have is special? Maybe you can't remember it, but you have to feel it." He gently brushes his fingers along the line of my cheek. The touch of his skin on mine burns like a flame.

I shrink back a little. Auden is quiet for a moment. We both turn to look out at the small pond in silence. Then he gets a strange tremor in his voice. "I've given this a lot of thought, Shelby. We need to go. We need to get out of Orchardview. Today. Right now."

I turn to him sharply, shocked. But his expression is deathly serious.

"If you really want control of your life and your mind, you have to reach out and take it. Your mother won't willingly let you have it. Right now, she has control over the narrative. And she always will. Unless you break free."

"What would leaving Orchardview accomplish?"

"Everything!" Auden exclaims. "Listen to me, last night, I didn't sleep at all. I kept thinking about how I got a second chance with you and everything I did wrong. Trying to make you remember was a mistake. There's too much working against us here. We have to put our past aside for a fresh start."

His eyes are bright with a mixture of desperation and hope. "We get in my car right now and drive to California, to Hollywood. We start living our lives. The memories you lost may be gone, but we can build new ones."

"We're not characters in some dramatic old movie," I say. "This is real life, and we're teenagers. We're not going to run off into the sunset together."

"Why not? What is keeping you here, Shelby?"

"My family, for one thing."

"A dominating mother who would rob you of the one thing no other human should be able to take from you—your mind."

"She's still my mother."

Auden scoffs. "She's everything I despise about Orchardview embodied in one person."

His words throw me. I knew he didn't like Mama, but I never heard him speak about her with such contempt.

"This is a small town," Auden says. "And I don't mean size or population. It's a small place filled with small people and small dreams. If you stay here, it will destroy you. You'll wilt in the smallness of it. The potential you have will be wasted, poured into some undeserving idiot who could never begin to understand what an incredible woman you are."

There's a lone mallard duck on the water, paddling in a quiet circle around the edge of the tiny pond. He goes around and around. My chest feels tight.

"I won't let that happen to you," Auden says.

Something in his tone makes me bristle. "It's not your decision to make."

"When are you going to stop being afraid to live your life?"

"I'm not afraid," I say, angrily.

"You are. You've always been afraid. And I don't blame you, growing up with a woman like your mother. You never even let yourself entertain the idea of stepping out of line."

I stand abruptly. "You know what? I'm sick and tired of everyone telling me what I think and feel. I know I don't remember everything from last year, but that doesn't mean I don't know who I am."

There's a painful hollow feeling in my chest and in my heart.

I start walking away, because I know that if I say anything else, I'll probably start crying.

Auden runs after me. "Shelby, wait."

"Leave me alone."

He keeps pace at my side. "I'm sorry. You're right. I shouldn't talk to you like that. I'm sorry, okay?"

I turn to him, arms folded. He hangs his head. "I run my mouth before I think things through. But I meant what I said about us leaving. It's the only way we can ever really get back our love. By starting again."

"I can't just pick up and leave. It's not realistic, and you know it. Even for a reckless, dramatic guy like you. We have no money. We don't know anyone in California."

"That's small-town mentality talking. Believe it or not, you don't *have* to know everyone who lives on your street in order to survive."

His condescending tone stokes my temper. "Well, I don't even really know *you*, the person I would potentially be living with, so that definitely makes it a terrible idea."

"Shelby—"

"What?"

Auden wordlessly searches my eyes. It's that same intense stare that first drew me to him. As if he were staring into my very soul.

"Forgive me. I know this is a huge request I'm making. And it probably feels totally out of left field for you…but it's really not. We *did* talk about this before. There was a time when you were ready to pack your bags and come with me."

The suggestion pulses in my mind, but I say nothing.

"Will you at least think about it?" he asks.

"I should get to school."

"Shelby."

I exhale. "Fine. I'll think about it." His body relaxes a little, and I point at him. "But I'll need space. You can't call me ten times a day."

"I can give you space."

"I'm not sure you can," I say, raising an eyebrow.

He covers his heart with his hand. "I promise. No more than two calls a day."

I widen my eyes, and he holds up his hands. "I'm kidding! You can be the one to call me first. I swear." Auden gives me outrageously effective puppy-dog eyes. "Can I at least hug you goodbye?"

"You're unrelenting," I say, but a smile creeps over my lips. Auden grins as if he's won an unspoken battle and pulls me into his arms.

Any resistance melts the moment he holds me. I won't tell him this, of course, but as his hands slowly tighten around me, I'm completely lost in the embrace. Lost in the best way.

As we break apart, he presses a kiss to my cheek. My heart pounds the entire drive back to school.

CHAPTER 22

I told Auden to give me space, but it proves a useless request. I think about him constantly, which is almost worse. There's no hanging up on or running away from your mind. And there, in the hazy regions of my imagination, I allow myself to wander into a hundred impossible scenarios.

Like getting my memory back. Challenging Mama with the truth. Breaking free and being with Auden in any way I choose.

It can never happen, of course. Auden was right in at least one respect—there's no point trying to fight to get my memories back. They are gone forever. I knew this from the start. The only reason I can remember that kiss by the lake is because it wasn't fully erased. That's why I saw the flicker of it during that last treatment. The other pieces of my past have been buried in the pristine emptiness thanks to the neural restructuring capsule.

The rest of the week crawls by slowly. Grace is avoiding me. Mama's extra busy at work. So I'm left alone with my thoughts. I would be lying if I said I don't check my phone regularly. I would also be lying if I said I'm not slightly disappointed that Auden obeys my command not to call or text. Each time I find my phone screen blank, I feel a little crestfallen. It's infuriatingly pathetic of me.

At least I honor my promise to him as well. I think about what he said. About getting in a car and not stopping until we get to California. I think about it more than I want to admit to myself. I can imagine us living in some ramshackle apartment in South Hollywood. I'm waiting tables, memorizing a monologue on my lunch break for the audition I have next week. Auden's going to film school on a scholarship. We stay up late together, eating Chinese takeout in bed and watching the movies he's been assigned as homework.

Another impossible scenario. And ridiculous too. It's a montage set to music in a romcom, not real life. I barely know Auden. And if Grace is right about us arguing a lot, living together could prove disastrous.

So why does my heart ache when I think about it?

At play practice on Thursday, I stand offstage watching the Romeo and Tybalt fight scene. Cam and Peter Jones are using rulers for swords because the techies haven't finished making the actual props yet—cardboard swords spray-painted silver. They're not exactly realistic, but it's what the budget allows. Mr. Lyman has always had to fight an uphill battle when it comes to funding for the theater program. Probably because theater has always been one of the last things anyone cares about in Orchardview.

That's when it hits me. Performing in this play will be the highest point of any theater career if I were to stay here. This small stage with its ancient curtains and creaking lights and two-dimensional sets, painted by ninth grade art students. This is as good as it will ever get.

I peer out at Mr. Lyman, who watches the scene from the front row of the audience. Maybe it's my imagination, but I could swear I see resignation in his eyes. He's given in to weary disappointment. The sight of it makes me shiver. He is a ghost of who I will become.

I linger on the stage after practice. It's partly to avoid Cam, who inevitably tries to get me to hang out this weekend. But I also can't stop watching Mr. Lyman. I'm gripped with a mixture of fascination and terror. I meander my way through the parting cast members until I'm sitting in the auditorium next to him.

He looks up from the notes he'd been making, and his eyebrows rise. "Something wrong, Shelby?"

We're mostly alone. Ana Guererro is passing out orders to a few techies about where to put the set blocks, but they are heading to the back room. I press my lips together and lean back.

"Nothing's really wrong. I just had a question."

Mr. Lyman removes his dark-rimmed glasses. "Shoot."

"You're not a local, right? I mean…you haven't lived here all of your life."

He blinks. I'm pretty sure he's taken aback by the question, but he tries to appear otherwise. "I'm not a local, no. But I grew up in Gainesville."

The information surprises me. Gainesville is another small Colorado town about an hour away. Like Orchardview, for the most part. Maybe a tad bigger. I process this information slowly.

"So…you've never lived in New York?"

He taps his script on his lap, as if he were straightening the pages, even though they're spiral bound together.

"No," he says. There's a note of shame in his voice, and I instantly regret asking.

"I'm sorry, I—"

"Nothing to be sorry for." Mr. Lyman turns up a tight smile. "It's on the bucket list. All I need is a big raise from Principal Nelson."

A heavy silence falls between us. The way Mr. Lyman looks at me, I'm almost positive that he understands why I'm asking. I dare to venture forward.

"If you could go back…If there had been a chance for you to get out of Colorado, to go after your dreams…would you?"

"Do you want to get out, Shelby?"

My throat tightens. "I was just wondering."

Mr. Lyman ponders for a long silence, then he leans forward. "Listen to me, Shelby. I've built my life here. There's no point in me looking back. That's not really what you're asking anyway, is it? You've seen your life here in Orchardview, and you're asking if it's worth the risk to leave everything you know, every comforting and predictable thing that's surrounded you since you were a child."

My eyes sting, and I nod.

"I can't answer that question for you," Mr. Lyman says, standing. "But you should answer it for yourself soon so you can apply to schools that will give you the kind of college experience you dream of. So you don't end up forty-five and wishing you had pushed yourself to explore a different path."

Mr. Lyman gives my shoulder a little squeeze and turns to leave. He thinks I'm talking about college, but his words still cut right to my heart. As I watch him go, two tears escape and slide down my cheek.

Words have a way of rooting themselves in your heart. Once they take hold, there's no shaking them. They grow deeper, more entangled in your reason and hope. Until a question becomes a decision. And a thought becomes a conviction.

Mr. Lyman's question rings in my ears for days. Is it worth the risk to leave everything I know? If Auden is telling the truth, I apparently thought it was worth it at one point. What made me come to that decision? Was it my love for Auden, for acting, or did it go much deeper than that?

Maybe I decided that the only way to finally be able to stand on my own was to leave Orchardview and everything I know. Maybe I believed that in California, I would find and become who I truly am, deep down inside. The real me.

At Sunday dinner, I find myself observing Mama and Blake in a way I never have before. I study each move, each shift of expression, each word they say to each other, each laugh, each touch.

They are fundamentally different from me. I can see it so clearly.

As an angry middle schooler, I imagined that I had been adopted. No way could Mama and I come from the same blood. I know that's not the case, of course, but maybe some traits run deeper than blood. There's more to who you are than the woman who gave birth to you and your hometown.

Mama sees how different I am, but I think she dismisses it as a teenage phase. She's never seen even a glimpse of the real me. She's never even tried.

I stab a fork into the slice of roast on my plate and sigh.

"Something the matter?" Blake asks.

"I'm tired. I think I'll go to bed early tonight."

I notice Mama and Blake exchange a glance. Mama sets down her beer and purses her lips for just a moment, in that way she does when she's about to lay down the law.

"I need you to clear your schedule this weekend, Shelby," she says, with calm authority. "Dr. Stevens has agreed to see you on Friday. We'll leave Thursday night."

I almost drop my fork. "What?"

"You heard me. Thursday night, we're heading to Denver. Tell your drama teacher you won't be at rehearsal on Friday."

I stare at her. "But…why?"

"For treatment," Mama says, cutting a bite of roast. "You're obviously not yourself lately. The panic attacks are back. After what happened during the last session, I'm convinced you've regressed. So I talked to Winonna, and she agreed that a thorough round of treatment sounds like just the thing you need. We'll hit those memories hard and make sure they're gone for good this time."

The air seems to have left the room. Did Grace tell Mama what she saw? With frantic eyes, I analyze her calmly chewing her roast. Unlikely. I know Mama, and if she knew she would have lost it the minute she found out.

Then where is this coming from? The panic attacks haven't been bad at all lately. If anything, I've tried my hardest to be as normal and cheerful as possible around them so they wouldn't suspect anything.

And then a terrible thought crawls into my heart. Mama doesn't care about my panic attacks. She only cares about erasing Auden and everything he inspired in me. With Auden, I dreamed of following my passion for acting, of going to California. *That's* what scared her. *That's* what she wants gone. It was never really about him. These therapy sessions are a convenient guise to help her scrub out the facets of my personality that she doesn't want. To wipe clean any thoughts of leaving Orchardview and the life *she* wants me to have.

Well, maybe I'm not going let that happen. I know who I am and what I want, and I'm not going to let Mama take that away from me. I stare down at my barely touched plate. Nausea roils in my stomach. It's time to make a choice.

∼

I look for Grace first thing on Monday.

We didn't talk all weekend, both of us too stubborn to be the one to cave in and call, I guess. But I need her more than ever now.

She's unloading books from her backpack into her locker. The sight of her makes my throat tighten with choked-back tears. I watch her for a moment before approaching.

Grace absently glances up as I walk over toward her, and her whole body stiffens. She crams the last two books in her locker, slams the door shut, and pivots on her heel in the opposite direction.

I rush after her. "Grace, wait."

"Gotta get to class," she says, shouldering her purse as she walks.

I grab her arm. "Can we talk?"

"I told you. I don't want to discuss Auden and whatever the hell is going on."

"I don't want to talk about Auden either," I say. "I just want to spend some time with you."

She visibly softens, but it's fleeting. She steels herself again. "I have class."

"What about lunch, then?"

"I'm going out with Brad."

This news makes me happy. "Things seem to be going really well between you two," I offer.

"Yeah," she says. "He's amazing."

"I'm happy for you, Grace. I really am."

She doesn't look at me. "I know. Thank you."

"Look," I say, softly. "I don't want things to be weird between us. I want my friend back."

"I'll always be here, Shelby."

We exchange a hesitant but genuine smile. I notch my head to the side. "Let's get out of here. Ditch first period. We'll go sit in the girls' bathroom in L wing and gossip while we fix our makeup, like we used to when we were freshmen."

Grace laughs. "Haven't we gotten a little old for that?"

"Do I look like I've matured since fifteen to you?"

"A fair point."

"Come on," I say. "One last time. For me."

Grace thinks I mean "one last time" until we are mature enough not to cut class hanging out in the girls' bathroom. But I'm thinking of something a little more permanent.

One last hangout with my best friend before I leave Orchardview forever.

CHAPTER 23

I'm ready to talk.

That was all my text to Auden said. I wrote at least ten different versions before I sent it. I need to be face-to-face with Auden before I share my new revelation. Maybe I'll take one look at him and realize precisely how absurd my plan seems. Maybe I'll feel more sure than ever. Either way, I figured it best to stay vague.

It takes him a full, agonizing minute to respond. Can we talk in person? Where are you right now?

I'm at home, but Mama's not going to let me out. It's way too late.

It's only 11.

I roll my eyes. Exactly. 11 p.m. on a school night. I bet Mama's already in bed.

Can't you make up a good reason to get out for a bit? You are an actress, after all.

I smirk. Give me a minute. I'll see what I can do.

Instead of coming up with an excuse, I go into the bathroom to check how I look. It's lame perhaps, but if there's a chance I might see him, I want to freshen up. I'm wearing a hoodie and pajama pants, and this afternoon, I stress-picked off my mascara. I run a touch-up coat over my eyelashes and shake out my hair. Thankfully, it looks wavy and messy in the beachy sort of way, not the sloppy, been-in-a-bun-all-day way.

Before I change clothes, however, I need to see if I can even leave the house at this point without getting grounded for life.

As I thought, Mama and Blake have gone into their room. I can hear the muffled sounds of their TV show through the walls. I hesitate at her door, racking my brain for a reason I'd need to leave. I *could* try to just sneak out, though with the position of Mama's bedroom, there's no way she wouldn't hear my car rev up and drive away.

My phone buzzes. Any luck?

I don't dare. Can't we just talk on the phone?

I'm coming to you, then. I've parked down the street. I'm walking to your house right now.

A bolt of electricity shoots through me. What??? I type.

I don't care about rules anymore. I have to see you.

I rush into my room and pull the curtain aside. The streetlight casts a faint glow over our front yard. I can't see anything other than bushes.

But then movement catches my eye. My phone buzzes with a text. I'm here. I'm coming up to the front door.

His tall outline materializes in the shadows, sending a flock of butterflies loose in my stomach.

Don't go to the door!!

I wave at him. With my bedside lamp on, he can probably only see my silhouette in the window, but he veers in my direction. My pulse beats in my throat. I cast a quick glance around my room. Do I dare?

Come to the window.

Auden approaches. His features become more distinct in the faint light cast. He seems hopeful and nervous all at once, which is just how I feel.

I hold up a hand, telling him to wait. After giving a final peer down the hallway and determining that Mama and Blake are in their room to stay, I pull my bedroom door shut quietly and click the lock.

Auden waits for me right in front of the glass. As a kid, I was afraid of these windows. It's so easy to take off the screen and crawl right into my room. At the moment, however, I'm pretty happy about it. Auden climbs in without so much as a creak.

We stand face-to-face for a moment. Instead of launching into my carefully planned explanation of my feelings, all I can do is gaze into those eyes of his. They seem to go on forever. Dark and mysterious but somehow brimming with warmth.

I take in every detail of his face. And once again, my intuition tells me it doesn't matter how much I remember. I know him now. And he knows me. The real me. It's right, whether or not it makes any sense.

Something unspoken passes between us. We both feel it. With a shaky breath, Auden grips my arms.

"Will you come with me?"

The room seems to spin around us, and all I can do is nod.

Without another word, Auden takes my face in his hands and kisses me.

I'm free-falling in this thrilling, perfect kiss. His hand tangles in my hair and tilts me back to deepen the kiss. I'm caught up in the moment, but then he releases his grip and steps back.

I steady myself, breathing hard. My face is flushed with heat. "Why did you stop?"

He closes his eyes. "I want to savor this moment."

I take him into my arms. It's so right, being close to him like this. Like wind. Like sunlight. I press my cheek against his neck.

"Are you sure?" he whispers.

"I'm scared of leaving," I admit. "But I can't stay here anymore."

He strokes my hair. "We'll make it work. It won't be easy, but we'll have each other. And we'll have our dreams. And one day, the world will know who we are."

My eyes are closed. I can picture the vision he's painting. I want it to be true. I want to believe that God or the Universe or whoever is out there will reward this leap of faith I'm taking by granting my greatest dream.

"What made you change your mind?" he asks, his breath soft on my face.

I almost hesitate because I don't want him to freak out, but the words push to the surface. "Mama scheduled another therapy session."

Auden steps back a little, eyes wide. "Are you serious?"

I nod, my throat tight, and he grips my arms. "I won't let it happen. I won't let them erase you."

My heart blossoms in my chest like a rose. Auden understands. He sees the real me, and he wants to protect it. I've never felt safer.

"I love you, Shelby. With every piece of my soul."

His words are summer rain on dry earth. This time, it's me who moves in for the kiss. I need the feeling of his lips. I need to close the distance between our bodies entirely.

Passion mixes with adrenaline. Our kisses grow more urgent. Our hands grab at each other hungrily. Auden lifts me, his lips still on mine, and carries me to my bed. We sit on the edge of the bed, swimming in the fervor of the moment.

"We'll never be apart again," he says, in between kisses.

"Never," I murmur.

His hands move along the curve of my hips, to my waist, up to my chest. He unzips my hoodie. I'm wearing a tank top underneath, but I pull back a little. I know we must have done this before, but it still feels new. I hesitate. Auden doesn't seem to notice. He rolls my hoodie off my arms, and it drops to the floor. Then he takes off his own jacket, and it falls to the ground as well. He is now breathing harder, and his lips begin to travel down my neck. He lays me down on my pillow. My head spins. Auden's hands canvass every inch of my body, and I can barely breathe. I push him back, gently but clearly.

Auden blinks, as if coming out of a fog. "What is it? What's wrong?"

"Nothing." I swallow. "I mean…this is all moving a little fast for me."

He squeezes his eyes shut. "You're right." He sighs and runs his hand along my arm. "It's just so wonderful to have you back like this, like the way it was before."

I smile shyly. "It's not that I wasn't enjoying it."

Auden brushes a hair from my eyes. "You can feel it, can't you? When we're like this? We have something special. Something so real. So pure."

I nod, my heart skipping. His intensity of feeling still surprises me. I've never met anyone like him. Frankly, I didn't think guys like him actually existed outside of movies and books.

"This feels familiar," I say, glancing around my dark room. "You sneaking into my room to make out with me."

Auden smiles. "It should."

I suddenly realize the implication. I think about the way he touched me, and heat rushes to my face. In my mind, I am still a virgin, but that might not be the reality.

"Auden," I say, my mouth dry. "Did we…Before, I mean, did we…?"

He studies my face, and then seems to understand. "No."

I'm taken aback. "We didn't?"

"You wanted to wait."

"That surprises me," I admit.

Auden sighs, stroking my arm again. "We might have. Eventually. If things hadn't gone the way they did."

I remember Karen's words at the gas station. *Not since last fall, when everything went crazy.* Once again, the longing to remember the missing pieces of my memory pulls at me.

"It's not that we haven't gotten pretty close. But never all the way."

"So I *am* still a virgin," I say.

He gets a mischievous glint in his eye. "For now."

"You're trouble," I say with a wink.

"What? You don't trust me?"

"Not in the slightest. In fact, I'm going to sleep with one eye open from now on."

I nestle into the warmth of his body, resting my head against his arm. He kisses my forehead, then sighs, tightening his grip around me.

"Are you?" I ask, after a moment. "A virgin, I mean."

He purses his lips. "No. Don't be mad."

Even though I know it shouldn't, hearing this confession stings. I try my best to seem nonchalant. "Actually, I assumed as much." Then I give him a sidelong glance. "You're too handsy to still be a virgin."

"I only have hands for you," he says, grinning.

"Whatever. I bet you've been with tons of girls."

His expression turns serious. "I never felt for them even a fragment of what I feel for you. Even if you and I were never to be with each other in that way, I'd still choose you a thousand times over any one of them."

His words are so lovely, it almost makes me ache. I kiss him hard on the cheek. He turns his face down to meet my lips. We fall back into the same tide of passion—ardent, like two wanderers in the desert who have found an oasis.

"Let's go. Tonight," Auden murmurs into the kiss.

"Hm?" I ask, still drunk on his sweetness.

"To California. Let's go."

I pull away. "Tonight?"

"Yeah. Why not?"

"I'm not even packed."

"I can help you. What do you really need, anyway? A few sets of clothes, a toothbrush, and we're on our way."

It's so reckless and so very Auden of him. "We haven't made any arrangements. We don't have money for gas and food or a place to stay once we get there."

"We can figure that out as we go. Besides, you said your mother was taking you back to therapy. We have to go before that happens."

"I know, but that's not until this weekend—"

His eyes widen. "This weekend? I can't wait that long."

"Of course you can," I say with an amused smile.

"I may die, Shelby."

I roll my eyes. "Calm down, Romeo. Mama said we were leaving Thursday after school. I'll need until then to be ready. But that's only three days away."

Auden presses a kiss to my forehead. "It will feel like three years, but it'll be worth the wait."

I gaze into his dark, beautiful eyes. "I think you're right."

He kisses me again. The sensation of his lips on my throat sends a surge of fire down my back, and I let out a shaky breath. Auden's kisses move down to my collarbones.

A quiet bang, like the sound of a door closing in the hallway, makes us both jump. We stare wide eyed at one another.

"Mama," I whisper, panicked.

Auden scrambles out of bed. "I'll hide."

"No," I say, jumping up after him. "You have to leave. Right now!"

I rush to the window, and he helps me open it as carefully and quietly as we can. He's about to climb through, when he hesitates.

"Will you call me tomorrow?" he asks.

"Of course I will."

Auden's gaze is filled with a mixture of desperation and hope. "Three days is a long time. You won't change your mind in between now and then?"

"Impossible. Now go. Hurry."

He kisses me one last time. "Three days," he says.

The words send a thrill of nervous energy through my entire body. I echo him breathlessly. "Three days."

CHAPTER 24

I float three feet above the ground. The sounds and smells of high school ebb and flow around me, but nothing touches me. In my heart, I'm already on my way to California, the wind in my face and the Pacific coastline cresting on the horizon in front of me.

As excited as I am, I also feel the weight of responsibility to say goodbye to Orchardview properly. I want to dig my fingers into this small-town earth one last time. I make a point to talk to everyone I can, even if it's just exchanging a sentence or two. I thank my teachers after each class. I'll remember this place. It may not be where I belong, but I won't forget the memories I made here.

Then I get the idea to film it all. A moving snapshot of Orchardview High to keep with me when I feel homesick. As class historian, I can easily convince people that I'm working on a project for school. I wander the halls before school starts with my official video camera, taking in every detail and face and interaction I can.

Two of my friends from drama stand in a small cluster of people near the gym. As I approach, Bailey Perkins squeals and hides her face. "What are you filming for, Shelbs? I'm having a terrible hair day."

"It's a farewell video for the seniors," I say, pointing the camera at her. "Say your goodbyes. They'll always remember your awful hair."

As I film the boisterous group, my eyes fall to one of the girls who has stepped out of the circle a little. She's glaring at me. Barely trying to hide it. It takes me aback a little. I try to pretend I don't notice but mentally try to place how I know her and why she'd possibly be angry with me. She's a sophomore. We barely know each other. I think her name's Sara Drake, but that's about all I know.

Luckily, the first bell rings, and the crowd disperses. Sara Drake disappears into the crowd of students heading to class. I walk back to my locker to put my camera away. I guess I need to say goodbye to it as well. After removing and pocketing the SD card, I gently place it back in its carrying case. Maybe it's silly, but I've loved being historian. That's one of the few perks of going to a tiny school like Orchardview High. It's much easier to be a big fish in this small pond.

And ponds don't get much bigger than California. I'll be a pretty puny fish there. The thought makes me nervous and a little sad.

The feeling lingers the entire day. After school, I walk through my empty house with a tightness in my chest. Maybe it's just a sudden rush of nostalgia, but wish I'd brought my camera to film my house. The living room, where I watched my movies in the early days, sitting cross-legged on the carpet. The kitchen, where I ran lines with Grace for my first school play. My bedroom.

I smooth my hand over the dingy wallpaper and try to push this feeling down. But in the back of my mind, I'm aware that this will be my last night sleeping in this house.

Tomorrow is Thursday.

I'm in a daze at school the next morning but not in the way I was just two days ago. I'm not floating and dreaming of California. I'm scanning the halls and faces, trying not to freak out at the thought that I am about to leave everything I know.

At lunch, I carry my tray to my usual spot with heavy footsteps, expecting to be alone again. But to my surprise, Grace and Brad Corbin are there. She's sitting with her legs across his, laughing at something he said. When she sees me, her smile softens. Something about that simple gesture strikes me right in the heart.

"Didn't expect to see you two here," I say, walking over.

Grace shrugs. "I told Brad we should eat at school more often."

Brad gives me a wry smile. "She thinks you and I could get along. Apparently, we're both sarcastic."

"Perfect," I say, with a short laugh. "Now we can join forces and annoy her twice as much."

I sit down beside Grace. She moves her legs off Brad and faces me. "We think you should join us this weekend for homecoming."

I'd been vaguely aware that was this weekend, but for obvious reasons, I hadn't paid much attention. I press my fork into the wilting side salad that came with today's lunch, hoping she doesn't see the twitch in my expression.

"I'll think about it."

Grace sets her hand on my arm. "Come. There're going to be a whole group of us. We're going to dinner in Riverside. And then up to Kelly Brewer's parents' cabin after the dance. It's going to be really great."

"That sounds fun," I say, trying to sound as sincere as possible.

And it *does* sound fun. In that moment, I'm struck by how little I've actually seen Grace in recent weeks. And now I'm leaving. The thought twists in me. We should have done so many things. One last trip to get milkshakes and onion rings. One last night talking in my room until two in the morning. I even wish I could go to one last school dance.

But I won't be here Saturday, of course. By tomorrow morning I'll be in California.

"So, you'll come?" Grace asks, her expression hopeful.

"Sure," I say. "Count me in." But I can't meet Grace's eye.

"Yay!" She reaches over to give me a hug and speaks words for me only "I just want my best friend back."

The lump tightens in my throat. "Me too."

Grace pulls away and carries on telling me about their awesome plans. Brad chimes in with the occasional sarcastic remark, as promised. Had this lunch taken place a few weeks ago, I'd have thoroughly enjoyed myself. Today, however, knowing everything I know, it fills me with an overwhelming sense of melancholy.

Grace gives me a quick, one-arm side hug on her way to class, completely unaware that she might never see me again. I almost reach out to her to say something. I almost tell her. *I'm leaving to go to Hollywood, Grace. Tonight. This is goodbye.*

But I can't do it. And maybe it's better this way. I'll call her tomorrow morning when Auden and I are on the road and miles from Orchardview.

I carry my somber mood to rehearsal. On Wednesday's practice, the sight of Mr. Lyman only confirmed my choice. Today, his resigned half smile twists the knife deeper. He'll find another Juliet—I'm pretty sure Bailey Perkins knows the part. It's more of a feeling that I'm betraying him by getting out when he never could.

When he sees me, however, his eyes brighten and he motions me over.

"What's up, Captain?"

He grins. "I have some news for you. But you'd better sit down first."

I lift an eyebrow but do as he suggests. He glances around to make sure no one else is listening, and then turns to me.

"I couldn't stop thinking about our conversation last week," he begins. "About you, actually."

"Really?"

He nods. "You have talent, Shelby. Real talent. Maybe I never went and lived my dreams in New York, because I knew this was the level of work I'm suited for."

"That's not true—" I start, but he holds up a hand.

"It is. But we're talking about you. You're meant for bigger things than Orchardview. We both know that. And though I may not have lived in New York or LA, I do have connections. I went to a theater convention a few years ago in California. Long story short, I have a friend who works out there as a talent scout. He's got some pretty significant clients and connections with major studios and casting directors. Anyway, I gave him a call. Told him all about you. And…" Mr. Lyman loves to pause for dramatic effect.

"And?" I ask, my mouth going dry as sand.

"And he's coming to opening night to scope you out!"

I'm speechless. Mr. Lyman raises his eyebrows. "Well?"

"Wow. I'm shocked." And terrified. And dismayed.

He smiles. "This is big, Shelby. There are no guarantees, of course, but he's the real deal. Impress him, and you could have some serious opportunities."

All I can do is stare. My brain's going a hundred miles an hour. Then Ana Guerrero informs Mr. Lyman that we'd better get started. He calls the cast to the stage. I follow, but I'm lost, falling in a downward spiral of my own thoughts.

I don't want to see it. I don't want to feel it. But I can't deny that doubt is crawling into my heart.

After rehearsal, I gather my things in a daze. As I shoulder my backpack, my phone buzzes. I pull it out just in time to miss the call. There are two other missed calls from Auden. And several texts. My hand tightens around my phone. I suddenly feel like I going to be sick.

Cam comes up beside me, and I jam my phone back into my bag.

"Geez, Shelby," he says, with the tang of irritation on his voice. "You were really out of it today. What's wrong?"

"Nothing… I've got a lot on my mind, that's all."

"What else is new?" He mutters under his breath.

I scowl at him. "What's that supposed to mean?"

"I'm sorry, but it's true. You've been in your own little Shelby world for a few weeks now. You never want to hang out. You always rush away right after practice. What's going on?"

Having this conversation is officially the last thing in the world I want. "I'm having monthlong PMS. It's a rare medical condition."

"Oh," he says, taken a back. "Sorry, I didn't know."

I almost break my eyes from rolling them so hard. "I was being sarcastic, Cam."

After a beat, he says, "Right."

I can't help laughing, and thankfully, he sees the humor and joins in. I hate to say it, but I'm going to miss this guy.

Instead of heading straight home, I drive through the shady streets of my town. One last time. My hands feel clammy as they grip the steering wheel. Everything around me suddenly seems too good to leave. Orchardview. Grace. The scout. Cam. My street. My house. Even Mama.

Maybe I'm not ready. Maybe I don't really want to leave.

Not yet anyway. Maybe Mr. Lyman has presented me with the perfect compromise. If this talent scout likes what he sees and wants to work with me, I won't have to go to Hollywood with only a hope and a prayer. I'd have real work.

Or maybe the talent scout won't think I'm good enough, and I'll be stuck here, never getting the chance to leave. And besides, going to California isn't just about living my dreams. Or even being with Auden. It's a fresh start for me in a new place—a place where no one will try to change who I am.

I must be having cold feet. That's perfectly normal before making a major life change, right?

It's like I'm moving through wet cement as I walk up to the front door of my house. The weight of this decision hangs on me, and I'm stuck.

"Shelby." Mama's voice comes from the dining room. I jump, dropping my keys. Brow furrowed, I peer around the dividing wall.

"Mama? What are you doing home?" She wasn't supposed to be here for at least two hours.

Seeing her face, an alarm immediately goes off in my heart. She sits at the kitchen table, her fingers laced together, eerily calm…

"Come here," she says.

"Is everything okay?" I sit carefully on the chair across from her.

Then I see it. Auden's jacket. The one he took off the other night as we kissed on my bed. Mama lifts it from the floor beside her and sets it on the table.

"Saw this on the floor of your room the other day. Didn't know quite what to make of it."

Breath evaporates in my lungs. He left in such a hurry. How could I not have seen it? He must have accidentally kicked it out of view when he scrambled off my bed. I stare at Mama.

"There was this little voice in my head when I saw it. And I knew I had to look into it."

The jacket lies there on the tabletop like a rattlesnake about to strike. Mama's expression darkens.

"I made a few calls and it seems he got out early on good behavior."

I have no words to give her, but I'm sure my face must say it all.

Mama leans forward and speaks in a chillingly calm voice. "How long have you been seeing Auden?"

CHAPTER 25

When it comes to fight or flight, with Mama, I always pick flight. Apologize. Say what she wants you to say, and get out of there.

But in this moment, I can't move. Or maybe it's that I *won't* move. I'm tired of giving in, of taking my lashes and keeping quiet.

"Answer me," Mama says through gritted teeth.

The irony of her demand causes a harsh, bitter laugh to escape my lungs.

"*You* want answers from *me*?"

Mama's brow furrows, but I'm emboldened.

"I've had nothing but questions and confusion for the last month, and *you* are the reason why. And yet there you sit, furious, demanding answers from *me*?"

She starts to respond, but I talk over her.

"Okay, I'll answer your question. How long have I been seeing Auden? I believe it's been two years."

Her lip curls slightly at my tone. I lean forward, pushing my hand on the table. "Isn't that right, Mama? Or did you mean how long have I been seeing him since you erased my memories?"

"He hasn't wasted any time filling your head with lies," Mama says, shaking her head.

"So it's a lie that we dated for two years?"

"I'm not trying to say it was."

"Then is it a lie that you had my memories of him erased without my knowledge while I thought I was only having the accident erased?"

Her eyes flash. "Yes, that *is* a lie."

I push myself away from the table. "Oh please. Are you suggesting the memories vanished on their own? Or that Dr. Stevens decided to throw that in for fun? A bonus package? Two major life events erased for the price of one!"

"Sit down," Mama snaps.

My fists clench. "No."

"You don't understand what's going on."

"You're absolutely right about that, Mama. That's the most accurate statement I've heard in weeks."

Mama stands. "You want truth? You won't get it from that boy. I bet he's conveniently avoided telling you that he spent the summer in prison."

"He *did* tell me that, actually."

"And he told you why?"

"Yes."

Mama's smirk fades. "He did?"

"Yes, don't be so surprised that someone would be completely honest with me. I don't judge him for running away. Who can blame him for wanting to leave this stupid town?"

Mama sighs heavily. "Oh, Shelby." The sympathy in her voice makes me squirm. She shakes her head, her expression hardening. "That's not why he went to prison. He lied to you. That's what he does."

My anger burns strong. "You're just saying that. You'd say anything to turn me against him."

"I can prove it." Mama's eyes are dark. "Auden went to jail for a hit-and-run. He killed someone. Edmund Drake. You were in the passenger seat when it happened. That was the accident we erased during treatment."

Her words are like lightning, striking me right in the heart. My skin burns from contact. My vision blurs. All sound fades aside from a sharp ringing in my ears. I take a staggering step backwards.

"I don't believe you."

"Auden is the one who would say anything to get you on his side," Mama says.

My legs feel weak and shaky. "You're lying," I stammer. "You're just trying to scare me."

Mama sighs heavily. "I thought this moment might come. I checked with Dr. Stevens first, and he said it would be okay to show you, if you ever regressed, just so long as you don't look at them for too long." Without another word, she walks into her room and comes back with her laptop in one hand and a file folder in another. She tosses the file on the table and flips it open.

Black-and-white newsprint glares up at me. My eyes go to the headlines of two clipped articles. LOCAL MAN KILLED IN HIT-AND-RUN ACCIDENT

And then: RECKLESS TEEN CHARGED IN DEATH OF ORCHARDVIEW MAN

There's a picture with the second article. Even in the grainy newspaper image, it's easy to see Auden being led out of a courtroom, hands cuffed behind his back.

And lightning strikes again.

But this flash is undeniable. I've seen this exact moment. I was there as they led him away.

I remember.

I stare up at Mama, open-mouthed. She sighs, opening her laptop.

"Contrary to what you might think, it doesn't give me any pleasure to dig this up." She seems to be searching for a file on the computer. "There's a reason we took the extreme measures we did to erase all of that for you. I didn't want you to suffer like you were. Blake and I agreed that we would talk about the accident and your life before the treatment as little as possible. Anything to prevent the memories from coming back."

She turns the laptop screen toward me. I half expect to see bloody images of a crash scene. Instead, it's a video. From Mama's phone, I assume. I'm sitting across from the doctor's desk, looking completely broken.

She clicks play, and the sound of my own voice, weak from crying, sends a chill down my spine.

"I want it all to go away," Video Shelby says.

Only Dr. Stevens's hands are in the camera angle. "Now, you understand that this memory erasure is permanent. There's no going back."

I nod shakily, wiping my eyes. "I want to forget him. I want to forget everything."

Video Mama says something to Dr. Stevens, but the audio is too muffled to make out. Then the footage ends.

Mama closes her laptop slowly.

"The day of the accident, you were in a terrible argument. You were trying to break up with Auden. Grace was at the same Halloween party, and she saw him yelling at you. You were trying to leave, but he wouldn't let you. He made you drive with him. He was so angry that he didn't watch where he was going and didn't see Mr. Drake until it was too late."

All I can feel is the *bang, bang, bang*ing of my heart against the walls of my chest. I shake my head, backing away.

"You wanted to forget him, Shelby. After what he did to you. After what he did to that man. You begged for us to erase him."

The room spins around me. Darkness seeps into the corners of my vision until there's only a tunnel ahead. My knees give out, but I don't even realize I'm falling, until I catch myself on the back of the couch.

Mama's on her feet, her eyes wide. I hold out a hand to her. Not to beckon her closer, but so she doesn't come any closer.

"I only wanted to protect you, Shelby. I would never have stirred all of this up if he had kept his distance."

Almost as if he could sense what was going on, Auden calls my phone. I know it's him without even having to look. Mama does, too, and has her hand in my bag before I can even straighten myself.

"Mama," I say, my voice strained.

She pulls out my phone and lifts it to her ear. I'm shaking, but no words come out.

Auden's muffled voice speaks my name before Mama cuts him off.

"This is LouAnne. I'm going to give you one warning, and you'd better listen good. Right now, by calling her, you are in direct violation of Shelby's restraining order."

She shakes her head, glaring. "No. Not a chance. No, you listen to me. This ends *now*. Don't call her. Don't try to see her. And if you come within one hundred yards of her or this house, I will turn you in so fast, it'll make your head spin. Because that would be in violation of your parole, wouldn't it? Do you want to go back to prison, Auden?" She pauses for emphasis, and then sets her jaw.

"Stay away from my daughter."

CHAPTER 26

The dream returns that night.

Once again, I'm surrounded by complete, suffocating darkness. And just as before, the only thing I can see is blue.

A small, round light appears in the blackness, moving gently in short waves, up and down, up and down. But it's too high. Too close.

An awful sense of foreboding presses down over the entire scene. It's all wrong. So wrong. So terrible and wrong. I scream, and then…the light is gone.

I wake with a start. I'm on my stomach, my face pressed into my pillow. I fight to draw in a breath. Only then do I realize I'm sobbing once again.

I push myself out of bed and out of my room. Almost by habit, I find my way to Mama's chair. Wrapped in my blanket, I curl myself into a ball in the soft fold of leather. I squeeze my eyes shut and will myself to fall asleep. I need to sleep before I start thinking. If I start thinking, I'll start crying again.

But it's too late. Fresh tears burn my already dry, swollen eyes. I bury my face into the arm of the chair, my shoulders shaking with silent sobs.

I guess this is what happens when everything you thought you knew turns out to be a lie.

Mama finds me in her chair the next morning. Her hand gently shakes my shoulder. My face probably looks awful after a restless night of nightmares and crying, because her expression is soft.

"Oh, my Shelby girl."

Her tenderness breaks the thin barrier holding back my emotions, and I start crying again even though my whole face hurts. Mama shushes me gently, stroking my head.

"I'll call you in sick today," she says, quietly. "You go on and get back in bed."

I obey, even though I don't want to be in my room. Lying in my bed, I'm open and vulnerable to more thoughts. Thoughts about that night here in my bed with him, in his arms, planning our future in California. But those starry memories are immediately marred by the dark reality. The accident that started all of this—my panic attacks, the lies, the erased memories—is because of Auden. And worse, an innocent man was killed in the crossfire. No wonder he tried so hard to hide it from me. No wonder he lied.

The thought makes me bury my face in my pillow and sob more. There's nothing else to do. I've never felt so completely miserable in my entire life.

Later that morning, there's a gentle knock at the door. Mama took the day off work to be here for me. Or to keep an eye on me and make sure I don't run to Auden? She peeks her head in the door and sees that I'm awake.

"Brought you a little something," she says. I'm not accustomed to this sweet tone in her voice. It seems like forever since she spoke to me that way.

She steps into my room and presents me with a huge fountain Dr Pepper from my favorite gas station. "A little medicine for what ails you."

I smile weakly. "Thanks, Mama."

She sets the drink on my nightstand and sits beside me. "Did you get a nap?" she asks, resting her hand on my leg.

I nod, even though it's a lie.

"That's good. When life hands you garbage, sleep it off. That's what I always say." She's quiet for a moment, perhaps searching for the right words.

I stare at the condensation on the soda cup. A droplet slides down, like a tear.

"Look, Shelby, I know this isn't easy. Heartbreak. Finding out that the person you love isn't who they said they were. I've been there. It hurts like hell. But no storm lasts forever, you understand? You'll get past this. Quicker than you'd think."

She makes it sound so simple. I wish it *were* that simple. I'd give anything not to feel this way. Even now, knowing Auden lied to me, I'm tugged with the ache to see him. I tell myself that it's because I want to confront him, but deep down, I know there's more to it.

I stare at the ceiling for two solid hours that night before I accept that I'm not going to sleep any time soon. I can't.

Auden went to jail for a hit-and-run that claimed the life of Edmund Drake. You were in the passenger seat when it happened.

The words repeat over and over, running mercilessly through my mind. And the more I think about it, the darker the places it takes me.

I was there. And we were arguing? What about? Is it possible that I somehow contributed to the accident? Am I complicit in Edmund Drake's death?

The image of Sara Drake glaring at me on Tuesday in the halls burns like bile in my throat. My head feels like it's being squeezed in a vise.

I don't want to think about it anymore, but at the same time, I need to know more. I need to see everything in that folder. Mama will be asleep by now… Had she left the folder on the counter? I sit up slowly. My head throbs from spending almost two days in bed crying. I press my fingers to my temples. When it abates a little, I slip out of my room.

The kitchen is dark, and the ticking of the clock creates an ominous tension. But I can just make out the outline of a yellow manila folder on the counter. My hands go cold and clammy. Never has a simple folder filled me with more dread.

I touch the smooth paper. A simple flick of my wrist will reveal all of the information I require.

Panic swells within me. My mouth begins to water in that

sickening feeling just before you vomit. If I read these articles, what's to stop the panic from coming back? The PTSD? Everything I fought so hard to overcome? I can't even *think* about the accident without nearly passing out. What will happen if I come face-to-face with hard facts and details?

I pull my hand away. I can't do it. I need my strength—or what remains of it—now, more than ever.

And does it really matter how the accident happened exactly? A man was killed. And Auden has openly lied to me about it. That's really all I need to know.

I go back to bed and manage to sleep until the early afternoon. I guess my body finally had enough. When I wake, I lie in bed, staring blankly. At least I've stopped crying. Maybe I finally ran out of tears. They've been replaced with a throbbing headache. After guzzling some Dr Pepper with a few Tylenol, I'm finally feeling good enough to rummage through the refrigerator for epic amounts of snack therapy.

Blake is sitting in his armchair, flipping through the newspaper. He looks up when I emerge, and a smile brightens his face. "Nice to see you up and about, Shelbs."

I give him half a smile. "I need chocolate. And ice cream."

He chuckles. "Help yourself, dear."

I've just filled my arms with options when there's a knock at the front door. Mama sweeps out of her room. "I'll get it."

I stack one more string cheese on my pile of treats when a familiar voice makes me freeze. I spin around.

Sure enough, Grace is standing in my doorway, carrying a

large garment bag in one hand, a duffle bag in the other, and a big (and somewhat strained) smile on her face. Mama has a satisfied grin.

"Hey Shelbs," Grace says, with a notch too much perkiness. "I'm here to get ready for homecoming with you."

I almost drop the food I'm holding. "What?"

"Homecoming is tonight, remember? Dinner in Riverside? Kelly's parents' cabin after the dance?"

"I remember. I just can't believe you think I'd still want to go."

Grace shoots a quick "help" look to Mama, who takes over, planting her fists on her hips.

"We talked about this, Shelby. You can't sit in your room crying forever. You need to get out of the house and get on with your life."

"Fair enough," I say, sharply. "But the fact is, I *have* been crying in my room for two days, and the last thing I feel like doing is going to homecoming."

Grace's shoulders sink. "I understand," she says, her voice finally sounding normal again. "I really do. But I also agree with your mom. You need distraction right now. Come on. You *know* it'll be fun. You can come back and cry in your room when it's over. But tonight, allow yourself a few hours to get your mind off it all."

I look back and forth, from her to Mama. It strikes me that while I am freshly processing the awful truth about Auden, it's nothing new to them. And what's more, they have seen me go through this mourning process once already. They want me to be happy, even if they are anxious for me to move on faster than I might be ready for.

"I don't have a dress," I say, offering a weak argument.

Grace gives the garment bag a little shake. "I brought one of my backups that I was planning to return. It's really cute."

"Well, I don't have a date either. Obviously."

Grace winks. "You're going to make Cam Haler's night."

"Oh gosh…"

She squeezes my hand. "Please, Shelby? For me?"

And just like that, I crumble. Grace doesn't need to hear me say the words to know I'm giving in. She lets out a happy little squeal. "We're going to have so much fun!"

CHAPTER 27

Grace wasn't wrong. Getting ready for homecoming with her is a blast. It's like old times. Like when she would spend the night in middle school and we'd do elaborate makeovers on each other, getting dolled up like the Harajuku Girls and then testing our looks out on the shoppers at the grocery store, giggling like crazy.

Grace's spare dress is gorgeous. It's a flowy teal Grecian-style dress. Grace pulls my hair into a curled updo with a gold headband and applies shimmering eyeshadow to my eyelids.

She wears a daring red dress. The kind of dress that will probably make Brad Corbin's eyes pop out of their sockets.

We stand side by side in the mirror, examining ourselves. Grace puts her arm around my waist. "Geez, we're so hot."

I smooth down my hair. "Not sure the boys can handle this."

Like a hidden snake striking, I suddenly think of Auden. I wish he could see me all dressed up like this. I can almost imagine his reaction. No doubt it would be fairly dramatic and poetic. An involuntary smile tugs at my lips just thinking about it. But it's followed by a crush of sadness. In a perfect world, Auden would be my date to homecoming. But the world isn't perfect. It never will be.

I'm starting to worry that I'm going to carry this heartache with me all night, but leave it to Cam to cheer me up. When he arrives to pick me up, upon first seeing me, he falls to one knee and presses a hand to his heart.

"Did my heart love till now? Forswear it, sight! For I ne'er saw true beauty till this night."

It's such a quintessentially Cam moment. I roll my eyes, but I appreciate it. I have to admit, it's nice to spend time with him again. He's a lot of fun when he's not shamelessly flirting with every girl in the group. Or maybe that's partly why I don't mind being his date. There's no fear that he's actually in love with me. It's completely relaxed and casual.

In fact, as the evening wears on, "relaxed" is the perfect word to describe the whole event. How can you not be relaxed with the friends you've had since elementary school? We all know the same people, the same places, even the same inside jokes. We can reference something that happened seven years ago, and everyone understands. Hanging out with them is easy. And fun. And uncomplicated.

The only moment of discomfort comes when Cam finally insists on a slow dance. I've been successfully avoiding it so far, but when Aerosmith's "Crazy" comes on, his brow sets with resolve.

"You have two choices, Seashell. You dance with me now, or I drag you by your pretty little strappy sandals onto the stage for a lip sync of this song."

I sigh wearily. "Fine. I'll dance."

Cam dramatically kisses my hand, and we step out onto the dance floor, which is really just the gym with some balloons and tissue paper added. I put one hand on his shoulder and hold my other out for his. He raises an eyebrow. Placing my other hand on his shoulder, he wraps his arms around my waist and pulls me closer.

"This is how we dance to Aerosmith," he says in my ear, his breath tickling my neck.

My stomach clenches. It feels wrong to be in Cam's arms like this. Like a betrayal.

"I wasn't aware there was an instruction manual," I say, deadpan.

Cam nods. "Very strict code, actually. For your information, when the song ends, I am obligated to spin you out, spin you back, dip you, and then kiss you on the lips."

"If you even try it, you're going to lose your front teeth."

Cam laughs. "Oh, my sarcastic little Seashell." He's quiet for a moment. "It's good to have you back."

I squirm a little. "I didn't go anywhere."

He analyzes my face, then says, "Maybe not physically, but in your head. I don't know what was going on, but I'm glad you are okay and it's over now."

Over now. The perfect phrasing, even if hearing him say it makes my heart sink. I rest my head on Cam's shoulder to avoid his gaze as my eyes go wet with tears.

As the song ends, the DJ's voice echoes through the gym. "And now we have a special request, made by a secret admirer, no less."

The crowd ripples with cheers and excitement, but my heart stops a little. *Auden?*

"This one goes out to Grace Bellingham."

The opening strains of some cheesy pop love song drift through the speakers, and I'm about to mentally bring Brad down a peg for his bad taste in music when I meet eyes with Grace.

Her face is ashen. I know that expression. It's the same one she had when I picked her up on the night Mike Jasper took the wheels from Brad's car.

I break away from Cam's grip and run to her.

"It's our song," she says. Breath seems to be difficult for her. "He's here. I know it."

Brad glares at the DJ. "I'm going to find out where. Right now."

I put my arm around Grace as Brad leaves. "We can go," I say. "I'll have Cam take us."

Grace's eyes are on Brad. For a long moment, she doesn't say anything. And then, all at once, a look of steely determination settles on her face. She turns to me sharply. "No. I won't let him do this. I won't let Mike ruin my night. He doesn't get to affect one more minute of my life." She narrows her eyes. "I know where he is." Then she grabs my hand. "Will you come with me, Shelbs?"

"Of course I will."

We slip out of the dance quickly, before Brad can question Grace's choice. Unlike the night of the bonfire, tonight the darkened school's walkways are empty. I nervously check Grace out of the corner of my eye, but she's not crying like I expected her to be. She's calm and strong. The only time she stops her determined pace is to pull out her cell phone and open up the voice notes. She presses record and puts it back in her purse, leaving the top open. She meets my impressed gaze with a smile.

"Let's do this."

I recognize Mike Jasper's tall frame as we round the corner of the auditorium. He's sitting on one of the picnic tables near the track field. He looks older, more worn down. The last few years don't seem to have been kind to him. When he sees Grace, the hopeful, almost desperate flash of love on his face reminds me of Auden, and it sends a cold chill over my whole body.

"You came," he says.

Grace stops, several yards away. "I came to put a stop to this, Mike. It ends now. Tonight."

He scoffs. "You don't just *end* something like this. There are two people involved here, Grace. Two hearts."

"Your heart isn't my concern anymore. And it never will be again. I've taken out a more extensive restraining order against you. If you try to contact me in any way, if you get involved in my life in any way, I am going to turn you in. No hesitation this time."

Mike's eyes blaze. "You think I care about a piece of paper? That's not going to stop me. You can't get rid of me that easily."

His rage only enhances her perfect calm. A little smile comes to her lips. "Actually, I can. I'm not afraid of you anymore, Mike. Or your heart. That's what I came here to say. To give you a warning to stay away. But even if you don't, even that's not my problem anymore. That's for the police to deal with." She slides her hand over her purse. "I've recorded this conversation, so it shouldn't be difficult to convince them that you're a threat to me."

Mike stares at her, speechless. Grace takes my hand again. "Come on, Shelby. I'm done here."

Without so much as a glance back, she turns and walks away. I can feel her pulse beating fast as we head back to the gym. Emotion unexpectedly chokes my throat.

"I'm so proud of you, Grace. You were amazing."

Tears glisten on her eyes, in spite of the determined smile. "I'm not afraid anymore. I never will be again."

For a moment, I envy her resolved strength. Grace has taken control of her life. And she didn't have to run away to another state to do it. She simply made up her mind and stood her ground. Maybe I need to follow her example. Maybe I've been overthinking everything, as I always do.

Maybe the answers have been here in Orchardview all along.

~

We don't make it to Kelly's parents' cabin. I'm not worried about Grace. She's earned a perfect night, and truth is, that means her being alone with Brad Corbin. I talk Cam into bringing me home early. He drives me to my house and parks in the driveway. His tie rests undone around his neck, and I'm wearing his jacket to ward off the chill in the air. It's a perfectly comfortable moment, so of course Cam goes and ruins that.

Faking a yawn, he stretches, and then slides his arm around the back of my seat. Just like he used to during our brief relationship. It was charming then. Not so cute now.

I give him a look. He waggles his eyebrows, and I push him away. "Hands to yourself, Haler. You get plenty of action with me during play practice. Now, walk me to the door like a gentleman."

Cam sighs but obliges. At the doorstep, I can't help comparing him to Auden. They're different in so many ways. Cam's like my brother. I've known him since the fourth grade. Maybe that was part of Auden's appeal. He was a mystery to be discovered. Cam's the open book I've read a thousand times.

"I did have fun," I say. "So thank you."

He takes my hand. "It was a pleasure, my lady."

"Guess I have to give you your coat back, huh?"

Cam smiles and holds his hands out to help me. I turn, and he slides the jacket from my arms. And then, in a swift and smooth movement, he spins me around, slides his arm around my waist, and kisses me.

One quick peck on the lips, and then he steps back, grinning. I stare at him. "What was that?"

He blinks. "Just an innocent kiss between friends."

"No, Cam. Friends don't kiss on the mouth. I've never kissed Grace on the mouth."

"Well, maybe you ought to try it some time. And, uh, let me know when that's going to happen."

I glare at him and he rolls his head back.

"Okay, okay. I'm sorry."

"I'm not one of your conquests, Cam. And this isn't rehearsal. You don't get to kiss me without asking."

His eyebrows raise hopefully. "So you'd say yes if I asked?"

"No. I absolutely would not."

"Even if I said I was overcome by your enchanting good looks?"

I smile in spite of myself and shove him. "Go on, get out of here. And maybe I'll let you keep your front teeth."

"Can't blame a guy for trying." He bows low. "Good night, good night. Parting is such sweet sorrow."

I'm still shaking my head as I close the front door behind me. He can be infuriating, but he's not a bad guy. Knowing Cam, he's probably off to be the king of the theater crowd's after-party somewhere. And I'd bet ten bucks he kisses another girl before the night is out.

Mama's dozing in her chair. She hasn't waited up for me in years. I come into the living room and give her arm a tiny shake. She opens her eyes with a startled half snore, half gasp.

"I'm back," I say, softly.

"Did you have a nice time?" She asks, her voice heavy with sleep.

"It was a lot of fun. Thanks for convincing me to go."

She smiles. "I'm so glad, baby."

I pat her arm. "Go on back to bed. I'm home safe."

She nods, and I help her out of her chair and into her bed. Back in my room, I shut my door with a sigh. A surge of negative memories from the last few days spent crying greet me. It doesn't seem possible to escape.

My eyes fall to my window. Blake securely nailed on the screen this morning. No more late-night visitors for me. Except a flicker of movement outside catches my eye. Goose bumps rise on my skin. I take a step to the window, but I hear him before I see him.

Auden. Standing on the front lawn, calling my name at the top of his lungs.

CHAPTER 28

He calls my name again, probably waking half the neighborhood. I run for the front door, not certain if this is reality or a bad dream. I know it's not a dream when I see Mama and Blake fly out of their room. I've never seen so much rage in Mama's eyes.

"Blake, get your shotgun."

"What? Are you crazy?" I screech.

She has her phone in her hands. "I'm calling 911."

I grab her arm. "Mama, please! Don't. I can handle this."

"You won't be saying a word to that boy." Mama shoves past me. I cast a pleading look to Blake, but he just follows Mama, his brow deeply furrowed. All I can do is run after them.

The picture that waits for me on the front lawn is like something out of my worst nightmare. Mama and Auden, face-to-face, screaming at each other. Mama looks like she's going to rip his eyes out. Auden looks awful, like he hasn't slept in three days. And he probably hasn't.

"I warned you," Mama screams. "I told you to stay the hell away."

"She's not your property," Auden yells back. "She's free to decide who she loves."

"She could never love a *murderer* like you."

Now it's my turn to scream. I pull at Mama's shoulder. "STOP THIS!"

Mama's eyes burn past me, pouring molten rage on Auden. "I'm calling the police. You'll never see her again, because you're heading back to prison."

Taking advantage of Mama's distracted fury, I lunge and pull the phone from her hands.

"Shelby!"

"You're not calling the police," I say.

"Don't be an idiot. Blake, give me your phone."

I turn to him. "Let me talk to him first. *Please.*"

"Blake," Mama snaps.

Tears well in my eyes, prickling in my throat. "I'm not going to go back to him. It's over between us. But let us say goodbye."

I can't look at Auden as I say this. I don't think I could bear the pain on his face.

Blake sighs and then gives Mama a single nod of reassurance. She's breathing hard, red in the face, but she relents to his judgment.

"You have five minutes," she says to me. "Say what you need to say, and if he's not one hundred yards away in five minutes, so help me God, I will have the police drag him away in handcuffs."

She storms back into the house, Blake following behind her. The sound of the front door slamming makes me flinch. I stare down at the grass. I want to run from this moment, erase it from my memory forever.

"Not one call," Auden says, his voice low, trembling. His tone cuts me right to the heart. "Not one text. Is that how you say goodbye, Shelby?"

"Mama took my phone. She's had it all weekend."

"And you couldn't steal it? Demand she give it back?" Auden swears and scrapes a hand through his hair. "Maybe you didn't care. You sure seemed your usual cheerful self tonight."

My face snaps to him. "*What?*"

His eyes blaze with a mixture of pain and anger. "I saw you kiss Cam Haler."

"So you were here?" I seethe. "Have you been stalking me this entire time? Watching my every move?" Grace's words flashing through my mind about Mike Jasper stalking her. Maybe he and Auden really are alike.

"No, of course not," he says, letting out a frustrated growl.

"Oh, so you just happened to be in the neighborhood at eleven thirty at night, strolling by my house at the exact moment?"

"I had to find *some* way to contact you, okay?"

"By stalking me?"

But instead of another furious outburst, Auden falls to his knees. He pounds his fist into the grass. "You have no idea what I've been going through," he says, his voice soft and strained.

"Auden…"

He looks up, his dark eyes glistening with tears. "You're tearing my heart out, Shelby."

I was barely holding on before, but his words break what little resistance I was holding on to. Hot tears stream down my face.

"I'm sorry, okay?"

"Why, Shelby?" he asks, in a strained voice.

I just shake my head. He presses again, his voice trembling. "Why? Why are you doing this?"

"You know why."

"I don't."

I wipe my eyes furiously. "You lied to me about your prison sentence. And about the accident. A plain, bold-faced lie."

"I didn't mean to—"

"You did. Don't make it worse by trying to justify it. You lied. And who knows what else you've lied about."

"It was only a half lie," he says, miserably. "I really did try to run away and steal my dad's credit card. And he did let me spend a night in jail. It really happened, it just…"

"It doesn't matter," I say. I shake my head. "I'm tired of not knowing what's true. I'm sick to death of it. I have to trust what I know. *Who* I know. Mama has her issues, but she loves me. And Grace too. And they both think you're bad for me."

"Of course they do," Auden says fiercely. "They want you to fall in line and become who *they* think you should be."

"I could just as easily say the same about you."

He stares at me, stunned. "Shelby…how can you even say that? You *know* that's not true. You know who you are, who you were before you met me. Why do you think we were so drawn to each other?"

He jumps to his feet. There's a desperate glint in his eyes. "Don't let them do this to you, Shelby. Don't let them break you."

He reaches for my arm, but I back away. "Don't touch me."

My words freeze him in place. He drops his hands to his side, staring at me as if I were about to swallow poison. And in some ways, he's not wrong.

"It's over," I say through the tears. "I can't do this anymore. I don't want to."

"What about your dreams? Forget me if you want. What about acting? What about Hollywood?"

I hug my arms around myself, suddenly aware how cold and utterly exhausted I am. "It's not realistic and you know it."

"I *don't* know that, Shelby. You have an amazing talent."

"It's a pipe dream," I say, cutting my hands through the air. "I wouldn't last one week in Hollywood. Because I don't belong there. At least here in Orchardview, I mean something to people."

His expression is one of complete disbelief. "So…you're giving up? Just like that?"

That question stabs me deepest of all. I can't bear even one more minute of this. Reaching deep within myself, I look up at Auden.

"This is goodbye. Please don't try to contact me."

"Shelby," his nostrils flare with emotion. "No."

"I won't keep Mama from calling the police if you come back."

It takes all of my strength to turn back to the house.

"Shelby, *please*."

The raw pain and desperation in his voice almost make me stop, but I force one foot in front of the other.

But I can't stop myself from glancing back at him.

Our eyes meet for a final time. In spite of all the anger, I can't deny how much I still care about him, as foolish as that seems. I wish I had the strength to offer parting words, something beautiful and true. I wish he had some poetic words for me to remember instead of this terrible pain.

But I step into the house and close the door, sealing Auden Keplar out of my life forever.

CHAPTER 29

No one speaks the next morning at breakfast. Or all that day. Mama and Blake wisely leave the house. They know I won't go running back to Auden now, but they also know that it's best for me to have my space.

Sometime after dinner, they return and quietly present me with a new phone. A fancy new phone, the newest model you can buy. Complete with a new number.

Then Mama goes back to normal life as if nothing happened. Maybe it's because I'm not crying my eyes out in my room. Auden isn't calling nonstop or showing up in the yard. And I try—I really try—to feel normal. If you could force yourself into a certain emotion by sheer power of will, the world would be a happier place. Nonetheless, I proceed with the life that Mama and Grace tell me I want. I go to school and rehearsal. Hang out with Grace. I watch TV with Mama and Blake.

But there's an emptiness inside me. An ache. And to make matters worse, my panic attacks resume. When I'm taking a test. Or walking to my car after school. Moments that have nothing to do with Auden or Mama.

It's always the same. A shortness of breath and racing pulse, accompanied by that dark feeling of dread. Something isn't right. The words peck at me like birds.

Something isn't right.

One day after school, I'm listening to music on my bed, trying to ease out of another such attack, when I hear a distinct tap on my window. The noise puts my whole body on alert.

My heart rate picks up even more. I stare at my dark blue curtains. I've taken to keeping them closed, cocooning in my room. Pressing my lips together, I pull them open.

A box balances on the window ledge, resting against the glass. It's Auden's memory box. The one we spent all those afternoons sifting through.

I cast my eyes out over the yard, but he's gone. I press my forehead against the window.

It's been more than a week since that awful moment out on the lawn. For days, I moved about with both a fear and a hope that Auden would try and contact me. That he would try to convince me to change my mind. I expected him to fight for me. The fact that he hadn't was a relief, but also a source of pain.

And now this.

Swallowing down the lump in my throat, I go outside to retrieve the box. Thankfully, Mama's at work, so I don't have to sneak. I sit on my bed, placing the box in front of me. Only then do I see the note tucked into the folded flaps. With trembling hands, I slide out the small piece of paper.

Auden's handwriting makes my heart leap with hope. But then I read the words:

IT'S CLEAR THAT YOU'RE ABANDONING WHAT WE HAD. I CAN'T LIVE WITH THESE MEMORIES, BUT I DON'T HAVE THE HEART TO DESTROY THEM. SINCE YOU ARE IMMUNE TO ALL THAT OUR RELATIONSHIP ONCE WAS, WOULD YOU DO ME THE FAVOR OF DISPOSING OF THEM?

～

"You know," Grace says at lunch the next day. "I'd act surprised, but I'm totally not. That is the exact kind of crap that Mike would pull. He's manipulating you. He's trying to make you feel bad and come apologize to him."

Watching her fume I can't help but smile. She always was good for a rant session. And lucky for me, Brad's out hunting with his dad and uncles this week, so I have her all to myself.

I stab my fork into the fruit cocktail. "I don't blame him for being upset."

"Oh, like it's *your* fault? Please, Shelby. Don't fall for this."

I sigh. Grace frowns. "Okay, you know what? I say you do it. Let's go out to the lake after school and burn that box."

I give her a look, but she's completely serious. "Why wouldn't you?"

"It's not mine to destroy, Grace."

She widens her eyes, incredulous. "He *told* you to destroy it. You would just be doing what he asked."

"I don't know…"

Grace is quiet for a moment, and then she pushes her lunch tray aside. "We'll go together. I have something to burn as well." When I give her a dubious glance, she suddenly loses a bit of her spark. "It's some papers. Chats. Between Mike and me. I…would always print them out after so I could save them for our future kids."

The information floors me, but I try not to show it. "And… you still have them?"

She bites her lip and shrugs. "At first I didn't really have the heart to toss them in the trash. But I also didn't want my mom to find them."

In that moment, I see how deep love can cut. Even after years of pain, even after fully moving on, the scars will always be there. I simply nod.

~

Grace and I are quiet as we drive out to the lake. I almost suggest we pick another spot. Any other spot. But it's fitting to do this here. End these memories where they began.

We carry our items to a fire pit near the picnic tables, me with the box, Grace with a full manila folder. After starting a small blaze, there's a moment of hesitation between both of us.

I sit down on one of the worn stumps that form a circle around the pit.

Grace purses her lips. "Here we go." She holds the manila folder over the flames and then drops it in without ceremony. The moment the pages hit the fire, she lets out a breath. I offer her a little smile.

"I'm proud of you."

"It feels good. I should have done that a long time ago."

My turn now. The box feels irrationally heavy on my lap. Like it's going to crush my bones. I struggle for a good breath. *Not here. Not now.* I squeeze my eyes shut for a moment and try to push back the panic. *Not now.*

Drawing in a shaky breath, I open the box. Pictures and letters stare up at me, accusing and sad. Auden and I went through the whole box over the course of a few days. I may not remember the events the items in the box record, but the memories of those hours with Auden beat fresh in my mind.

"Do you want me to help you?" Grace asks.

I shake my head and pick up a stack of pictures. It's impossible not to look through them one last time. These memories and moments that don't belong to me anymore. They paint a lovely scene, though. Two people in love. You can tell Auden has a filmmaker's eye. So many of the pictures are like stills from a movie, playing around with interesting angles and lighting. Most of them are pictures of me.

One picture of the two of us stands out. We're arm in arm, in full Renaissance costume, standing by a large bonfire. I frown at the image. It's not so much a memory but knowledge. This is a Halloween party. And Auden and I are supposed to be Romeo and Juliet.

Where did I get that gorgeous blue dress? And why don't I have it anymore? It would work perfectly for the play…

Auden and I are both smiling for the camera, but somehow…somehow I know that we were fighting just before they took this picture.

"Shelby?"

"What is it about this picture…" I say, not looking up.

The smell of smoke from our little fire tingles my nose. Like the flicker of flames, I see Auden talking to me by the bonfire. He's upset but not angry. He's trying not to let others around us hear our argument. An argument at a Halloween party…

"What's wrong, Shelby? You're kind of freaking me out."

I hold up the picture for Grace. "When was this taken?"

She shrugs, claiming she has no idea, but I don't hear her words. She knows.

In that moment, I realize three very important things. First, even Grace lies to me. They all do. Grace. Auden. Mama. It's so clear to me now. They want to protect me, yes, but they also want me to see things the way they do.

They all have their own versions of the truth. Their own perceptions of me and my life are colored by their own experiences, their own hopes and fears. Their opinions of my love for Auden say more about themselves than our actual relationship.

But it goes beyond that. My second realization is more of a

confirmation of a nagging impression I've had ever since I left Denver. There's something more to the story of what my treatment made me forget. There is something that someone isn't telling me. I don't know if it's Auden or Mama or Grace who is withholding the information. Or all three. But there is a piece missing. I can feel it in the very depths of my heart.

And that leads me to the final realization: I am the only one who can find my own truth. This whole time, I've relied on others because I thought that my erased memories made me helpless. But that's not true. My erased memories make me pure. I can piece together every opinion to discover unvarnished truth.

The only person who can help me get my memories back is myself.

"Aren't you going to burn that stuff?" Grace asks, coming to sit by me. "This wasn't going to be a reminiscing session."

"You're right." I hold out the picture over the fire, and the relief on her face is palpable. I study the picture a final time, making a mental copy of it, and then I drop it into the flames.

CHAPTER 30

With just over a week to go before opening night of *Romeo and Juliet*, the stage and auditorium are a flutter of activity after school. Techies test out lights. The art students paint finishing touches on the set. I expect a crowd in Mr. Lyman's office. He always has an open-door policy for students, and as such, it's always been a popular hangout for theater kids.

Thankfully, as I peer my head through the door, an empty office greets me. Mr. Lyman sits at his desk, listening to some modern, avant-garde jazz music and eating a green apple as he grades papers.

"Just the person I was hoping to see," he says.

"I am?"

He smiles. "I talked with Justin Regel last night. He's definitely coming, Shelby. To see you."

My heart drops. I'd forgotten all about the talent agent. I sink into the chair in front of Mr. Lyman's desk, quietly reeling from the reminder. It's one more thing I'm giving up to live the quiet, safe life in Orchardview.

"Something wrong?" Mr. Lyman asks with a frown.

"Just a little nervous," I say, scraping for the best smile I can manage.

"Don't be. You'll knock his socks off."

I muster another weak, barely believable smile.

Mr. Lyman takes a bite of his apple. "So, what's up, Shelby?"

I've always seen Mr. Lyman as a mentor and even a friend. I'd like nothing more than to unload my troubles on him, but something holds me back. Instead I say, "I have a question for you. A costuming question."

"Okay, shoot."

"I'm looking for a dress that I'm pretty sure is school property. It would work for Juliet. It's blue with gold accents. It came with a shimmery blue veil. Do you know where it is?"

Mr. Lyman's face slowly drains of color. He stares at me, and I know that my suspicion was right.

"I borrowed it about a year ago," I say, pressing further.

His lips part, but he doesn't speak. "You did," he says finally. "For Halloween."

"Did I not bring it back?"

He shakes his head, looking quite pale. "Shelby, that was the dress you were wearing the night of your accident. It was...damaged."

Even though I suspected as much, hearing Mr. Lyman say the words is intense. I sit back in the chair, feeling suddenly cold. "What happened that night, Mr. Lyman? I know you know."

"Shelby…"

"And I know they erased my memory. I suspect someone told you and maybe tried to convince you to keep that a secret. Well, I know, and now I want to know the whole truth."

Mr. Lyman presses his hands together. "Some things belong in the past. You've been given a remarkable second chance. One most people don't get. A chance to truly start fresh."

I lean forward. "But it's not forgotten, Mr. Lyman. All that therapy did was hide the past from me. But it's still there, banging on the walls, somewhere deep in my mind. The past won't let me escape, so I might as well turn and face it head-on. And I *want* to. I want my memory back—all of it. I need my truth. The good and the bad."

Mr. Lyman considers me for a long moment, and then he sighs. "I don't know more than anyone else."

I can't tell if he's lying. He's an actor, after all. He taught me everything I know.

"Please," I choke out.

"Listen to me, Shelby—"

His office door opens, and I glance over my shoulder to see Auden standing in the doorway.

It takes me a moment to process his presence. A surge of emotions clashes inside me. Surprise, confusion, anger, and unwelcome elation. His expression shows only pain. I stand and turn to face him. Mr. Lyman also gets to his feet.

"What are you doing here?" I demand of Auden.

"Mr. Lyman is my friend too," he says, tense.

I scoff. "No he's not."

"Actually, I am," Mr. Lyman says, coming between us. "You may forget, but you two used to come hang out in my office all the time. Before…"

"Why are you here?" I demand, my throat tight. "What were you going to talk about? About us? Were you going to tell him what a horrible person I am?"

Mr. Lyman sets a friendly hand on Auden's arm. "Why don't you come back another time?"

"No," I say, grabbing my bag. "Don't let me keep you from your visit."

Auden remains silent. Mr. Lyman calls out my name, but I storm out of the office. I'm halfway down the hall before Auden comes running after me.

"Don't bother," I say, not turning around. "Unless you're going to tell me why you were in Mr. Lyman's office."

"Why were *you* there?" he asks.

"Maybe because I go to this school? Or because he is the director of the play I'm in that starts next week? Pick a reason."

"I know that's not why. The energy was too intense when I interrupted."

I fold my arms tightly across my chest. "Fine. If you must know, I was asking him about the accident."

He stares at me. "What? Why?"

"Because I'm sick of not knowing the truth! I'm sick of not

knowing what happened to me and why. And you and Grace and Mama—all you do is tell me what you want me to believe."

"That's not—"

"There's something more to this story, Auden. Tell me what it is right now, or you will confirm exactly what I just said."

I've struck a nerve. I can see it all over his face. "Tell me," I demand.

"Shelby, I…you have to give me time to explain."

"No. I don't want the carefully polished version. Just tell me."

He's breathing harder. "It's not…that simple."

And there it is. That hesitation tells me everything I need to know. After everything that has happened, he *still* won't be completely honest with me.

"Forget it." I turn so he doesn't see the tears forming in my eyes. "I'll find out on my own."

I run from him as fast as I can. He calls my name, but he's at a disadvantage as he tries to follow me. He doesn't know that there's a hallway connecting to the science wing. I lose him easily.

Driving back home, I have a good cry, but nothing feels good about sobbing alone in your car. I'm just grateful that Mama isn't home this afternoon. First, because she won't see me crying, which will inevitably lead to questions. But also because I will have easy access to Mama's things.

I can't hesitate anymore. I have to know. Even if it brings back the panic attacks.

Storming into my empty house, I don't waste a minute. I

head right for Mama's room and rummage until I find the file folder she showed me when she told me about Auden. Sitting down on the couch with the folder in my lap, my heart pounds so hard I feel it in every part of my body. I close my eyes for a moment with my hands pressed on the truth.

Breathe. Just keep breathing. You can do this.

I open the folder.

The same dream haunts me. Darkness and pain. The color blue. Crying.

The small round light moves up and down, up and down. Too high. Too close. And then, it goes out. A scream fills my ears. Only this time, as I jolt awake, the scream is ripping from my own throat.

It takes me longer than ever to calm down. Maybe because now I know that it's not a dream.

It's a memory.

I bend over on the edge of my bed. It feels like someone is smashing my head in between two rocks. Like I'm being slowly burned from the inside out.

Pieces of my worst memory are clawing their way out of the recesses of my mind. The dream matches up with everything I read this afternoon.

The color blue, for example. It's my dress. My Halloween costume.

The accident took place on Halloween night. The perpetrator had been attending a party in the barn house a few blocks away. He maintains that he was not drinking, though the validity of this is impossible to determine, as he turned himself in after a toxicology report would have been effective.

That light. The strange, small light moving up and down.

The victim, Edmund Drake, age 59, had been out for an evening jog on K Road. The sky had darkened significantly, but he was wearing reflective gear as well as a headlamp.

The scream. Is that my scream as Auden swerved too far off the road?

The perpetrator maintains that he lost control of his vehicle in the darkness and didn't see Mr. Drake until it was too late. He struck Mr. Drake from the side, swerved, and then crashed his vehicle into a telephone pole.

The only part I can't place is that dark, horrible feeling that something isn't right. It grips me now, even as I bend over, trying to breathe.

I'd think it was the same feeling that I had at the scene of the accident. Leaving Edmund Drake bleeding in the ditch on the side of the road. But I wasn't awake for that.

His passenger, sixteen-year-old Shelby Decatur, was knocked unconscious upon impact.

So what is this feeling? I still can't place my finger on it. Reading the details of the accident caused an undeniable shift in my mind. The facts I read crawl around in my mind, like spiders, ripping open the hidden pockets of memories. Tiny details seep out. But still, there's something missing. Something terrible. It looms in the back of my mind like an oncoming storm.

The dark cloud only pulls closer. Stepping out of my house in the morning, I swear I see Auden's car round the corner. Then, as I open the doors to the school, a girl dressed in a witch costume brushes past me. I'm about convinced that I've gone crazy until I spot Mr. Harwood, one of the school counselors, dressed as a vampire, stapling a sign to a bulletin board. Two freshman girls walk by in matching Tinker Bell costumes, each talking on their cell phones.

Tomorrow is Halloween. This can't be a coincidence. The past, it seems, refuses to let me go. And I have to find out the truth. I can't wait even one more day. I'll have to figure it out myself, the only way left. By visiting the site of the crash.

By the time the late bell rings, I'm at my car. My hands shake as I turn the key in the ignition. Auden was right. My memories weren't erased by Dr. Stevens. They were simply hidden, blocked. A fragile dam created by the therapy. But the weight of those suppressed memories push against me now. The dam won't last long.

~

The location of the accident is a remote country road, a slice of asphalt in a sea of yellowing fields. It's peaceful yet I am anything but calm. I'm panting, gasping for air. My heartbeat shakes my entire body.

Just ahead, I spot a white, wooden cross in the grass off the side of the road, covered with flowers and a small, weathered American flag.

The earth seems to shift around me. It was there.

And then, in the rearview mirror, I see Auden's car. He's pulling up behind me at a desperate pace. Unless this is some kind of hallucination. I honestly don't know.

I watch him draw closer, eyes wide, my entire body trembling. My phone starts ringing. The sound echoes in my ear. I don't have to look to know it's him.

In my rearview mirror, I see Auden flash his lights for me to pull over. My breath stops. The ringing, the flashing lights, the panic—they overwhelm me. My foot slams on the brake. Auden's brakes squeal to avoid a collision as my car jolts to a stop. I hit the steering wheel. And a scream rips from my throat.

It all comes back. All of it. Rushing into my being like a flash flood. The dam has broken.

CHAPTER 31

Brooklyn Belnap has a Halloween party at her family's barn every year. It's so far out in the middle of nowhere that there're no neighbors to complain about the noise. And I think the Orchardview parents simply agree to turn a blind eye and let the kids do whatever they want for one night.

It was cool the first few years. Grace and I would go all out on costumes, arrive fashionably late, and stay long after the fun had dwindled. Being invited was a sign that we had arrived. This year, however, we aren't even hanging out together. She's off, who knows where. Probably with Mike. Why she keeps getting back together with him is beyond me.

I'm over it. All of it. Auden and I arrived less than ten minutes ago. It's not even dark yet, and I already want to go home. There's nothing like an argument with your boyfriend to kill your party mood.

Standing by the bonfire, I brush the dust from my blue Renaissance gown and grimace. Mr. Lyman will kill me if I ruin this thing. Besides, I think I have finally talked him into doing *Romeo and Juliet* next year, and it's the perfect costume to play the lead. The plan was to get Auden cast as Romeo, but I'm suddenly not so sure if we'll even be together next fall. Not if we keep arguing about California.

Auden comes to my side and presents a red plastic cup filled with water. "Sorry. No soda. This is your only option if you don't want booze."

"Thanks." I take the cup, my gaze still on the fire.

We're silent for a moment, and then he sighs. "Look, can we just pretend I didn't bring it up? There's no reason to ruin our whole night arguing over this."

I sip my water. "Too late."

He bends his head back, looking up at the sky. We've had this fight before. A few times. Ever since the night I backed out.

I had my bags packed. The car filled with gas. I wanted this so badly. But when the moment came, I couldn't go through with it.

At first, Auden said he understood. He apologized, even, for pushing me before I was ready. But as the days passed, it found a way to creep back into our conversations, usually at times like tonight when I just want to enjoy myself and forget the drama and weight of Auden's hopes and expectations.

"I can't believe you'd accuse me of not loving you," I whisper, angrily. "How dare you even say it?"

"That's not what I said."

"Oh, please. It is."

Brooklyn skips up. "Hey guys! Say cheese!" Auden and I both force a smile while she snaps a picture. As soon as she's out of earshot, Auden turns back to me.

"It's not what I meant," he says, softly. "All I said was that I wonder what I am to you. Am I some kind of novelty? A fun, unique experience to try out for a while before settling back into the comfort of the life your mother planned for you?"

"You know that's not true," I snap, a little too loudly. Two people nearby us look up and exchange glances with each other. Auden moves closer, self-conscious.

"That's the problem, Shelby. I *don't* know that. I've given you my heart and soul, with the understanding that we would be together forever. But sometimes I look into the future, and all I see is my own shattered dreams."

"You ask too much," I say, exasperated, my chest tightening with the crush of impending tears. "I love you, Auden. And I want to see new places. I'm just not ready right now."

"If you're not ready now, you'll never be ready."

I stare at him, stung by his words. "You're completely unreasonable."

"Better unreasonable than afraid."

Our anger goes back and forth until we dig ourselves into a hole we can't get out of without hurting each other. Soon, we're in a full-blown fight in front of everyone. It isn't until I lock eyes with Grace across the crowd that the humiliation becomes real.

I storm away from the party, angry tears burning down my

face. Twilight has fallen, and I nearly trip over the hem of my dress in the dirt lot. Auden follows wearily, though I imagine he's tired of chasing after me. This thought makes me even angrier.

"Why do you always run away from your problems?" he calls out. "Talk to me. We can get through this."

"I'm tired of arguing with you," I snap.

He pauses, and then his voice comes again. "Well, maybe I should leave you alone. Give you some space."

I spin around, glaring at him. "I wish you would." The words fall from my tongue like acid. "I'm sick of this, and I'm sick of you."

The look of pain on his face brings instant regret. I want to retract my words. I want to press the rewind button and go back to the start of the night. Try again. But it's too late. Swallowing the bile in my throat, I storm off and get in my car, slamming the door.

Auden stands frozen in place. He's a few yards back, but I can see him staring at me. I turn away, tears streaming down my face. I've never loved anyone as deeply as I love Auden. So why do I hurt him like this? Why does he hurt me? Why does it have to be like this?

Part of me is begging to get out of the car. To let him hold me in his arms. I want things to be perfect between us again. But I know that's guilt talking. I love him, and I don't want to hurt him. I could get back out right now, and we would make up easily, but the problems would only come back later. They always do.

An inescapable train of thought charges through my heart. For the first time, I stare in the face the fact that I really do need space from Auden.

I have to break up with him.

Heart pounding with pain, I start my car. And immediately, my phone starts ringing. Ignoring it, I pull out of the dirt lot. Auden runs toward me, phone to his ear. The ringing echoes in the car, screaming in my head.

I keep driving. And the phone keeps ringing, ringing, ringing. And I cry. The road ahead blurs in a mixture of falling twilight and tears. Auden sprints behind me, almost keeping pace with my car.

A strange, small light moves gently in my peripheral vision. Up and down, up and down. In the midst of my own distress, I give one single thought to that light. It's too high to be headlights. It moves too strangely.

Auden screams my name. My eyes flash to the rearview mirror. Both of his hands are outstretched. His eyes are wide with panic.

I snap my gaze back to the windshield in time to see headlights illuminate a man. I slam on the brakes. But it's too late. *Impact.*

A scream rips from my soul and tears through me as the man's body flies out of view.

And then, as I swerve, the telephone pole comes toward me like a specter of death.

Images and sounds flicker in and out of focus.

I stumble out of the car, sobbing and shaking. Auden catches me from falling. His face is white as a ghost.

My words are slurred and frantic. "The man. The man. I hit him."

Then, I'm lying on the grass, trembling. So cold. So dark and cold. My head feels wet, and I know it's from my own blood, because the iron tang burns my tongue even now.

Auden's bent over the crumpled body of the man. On the grass, that small white light glares blankly from an elastic strap. A strap that's no longer around the man's head.

"I hit him. I hit him."

Auden's dialing a cell phone. His voice is low and shaky. "There's been an accident. Someone's been hit."

He pulls the phone away and looks at me, his eyes wide. I can vaguely hear the buzz of a voice on the other end. But Auden doesn't respond. With trembling hands, he sets the phone on the man's chest.

Then, I'm in Auden's arms as he carries me to the car. "Stay with me, Shelby. Stay awake."

"I hit him," I moan, quietly. "I hit him."

He shushes me and kisses my head. Blood stains his lips. He sets me in the passenger seat.

Auden climbs into the driver's seat. He stares forward for a long time. And then we drive away.

$\sim$

Auden's hand is the first solid thing I grasp as I come to. But I'm not in the car anymore. I'm lying in a bed. An antiseptic smell lingers in my nose, and the soft, persistent beep of a heart monitor breaks the silence.

Awareness of pain comes over me next. A throbbing, dizzying ache overwhelms every part of my body. I let out a weak moan. Auden's hand tightens over mine.

Auden.

I crack my eyes open slowly. He watches me. His face is still pale, though his eyes are red. He kisses my hand gently.

"Do you need more medicine? Are you in pain?"

I manage a nod, and Auden calls the nurse to bring in more pain meds. Hanging up the phone, he turns back to me, stroking my hair. His eyes gleam with tears.

"I'm sorry, Shelby," he whispers. "I'm so sorry."

My throat is dry as paper, but I croak out a few words. "What happened?"

"We were in an accident," he says, his eyes down. "I was distracted, and I lost control of the car. We hit a…" Tears stream down his face now. "We hit a telephone pole."

Searching the haze of my mind yields nothing but confusion. After the nurses administer more Vicodin, the haze only grows. As the pain melts away, so does my consciousness. The last thing I see before my eyes close is Auden's weeping into his hands.

I've never seen Mama angrier. The fact that I'm bandaged up, lying in a hospital bed doesn't stop her from practically screaming at me.

"Will this be what finally makes you see the truth about this boy? Or will he have to kill you before you realize how dangerous he is?"

I glare at the ceiling. "Accidents happen, Mama. He's not an evil person because he lost control of a car."

She scoffs, and then blinks at me, frowning. "You mean… you don't know?"

Blake sits in one of the chairs by the window, stormy faced but quiet. Something in his expression makes my stomach knot.

"Know what?" I ask, my voice small.

Mama straightens. There's righteous fury in her expression, but I swear I see a hint of triumph. "Auden is in police custody."

"What?"

"Shelby, your life wasn't the only one he risked. He hit a pedestrian when he swerved off the road. A jogger. A man Blake's age. He hit him, and then he drove away."

Mama's words flatten me. Because I remember. I remember my words, rasped over and over again as the tang of blood filled my mouth.

I hit him. I hit him.

"No…" I whisper.

"I'm sorry but yes," Mama says, misinterpreting my horrified expression. "The man died within hours of the accident."

Dead. An innocent man is dead. Because of me.

Mama thinks I'm delirious when I tell her I was driving. And I *am* delirious. Weak with pain. Fragile from injury. Cloudy from pain meds. Spiraling from shock and revulsion at what I have done. I protest so frantically that the nurses come in and sedate me.

~

Auden visits me his first night of freedom after the arraignment. His dad paid bail, so he's free until the trial. He comes to my window after Mama and Blake go to bed. I'd be furious with him if I weren't so distraught.

"Why?" I demand. "How could you do this?"

"It was my fault. I upset you and distracted you."

Closing my eyes, all I can see is the man's body, illuminated in my headlights, flailing through the air at impact, and then lying lifeless on the grass. My throat burns and I shake my head. "But I'm the one who hit him. I killed him. I killed an innocent man."

Auden pulls me into his arms. "Don't think about it, Shelby. Put it out of your mind."

"I can't." Tears flow, and Auden's grip tightens.

"I know," he says, his voice heavy with emotion. "I can't either."

We stay that way for a long time, crying, lost in the anguish of genuine guilt and remorse. No one meant for it to happen, of course, but it did. And a man's life is over because of it. And nothing we do can ever give it back.

"I deserve any punishment they give me," I say.

Auden shakes his head. "That's not going to happen."

"I won't let you take the blame for this."

He strokes my hair. "I'll do it for you. I'd do anything for you, Shelby."

"Don't you think I feel the same?"

He's quiet next to me, holding me gently so as not to hurt my injuries. His silence breaks my heart.

"I won't let it happen," I say. "I'm going to the police tomorrow morning to tell them I was the one driving the car."

He grips my arms and looks hard in my eyes. "No you won't. Swear to me you won't."

"I absolutely will. I'm the one who was driving. Not you."

"Listen to me, Shelby," he says, firmly. "I've given this a lot of thought. There's too much at stake. You can't throw your future away for this."

"And what about your future?"

He shakes his head. "I can overcome this. For you, this is all your mother needed to keep you in her control. You'd never get out of this town."

I don't know if what he's saying makes sense or not, but in my weakened state, all I can do is melt in his arms and fight back tears.

"Please, *please* let me do this for you," he says, holding me tightly.

"What will happen? You won't go to jail, will you?"

"No," he says. "My mom's boyfriend, Bryce, is a lawyer, and

he thinks that since I'm a minor with no previous record, I shouldn't have to do more than pay a fine and do community service."

I consider this for a moment, though the burden weighs on me, threatening to crush me. The image of the man lying on the road, his body limp and broken, flashes before me.

"Promise me you'll go along with this," he says, gently. He hooks his pinkie finger with mine. "Promise me you won't tell another soul what really happened."

My head hurts. I'm exhausted and broken. I know I should, but I can't fight Auden on this, not now. Maybe later, when I have more strength, when I'm not crying every single night. Before the trail. Satisfied with the weak compromise I've made in my mind, I bring the linked fingers to my chest. "I promise."

~

The days building up to the trial, and the trial itself, take a greater toll on me than I could have imagined as I watch the boy I love get dragged through the mud in the local news. There are accusations that he was driving drunk the night of the accident, that he saw Edmund Drake, but simply didn't care. The prosecution paints the picture of a depraved, entitled city boy raising hell in our small town and killing a beloved father and grandfather. The papers have a heyday with it.

Everyone treats me like a delicate flower who had barely

escaped the grip of death. An Orchardview lily nearly crushed by the evil boot of big-city ways. The town circles their wagons around me. Mama leads the charge, all protective and righteous in her indignation. The guilt of knowing that I am the one who actually deserves their scorn weighs me down with iron agony.

And every day, my anxiety builds as Auden is shamed and berated for the crime I committed. I can't carry this secret. I can't sleep at night. I break down crying. My hands shake. It's the beginning of the panic attacks.

I beg Auden to let me come clean, and he begs me to ride out the storm.

"It will all be over soon," he promises, again and again. "And it will all work out."

~

On the day of sentencing, the judge throws the book at Auden. The judge is fifth-generation Orchardview stock, white haired, and eager to preserve our "sacred way of life."

Two years in a juvenile correctional facility.

As I watch the police officer escort Auden, pale and wide-eyed, out of the courtroom in handcuffs, my throat closes with panic. Our gazes meet, and I try to call out, try to reach for him, but everything goes black.

~

Sobbing, shaking, I tell Mama everything. On my knees, I beg her to take me to the judge to the truth. She listens with an inscrutable expression.

The next thing I know, I'm lying in bed again. Blake stands on one side, his face ashen. Mama's holding my hand, and there are tears in her eyes.

"Oh, my Shelby girl. Look at yourself. Look what he's done to you."

"He didn't do this to me," I sob. "I did. I killed that man. And I'm the one who should be in prison."

Mama's eyes flash. "Stop saying that!"

Blake sets a calming hand on her arm, and then he moves a little closer.

"Do you think Auden would want to see you go to prison, Shelby?"

I stare at him, my frantic sorrow paused momentarily at the thought. Blake's expression shifts as the realization comes to him.

"He told you to let him take the fall, didn't he?"

The tears come in full force. "I can't lie anymore."

Mama sweeps me up into her arms and shushes gently while I sob. "We're going to fix this," she says softly. "We're going to make it all better."

~

When Mama and Blake approach me about the memory erasure, I flatly refuse. How could I take the easy way out? Run away from everything I've done and not take responsibility? Let Auden suffer for two years in prison? And what about Edmund Drake's family? Do they get to forget?

But Mama doesn't relent. Every day, she talks me through it. No more pain. No more nightmares. No more panic attacks. Something to help me get ahold of my own mind and control over my emotions.

And eventually, she wears me down. It's not too difficult. I'm weak, frayed mentally and emotionally from nightly panic attacks. Beaten down, body and soul. Sitting in Dr. Stevens's office for the first time, I'm at rock bottom.

"I want it all to go away."

Dr. Stevens folds his hands together on his desk. "Now, you understand that this memory erasure is permanent. There's no going back."

I nod shakily, wiping my eyes. What will it be like to not have to live this lie? To not to have to see Edmund Drake's body lying lifeless on the grass every time I close my eyes?

"I want to forget him," I say. "I want to forget everything."

CHAPTER 32

The weight of so many memories coming back all at once flattens me in the seat. Thankfully I have the presence of mind to slam my car into park.

I lift my hands to my face to make sure this is reality. In the present. The flashback was mere seconds, but I'm still spinning. Reeling. My hands shake on my cheeks. My skin feels ice cold.

Through the windshield, Auden stares at me. His lips form my name.

It suddenly strikes me as strange. We both wanted this moment for so long, for me to remember. Now I see what he didn't want me to remember. What Mama didn't want me to remember.

What I didn't want to remember.

I meet Auden's gaze. He's tense, completely on alert. He senses something has changed. He comes to the driver's side door. I stare at him, breathless, trembling, as he opens it.

He falls to his knees beside me. Tears shimmer on his eyes. "Shelby."

My name is both a question and a declaration. I nod slowly. "I remember."

Auden draws in a sharp breath and grabs my hand. He's squeezing his eyes shut, and his body shakes with a single sob.

My own eyes burn. He's carried this weight alone all this time. It's unimaginable. Unthinkable.

But I'm still overwhelmed. It feels as though I'll crush inwardly from this pain. I pull away my hand gently. "I need to be alone for a little while."

Auden nods.

I cast only one glance at him in the rearview mirror as I drive away. His tall frame stands in the road, bent with sorrow. I wait until I'm far away and parked the side of the road before I let myself cry.

~

It's nearly three in the morning before I go home. There's a police car in the driveway, and all the lights are on in the house. I expected it. After the fourth time Mama called me and the tenth text from Grace, I'd shut off my phone.

When I walk into the house, Mama cries my name. But one look at my swollen, tear-stained face and her expression fades. I walk past her and the police officer without a word.

"Shelby," Mama says, her voice fierce. "Don't you just walk by as if nothing's happened."

"My memory has come back," I say simply, though I can taste the venom in my tone. "I remember *everything*."

Mama is speechless, and I finish my march into my room.

Locking the door behind me, I sit on the edge of my bed, though I won't sleep. I can't even lie down. I sit in the darkness and stare numbly out the window.

One day bleeds into two. Two into three. Three into four. I lie in bed. I eat what is required, when required. I stand in an ice-cold shower. But I'm a zombie. Blank. Numb. Broken. Or so it seems to anyone who tries to come talk me out of my life-less state. Inside, there's only pain. And guilt. There's only the man whose life I ended.

Mama sends Grace to me. She knows better than to come in herself. Grace tries every tactic to get me up. *Everyone's so concerned about you. Your mama is just sick with worry. I've never seen her cry before. We all want Shelby back.*

It's an ironic statement. So many people, included myself, have talked about how they want me "back." Well, I've gotten myself back, in a way, and I hate what I've found.

"You can go back to therapy," Grace says, squeezing my hands. "You can make all of this go away again."

I cry that night, alone again in my room. But Grace's words linger. It strikes me that, in spite of the misery and regret I feel right now, I resist the idea of having it erased. This pain is a result of my actions, and it's my responsibility to carry it. And this pain is also part of me.

I sit up in my bed. The clock reads three. I can suddenly see so clearly what a mistake it was to agree to the therapy. I tried to escape what I've done. And now it's time to face it. No more running.

Enough despair and agony have been waded through. I'm sick of it. The only pain that really matters doesn't belong to me. And it is my responsibility to help deal with that.

As the sun pushes onto the horizon, I know what I have to do.

～

The Drakes' home rests in one of the oldest neighborhoods of Orchardview, hidden among the farmlands and shaded with large trees. As I pull my car in front of their neatly trimmed yard, the panic returns, as I knew it would. But I also know that facing Edmund's widow is the only way to stop it.

No more running.

I bend over, breathing slowly, trying to calm down. It takes me nearly a half hour, but my hands finally stop shaking, and I can breathe evenly. My legs seem unsteady as I walk up to the front door, but I ignore it.

My fist hovers over the dark blue wood door for a moment before I gather the strength to knock. A woman's voice murmurs from the other side. I nearly run. But I hold onto the pain. I make that pain nail my feet in place.

The door swings open. A brunette woman in her late fifties stands on the other side. Helen Drake. I recognize her from the news. She's silver at her temples and has a soft sadness in her smile. When her eyes fix on me, however, her smile fades.

"Mrs. Drake," I say with a shaky voice. "I'm so sorry to come unannounced."

She steps back. "What are you doing here?"

"I…have something to tell you. About your husband's death."

She draws in an audible gasp, and I'm certain she's going to slam the door in my face. For a moment that seems like forever, she stands in the doorway, staring at me. I am about to apologize for bothering her and leave, but then she opens the door a little wider and steps aside.

"Come in."

I follow her to their cozy, if dated, living room. The couch pillows look hand sewn, and there's a bouquet of autumn flowers in a vase on the coffee table. There are pictures of her two grown children and their families. I recognize Sara Drake in one of the pictures. It feels like someone has grabbed my throat. And on the mantel above the fireplace sits a picture of Edmund. I'm not sure I can make it through this.

Helen sits across from me. Maybe it's my imagination, but she seems so small and lonely in the large, empty house. Sorrow washes over me. A sorrow not for myself but for this family that is suffering so much more than me. And it's all my fault.

"What is it you came to say?" Helen asks.

I stare at my hands in my lap. "I don't really know where to start. So I'll come right out and say it."

She watches me with an unexpected tenderness that strikes me right in the gut. I close my eyes. "You need to know that Auden wasn't the one driving that night. It was me."

Silence pushes down on the room. Only the soft *tick, tick,*

tick of the grandfather clock in the corner invades the oppressive quiet. Then Helen lets out a trembling breath.

"I…I don't understand."

"I was driving. But after I crashed the car, Auden put me in the passenger side. He convinced me that it was him behind the wheel, and he turned himself in. When I finally remembered the details, he begged me to keep it secret. He took the blame, but the accident was my fault."

Helen seems floored by the information. She's silent, dazed. I force myself to go on.

"I haven't said anything until now, because…well, it's complicated. I haven't been myself in quite some time. I've been selfish. I tried to run away from the guilt. But I'm not going to do that anymore. And so I came to—" Tears well in my eyes, but I keep going. "I came to ask for your forgiveness." My voice catches. "I'm *so* sorry for what I did."

Helen covers her hand with her mouth and looks away from me.

I lower my face. "I'll never be able to forgive myself. I don't blame you if you can't forgive me. I had to tell you the truth. And I had to tell you how deeply I regret my actions. I'm going to make it right. I swear to you."

Having said what I needed to say, I press my face into my hands and weep. I feel another rush of guilt. I don't deserve to splash around my sorrow when Helen is the one who's truly suffering.

A hand touches my shoulder. Helen looks down at me, her own cheeks wet with tears.

"You're young," she says, gently. "Too young to give up on yourself."

I can't bear to look into her eyes. I don't deserve the kindness there.

"I wasn't ready to say goodbye to Edmund, but we all have our time on this earth. And there's no sense in destroying ourselves when someone we love is gone. It is no good for the living or for the memory of the person who died."

"But he didn't have to die," I say, through the tears. "It's my fault. If it weren't for me, he'd still be here."

Helen pulls me into her arms. Her body is frail and small, but her embrace is warm.

"Listen to me," she says, softly. "None of us know what's going to happen tomorrow. All we have is today. We have choices to make. There's enough pain and injustice in the world to make someone angry or sad their entire lives if they let it." She pulls me back to look into my eyes. "But there's so much good if we look for it. I choose to forgive you. And for today, that brings me peace."

I leave Helen's house feeling drained and undeserving of her tenderness. After the bitterness I've tasted, her sweetness is unfamiliar to me. But her words echo in my heart.

Every day is a choice. It's not just about what we do and where we end up but the emotions we embrace in our hearts. Somehow she knew the exact words I needed to hear.

CHAPTER 33

They say that sometimes you have to tear something down completely before it can be built back the right way. This is my life now. This is my goal. Complete destruction of the old Shelby so maybe the new one will get something right.

Within three days of visiting Helen Drake, I take down all of my movie posters and pack them away, along with all of my DVDs. I email Mr. Lyman and officially withdraw from the play. It's a formality. I'm sure he's already gotten Bailey Perkins in as Juliet. As I click send, an emptiness claws at my insides. Tomorrow is opening night.

A fantasy sweeps over me for a moment. A dream of what could have been. A world where Auden and I are still together and happy and the accident never happened. A world where I star as Juliet and Auden stars as Romeo. And Mama watches proudly from the front row.

I close my laptop. Such a world doesn't exist. *No more.* Chasing after fantasy worlds has only gotten me into trouble. This is my reality now, and I have to accept it.

I leave my room. The less time spent in there the better. Mama sits at the kitchen table, paying bills with a grimace of concentration. When she sees me, her expression softens.

"What are you up to?" she asks.

I don't have a ready answer. The new Shelby doesn't try to pretend that everything is okay anymore, but I also see no reason to constantly drag Mama into my sadness.

I know she sees it anyway. I know she's watching me carefully. Like always.

Mama considers my silence for a beat, and then goes back to writing her check. "If you have a minute, would you mind running to the grocery store for me? We're out of milk and running low on some other things."

I suppress a sigh and grab my keys. "Sure."

"I'll text you the list."

Thankfully, I make it in and out of the store without seeing anyone I have to talk to.

As I drive up to the house, however, I see something that makes me slam on the brakes. Auden's car. Parked in our driveway. Empty.

He's inside the house.

I find myself running up the front walk, though it feels like I'm moving in dream sequence slow motion. I swing open the door, fully expecting to hear arguing. Auden's voice does reverberate through the air, but it's calm. Auden and Mama are sitting across from each other in the living room.

They both look up when I come in. Auden looks how I feel. Exhausted and worn down. But a smile pulls at his lips.

"What's going on?" I ask, my voice louder than I intended.

Mama stands slowly. She walks over holding something out in her hand. It's the restraining order—torn in two.

"I called him here," she says, her voice tight with emotion. "I knew he was the only one who could get through to you. I want my Shelby girl back."

My pulse beats in my throat. "I *am* back. This is the new me."

"No. It isn't right. Look, I know I haven't always been that excited about your drama stuff, but I know you love it."

I feel both Auden and Mama's gaze on me, but I stare resolutely at the floor. I'm not going to cry. I'm not going to give in.

Mama comes forward. "Shelby. Listen to me. I brought Auden here because I know I did some things wrong. We all did. But I want you to be happy. And maybe that means being in drama…maybe that means being with Auden."

Forgiveness. The sweetness of the feeling washes over me.

"I love you, Shelby girl."

"I love you too, Mama."

I wrap my arms around her. We haven't hugged like this since I was a kid. A tear escapes my eye. It's not from sadness but wonder that two imperfect people can come together in spite of everything that happened between them. Mama and I may never fully understand one another, but these are our first steps to meeting in the middle.

Mama backs away and hurriedly wipes her eyes. She nods at Auden. "Go on now. I know you two have a lot to discuss."

Auden takes my hand, and we go to my room. Mama wasn't wrong. There's so much to discuss. Where to even start? I close my bedroom door and turn to face him. For a long time, we just look at one another. Sometimes the heart speaks in a way that transcends words.

Auden's hand rises slowly and rests on my face. I close my eyes, and we fall into an embrace. We hold each other in a way that was almost lost to me forever. More tears stream down my cheeks. I can't help it.

I pull back a little. We don't kiss. An unspoken awareness hangs between us that any move toward reconciliation will have to be made one step at a time.

Auden tenderly wipes my tears away.

"I can't believe you remember us now," he says.

"It was there. Just hidden. I don't think you can ever truly erase your heart."

He kisses my forehead. The feeling of his lips on my skin almost breaks me. I almost melt into his arms. I almost give in to the past.

But I can't. I have to keep moving forward.

Auden is quiet. "I think you know the reason your Mama sent for me…"

I'm quiet before replying, "Opening night."

"You have to perform, Shelby. The talent scout will be there. This is your chance. A *real* chance."

"How can I?" I ask, feeling the heaviness again in my heart. "After what I've done, how can I go on living my life, chasing my dreams? That Shelby only brought pain to others and to myself."

"So, you're going to give up everything, including your dreams? What will that help? It won't bring Edmund Drake back. It won't make you feel any better. You'll be throwing away your life over an event you can't change."

"I don't know, okay? It just doesn't feel right."

For a moment, Auden considers my response. "There's something else you should know." He seems hesitant, but he goes on. "I talked with Mr. Lyman and Cam Haler. If you agree to perform tonight, they'll let me join you onstage as Romeo for tonight." My eyes widen, and he takes my hand. "Just as it was always meant to be."

The news floors me. With Auden as my Romeo, I know I'll be able to give an amazing performance. With Auden, I can give that talent scout a show to remember.

My heart quickens. The guilt is still there, but Auden's right. Not performing doesn't help the situation. It's just more running away. And like Helen Drake said, I get to choose. I don't have to let this sadness consume me. I can *do* something about it.

An idea comes to me. I pull out my cell phone and find Mr. Lyman's contact information. He's probably running around like a crazy man before opening night, but I call him anyway. He answers immediately.

"Shelby?"

"Hi Captain, my captain."

He lets out a huge sigh of relief. "Please tell me this means you're performing tonight."

"Yes, but I have one condition. I want the entire proceeds of the night to go to Mrs. Helen Drake and her family."

~

Standing backstage in my wine-red Juliet gown, I peer out into the crowd. It's a full house. The sight of the filled auditorium sends a current of energy through my body. I feel more alive than I have in a very long time.

I realize Auden is behind me.

"You look incredible." He kisses my hand. "My Juliet."

Warmth flutters through me. "You don't look too bad yourself."

He smiles. "Are you ready?"

"I've never been more ready in my life."

Auden beams. "The talent scout is in the second row in the middle. Be sure to flash him just the right amount of leg."

I laugh and smack his arm. "Yeah, well, maybe it's your leg he'll want to see."

"May the hottest win then," he says, with a wink.

At that moment, the house lights drop, and a frantic Ana Guerrero comes running up. "Auden, you're on in five! Get on your mark!"

Auden blows me a kiss and runs into the darkness. I can't

keep the smile off my face as I close my eyes to get into character. I feel different now. I understand Juliet in a way I never could before. Her pain, yes but also her love. I embrace the darkness from the last year and carry it out onto the stage with me.

I give the performance of my life. There's no other way to describe it. Auden and I are perfectly in sync onstage, and the rest of the cast is swept up with us. I'm not Shelby anymore. I *am* Juliet. And Auden is my Romeo.

But when the scene calls for Romeo to kiss Juliet, I can feel Auden pouring every bit of his heart into it. In those moments, he is just Auden, and I am his Shelby.

As the curtains fall, the crowd goes crazy. Orchardview doesn't normally make such a fuss over a Shakespeare play, but I think everyone in the audience knew they'd witnessed something special.

Taking my second curtain call bow, I glance out into the packed audience. My gaze immediately falls to Mama. She's in the front row, standing and clapping with a bright smile on her face. And tears streaming down her cheeks.

Afterward, Mr. Lyman has to pull me away from a crowd to introduce me to Justin Regel. He's tanned and handsome and everything I'd imagine a Hollywood talent scout to be.

"Very impressive performance," he says, grinning. "Matt was right about you."

I'm afraid my heart will burst. Or that my huge grin will scare him away. "Thank you," I say, struggling to keep my cool. "And thank you for coming all this way. I know our town isn't much."

He smirks. "Oh, Orchardview has its charms. But talent like yours belongs in Hollywood."

I will not freak out. I will not freak out. "Thank you."

"Here's my card. Give me a call when you get into town." He winks. "I'm assuming that won't be too long after graduation."

I watch him as he saunters off, hands in the pockets of his immaculately tailored pants. When I turn around, I catch Auden's eye from across the crowd. He couldn't look prouder or happier for me. I feel like I'm flying.

In the quiet of my dressing room, I look in the full-length mirror. I hardly recognize the girl looking back at me. So much has happened. So much pain. So much joy. I'm not sure how my heart can contain it all.

I'm moving forward, but now I know the right way to do it. I feel that in every part of my soul. There's no point trying to re-create the past. It's over. But there's also no use trying to fight who I really am either. All I have are my dreams and today. And I get to choose where that leads me.

CHAPTER 34

The cast is going out to celebrate, but Auden and I slip away. We drive together, silently. Words don't need to be said. Not yet.

We go back to that country road. To the little wooden cross commemorating the place where Edmund Drake died. Auden carefully wipes the dust and grime away from the white wood, and I kneel before it, fresh tears streaming down my face. Mr. Lyman and Principal Nelson gave me a bouquet to celebrate opening night. A dozen perfect red roses. I place them on the grass in front of the memorial. Auden kneels beside me and takes my hand in his.

I don't need to tell him where to go next. He knows. When we get to the lake, he finds our exact spot and pulls a blanket from his trunk. It's an unseasonably warm night. We sit side by side on the hood of his car, wrapping the blanket around us for warmth against the cool night breeze and gaze up at the perfect shimmer of a million stars.

I hug my arms around my knees. "I'll never forget tonight."

"I won't either." Auden brushes some hair from my face and tucks it behind my ear. His dark eyes sweep my face, studying me. "Something's changed in you, Shelby. I can feel it."

"I told you. I'm not running anymore."

His brow lowers. "I'm not sure I understand...or maybe I'm afraid to ask."

My smile fades. "Auden...I'm going to turn myself in for the death of Edmund Drake."

He stares at me. "What?"

"I can't undo what happened, but I'm going to make it right."

"How will that make it right? It won't change anything."

I grab his hand. "It's as much for me as for anything else. I never should have let you pay the price for me. And I love you for doing that for me, for loving me that much. But I've given this a lot of thought, and it's the right thing to do."

"What about the talent scout? What about everything you've been working for?"

"Those opportunities will still be here when I come back."

He searches my eyes. "And what about us?"

My heart sinks. I'd been hoping to stall this conversation as long as possible. But Auden's not a fool. He senses it coming. I know he does.

"We can never be what we were, Auden."

He doesn't ask what I mean. His face is stricken with regret. "Is it because of your memory?"

"No. In a way, I'm grateful my memories were erased. It

gave me a chance not many get. A chance to look back with fresh eyes. Sometimes I think people get so caught up in their history and the emotions of those experiences that build, layer upon layer, that they can't even see what actually happened anymore. I got the chance to see us, Auden. As we really are."

He stares out over the dark lake. "And what did you see?"

"I saw a fire. Beautiful and bright and warm…but wild. Destructive."

He shakes his head, as if fighting what he knows is coming. "No…"

I grab his hand. "We love each other, Auden. Our feelings are real and powerful, but we can't contain them. Not here. Not at this point in our lives."

"How can you say that?"

I caress his face. "I know you see it. Just like you see that this town is too small for me. Our love is the opposite. It's too much."

"Don't do this," he says softly.

His pain burns into my chest like a brand. It will leave a mark. I kiss his cheek. "I wish it didn't have to be this way. I hate that I'm going to hurt you. If I could, I'd give you everything you wanted. But I can't. And you know I can't. You knew it all along. I need to be my own person, away from Mama. Away from anyone. Even you."

"We were going to do it. We were going to get out of this town and make a life together."

I shake my head. "It never would have happened. I was going to back out, but then everything exploded with Mama."

Auden wipes tears from his face. Seeing him cry crushes my heart with pain. I put my arms around him.

"I do love you, Auden. Never doubt that."

"I know," he whispers. "Will you ever be ready for this? Will you ever want to try again?"

I touch his beautiful, sad face. "When I've found myself. When I know who I am. Come to me then, Auden. I'll be ready for you then."

He smiles wistfully. "I'm holding you to that."

I latch my pinkie with his and press it to my chest. "It's a promise."

Auden and I hold each other. Together, we cry tears for everything we've lost, for everything we are about to lose. We stay together until the sun shifts into the watery light-blue of dawn. And then, as the sun rises, we drive to the police station and walk through the doors, hand in hand.

EPILOGUE

Even though it's nearly summer, the mornings are still cool and dark. I breathe in the chill, rich with the smell of oak and pine. I want to remember this, the smell of Orchardview. The smell of home.

I load the last bag into the trunk. Grace slams it shut. "You sure you got everything?"

"If I forgot something, it's too late now." I grin. "Besides, I think they have a few stores in California."

Grace laughs but then bites her bottom lip. Her eyes are already bright with tears.

"Grace."

"I know. I know. No crying."

"It's not like I'm dying. I'll be a flight away."

She nods, but I know the words don't comfort her.

I already hugged Mama and Blake in the house. Mama hates goodbyes, so we kept it brief. I promised to video call her every weekend. And to come home to visit every holiday. Grace is the only one who demanded to see me off. It was very generous of her to get up so early, since we had yet another graduation party yesterday that went late into the night.

Mama says it's too abrupt to leave like this, less than a week after graduation. But she had to have seen this coming. The day I finished my community service hours, I was packed. I only stayed for the graduation ceremonies and parties for Grace's sake.

Not that she really needs me. She and Brad seem to be joined at the hip these days. I'm a little surprised he isn't here right now. I grin as she goes to her car and pulls out a large, ice-cold Dr Pepper and our other favorite gas station snacks. You have to respect her devotion to ceremony.

"It's a little early for Dr Pepper, isn't it?" I joke.

"Take it," she says. "For the road."

I set it in my cup holder. "It's a long drive to California. I'm guessing I'll only need six or seven more of those along the way."

We both laugh, and then a silence falls between us. Grace runs her hand along my car.

"Do you think you'll see him out there?"

Auden moved back to New York in November to live with his mom. Right after *Romeo and Juliet*. That night on the lake was the last time we spoke. But then, in the spring, a single post showed up on his long-abandoned Instagram account. He had been admitted into the USC film school and would be leaving for California immediately.

"Don't know," I say, with a shrug, pretending not to feel the excited and nervous twist in my heart. "California's an awfully big state. I don't think you bump into people there like you do around here."

A funny little smile crosses Grace's lips. "I bet you'll see him."

"Maybe one day."

"If you're not too busy being a famous actress," she adds.

"True. I imagine my days will be booked with glamorous photo shoots and power lunches with famous directors."

Grace laughs, but her eyes shine. "You're going to make it out there, Shelby."

"I'm sure going to try."

She bites her bottom lip again. There's a knot at the pit of my stomach. In so many ways, I've longed for and dreaded this moment. I throw my arms around Grace in a fierce hug.

"Take care of yourself. And…I'm sorry I wasn't there for you when you needed me."

She hugs me back tighter. "Don't. You're the best friend I've ever had and ever will have." She breaks away and gives me a playful shove. "Now go. Get out of here. Go make your dreams come true."

I get into my car. Drawing in a deep breath, I push the key into the ignition. Grace waves from the driveway, then steps into the street. She waves until she's little more than a speck in my rearview mirror.

I roll down the windows and push my foot on the gas pedal. It doesn't hit me that I'm actually going until I'm out of

ACKNOWLEDGMENTS

Every time I write an acknowledgments page, I feel very aware of how lucky I am. And I feel so grateful to everyone who has helped me get to this point. First and foremost, a huge thank-you to my awesome agent, Jessica Regel. You saw the heart of this story and believed in it, and I will always be grateful for that.

Thank you to Annette Pollert-Morgan. It's so great to work with you again. Your insights always make my work stronger. I loved watching my story develop into all it could be.

I'm grateful to all the people at Sourcebooks and Foundry Literary + Media. Bringing a book into the world is a serious team effort, and I feel lucky to have such an awesome team on my side.

All the love to my writer friends (especially the esteemed members of the Sandwich Club): Kasie West, Jenn Johannsson, Charlie Pulsipher, Michael Bacera, Aaron Kawakami, Tyler Jolley, Natalie Whipple, Daniel Noyes, Candice Kennington,

Michelle Argyle, and C. K. Edwards. You're all a little crazy, but I think I've proven that I'm the craziest. At least we're all in this together.

Thank you to my beautiful friends who make me laugh and help me relax when I'm on deadline: Lisa, Aubrey, Susan, and Natalie. The next round of sodas from Maverick is on me!

Shout out to the Best Book Club Ever! I love you ladies and all your awesome support.

A special thank-you to the brilliant experts I consulted with to make sure I had the medical and legal details right: Bryce Lee, Esq., and Dr. Brian Belnap.

Love and hugs to my siblings: Jared, Sarah, Becca, Diana, Rachel, and Amy, along with your fun spouses and adorable kids. One day, when I'm famous, I'll treat us all to that Fam Bash on the beach!

As always, Diana, you have helped me in ways I can't even express. Not just in support with writing, but in life as well. I love you and feel incredibly blessed to have you as a twin sister.

Mom and Dad, I dedicated this book to you, because I truly feel that you have played an irreplaceable role in helping me get to where I am today. Thank you for always teaching me to explore and dream. Thank you for your love and support that has never wavered. I love you both so much!

Finally, a huge thank-you to my wonderful family. Amber, Logan, and Ella, you kids make me happy every day. I feel so lucky to be your mom. I know you think I'm joking when I always ask, "How did I get such good kids?" But I mean it! Some days I feel like I hit the kid jackpot.

And Ben. You are the one who sees it all—the highs and the lows, the moments of joy and the moments of stress and exhaustion. Thank you for loving me and helping me through it all. I truly couldn't do this without you. You're my best friend.

ABOUT THE AUTHOR

Renee Collins grew up in Hawaii, where she played Lady Capulet in her high school production of *Romeo and Juliet*. In college, she decided to abandon her dreams of being a famous actress to study history and become a writer, but she'll always have a soft spot in her heart for drama kids. Renee currently lives in Colorado with her family.

CAN HER LOVE SAVE HIS LIFE?
FIND OUT IN RENEE COLLINS'S

Until We
Meet Again

Prologue

The beach is empty. In the fading glow of twilight, the waves roll up to the rocks in sweeping curls of white foam. The sand glistens like wet steel. The grass bends low in the briny night wind. Always changing, yet always the same. I imagine the beach has looked like this since the beginning of time.

Stepping onto the soft terrain, I feel transported to some ancient evening, eons ago. Long before my uncle claimed this land as his own. Long before man even dared to taint these shores.

I wish the fleeting vision were true.

My gaze falls to the full moon's reflection on the water. It's broken into shards on the black sea, tossed about with each wave. A small, white shape catches my eye. It's in the glare of the reflection, so I nearly miss it.

I step into the wave break. A seabird, dead and limp, is rolling back and forth in the foam. Her wings are spread open, her white-and-brown-speckled breast exposed.

I lift the small creature into my palm. *What killed her?* I wonder. There's no sign of injury. Did she drown in the sea?

Pinching her brittle, fragile leg gently between my fingers, I notice a small metal band snapped around her ankle. The sight of it startles me. Examining it closer, I catch the faint impression of numbers and letters etched into the band, but something in me resists reading them. I can't say why.

What does it matter, anyhow? The poor creature is dead. And she reminds me that there is no going back. Time howls on, like the wind. And it is not only weaker creatures like this bird that succumb to it. Even the strongest man will fall before its crushing forward push.

I set the bird out into the water. As the tide pulls her away, I accept this truth. Soon the summer will be over. Too soon.

CHAPTER 1

Cassandra

Date: July 8.

Days at my mom and stepdad's new summer home: 22

Hours spent at the froufrou country club: 0

Hours spent on the fancy private beach: 0

Hours spent lying on the couch bemoaning my lack of a life: somewhere in the 100s.

Number of times Mom has told me to make some new friends and stop moping around: also somewhere in the 100s.

To paraphrase Shakespeare: Oh, for a muse of fire to convey how utterly and completely bored I am.

Given the circumstances, it should be clear that I have no choice but to try to sneak into my neighbors' yard and swim in their pool at 2:00 a.m.

My two accomplices are less than ideal. Travis Howard and Brandon Marks are local royalty of this ritzy, historic neighborhood slapped on the coast of Massachusetts's North Shore. Both have the classic all-American look—tall, sparkling blue eyes, and a crop of blond hair that's been gelled to scientific levels of perfection. But given the circumstances, they'll have to do.

Brandon can barely keep pace as we cut along the tailored brush that adorns the Andersons' back fence. Maybe because he's too busy shooting nervous glances behind us.

"We're being followed," he says.

Travis and I exchange a look.

"Chill out, dude," Travis says.

I sigh. "Seriously. I didn't pack my smelling salts, so try not to faint."

Travis holds out his fist for a bump.

Brandon is resolute. "At the very least, we're being watched. You think these people don't have security cameras?"

"No clue," I say brightly.

"Well, that's reassuring."

"I try."

I probably should have come on my own. Trouble is, I need a pair of hands to boost me over the fence. My little brother, Eddie, couldn't do it, since he's three. And for obvious reasons, I couldn't ask Mom or Frank. That left the only other person I know here: Travis.

He and I met at a garden party. How bourgeois is that? I was so bored, I was ready to claw my eyes out. Then I saw this crazy guy doing a chair dance, to the utter shock of the local hens, and I decided he might be okay. Travis is pretty cool. He reminds me a little of my friend Jade back in Ohio—a delightful troublemaker. Having Travis's buddy Brandon tagging along, however, has proved to be an unwelcome change of plans.

It's late, but humidity still hangs in the air. Not as oppressive as during the day, but enough to make the hair against my neck damp. Crickets chirp loudly in the surrounding brush, which makes me uneasy somehow, as if their incessant noise will draw attention to us. As if they're crying, "Look! Look! Look! Look!" to some unseen guard. Brandon's nerves must be contagious.

Luckily, I spy the edge of the fence before I can dwell on my uneasiness for too long.

"We made it," I say.

Gripping the bars, I look for a good spot to grab midway up. Travis helps me with the inspection.

"Right over here," he says, motioning. "The ground's a little higher on the other side, and those bushes will break your fall."

"Nice," I say, impressed. "You have a lot of experience breaking in to private property?"

"Yeah, except we usually go for cash and high-value items. Breaking in to go swimming should be a nice change of pace."

I smirk and he gives me a Mr. Teen USA wink.

"All right then," I say. "Hoist me up."

Brandon steps in between us. "Are we seriously doing this? You know, your stepdad's house has a huge private beach. If you want to swim so badly, can't we go there?"

"You're missing the point, Brandon."

"You never explained the point."

"Only a fool asks to understand that which cannot be grasped," I say, pretending to quote some ancient philosopher.

Travis blinks. "Dude. That was deep."

"I know, right?" I turn back to Brandon. "See? He gets it."

"This is really stupid," Brandon says, unamused.

I pull out my phone. "So, I guess you don't want to be in the group shot then?"

Travis comes to my side and puts his arm around me. "Sweet! Selfie time."

I hold out my phone, and he and I make an overly enthusiastic thumbs-up pose.

Brandon folds his arms impatiently across his chest. "Can we get on with this?"

"Well, look who's eager to have some fun," I say, giving him a hearty slap on the back. "About time you came aboard."

Brandon shakes his head and holds out his interlocked hands. Travis stands across from him. Together, they form the perfect ladder. Pushing off of their shoulders, I reach for the top of the fence. One push and my leg tips over the edge.

"Got it!" I shout. Perched on the top of the wall, I survey my target. The pool is lit, even with the Andersons away for the week, and it gleams an appealing turquoise blue in the dark night. If I had time and my stuff, I'd paint the scene. For now, however, an immersive, performance-art type of scenario will have to suffice.

"Let's do this," I say, hopping onto the grass below. I land firmly on my feet and unlatch the side gate.

Brandon remains frozen at the threshold. "Cass…"

"Let me guess. You don't think this is such a good idea."

Travis laughs. "Seriously, dude, don't be such a pansy."

He starts through the gate when Brandon grabs his arm. "Trav. You know why we can't."

Travis says nothing, but a shadow crosses his expression. I frown. "What?"

When Travis doesn't reply, Brandon exhales. "We could go to jail."

"Oh, don't be so dramatic—"

"No, seriously. We're both...kind of on probation."

He officially has my attention. "Explain."

Travis shakes his head. "It's not that big of a deal. Brandon's freaking out."

"Then tell me," I say.

His eyes shift away from mine. "It was me and Brandon and some of the guys from the lacrosse team. One night a few weeks ago, we were a little drunk. It was late. And we sort of...broke into a liquor store."

Brandon scrambles to explain before I can react. "It wasn't my idea. We never would have done it—it was really stupid, okay? Anyway, we got caught, but Austin's dad pulled some strings and got us off with a warning."

I nod slowly. "I see. So, you got Daddums to skirt the law for you?"

"It's not like that," Travis says, but I can tell he's really embarrassed.

Brandon sighs. "I can't get into trouble. I've got a lacrosse scholarship on the line, and my parents would murder me if I screwed that up. Trav's the same."

I'm not sure which is more irritating, the sham justice system in these ritzy areas or the fact that there's actually a legitimate reason to cut our little excursion short.

I fold my arms. "So after all this, we're leaving?"

"I never said that," Travis says, defensive.

Brandon glares. "Don't be an idiot, Trav. It's not worth it."

I can tell by the look Brandon gives Travis that he actually means *I'm* not worth it. Irritation flares up in me.

"Well, I haven't come all this way to wuss out now. You boys and your lacrosse scholarships are free to go back home."

"Fine," Brandon says. "I'm out of here."

He storms off without a glance back. Travis lingers, but I can tell he's seen the error of his ways and wants to go as well.

"Go ahead and leave," I say. "I'm over the fence. I don't need you anymore."

Travis sighs. "Brandon's right. We should probably get out of here."

I plant my fists on my waist. "Nope. I'm going to swim."

"Cass."

"Seriously, go. I can take it from here."

"I'm not leaving you alone at two in the morning. It isn't safe."

I laugh. "How very gallant, Travis."

"I'm serious. It isn't safe."

With only a smile, I turn and head for the pool. He calls my name in a sharp whisper, but I ignore him.

Little garden lights illuminate the path and surround the flagstone patio. The pool shimmers. You've got to hand it to the Andersons. They have a nice place here.

I circle the pool thoughtfully, then dip one toe in the water. "Ideal temperature."

No simple entrance into the pool will do. It's got to be diving board or nothing. With determination, I march to the elaborate diving area and grip the ladder.

Travis calls my name again. I glance over my shoulder with a sigh. He's in the shadows by the shrubs.

"You're crazy," he whisper-yells.

"Guilty as charged, Travis, my dear." I blow him a kiss and climb the diving-board ladder. My nerve ends tingle as I approach the long plank. It's a stupid little thing, but I feel more alive now than I have all summer.

"Okay. Here goes nothing. One…two…"

The porch lights snap on with the fury of midday sun. It startles me so much that I throw my arms up to block it and almost fall backward into the pool.

"All right, kids," a man's voice booms. "Fun's over."

Who knew an über rich, gated community would have twenty-four-hour guards on staff? Oh wait. I knew. I just didn't care.

A big man in a bouncer-type jacket strides in by the side of the deck, right near where I entered. To my left, Travis flattens against the house, trapped. If he runs, the guard will notice for sure.

The beam of a high-powered flashlight blasts in my face.

"Get down from there."

I shoot a look to the gently rippling pool water, then to Travis, then back to the guard. He's clearly not in the mood to screw around.

Something about this situation feels so symbolic of this whole summer. There I was, about to plunge into that film internship in New York. Or go to Paris with Jade. Or maybe the acting camp. I hadn't really decided. Either way, I was ready to start living and get out of Nowhereville, Ohio. And what happens?

Mom and Frank get the crazy idea to rent a beach house in Massachusetts. And because Frank can work remotely with his finance job, they don't rent it for a week like a normal family. They rent it for the entire summer. And of course, they insist on dragging me and Eddie down with them. To sit on my butt all day and to go to garden luncheons.

"Where are the two guys I saw you with?" the guard calls out.

Cameras. Of course there are cameras. The beam of the flashlight cuts from me to scan the yard. Travis's whole body tenses, and guilt washes over me. As much as I initially wrote him off as a rich jock, I actually kind of like the guy. He's been cool and willing to play along with my ridiculous little shenanigans. I can't let him suffer serious, long-lasting consequences.

Meeting Travis's eyes, I mouth the word "go" and then wave to the security guard with both arms. "It's just me, big guy. Me all by my lonesome."

The flashlight snaps up to me. My pulse races. What I'm doing, I'm not exactly sure. But the recklessness feels good.

"I thought I saw someone else," the guard says.

He starts to pull the light away to search the yard. I have to act quickly. Drawing in a breath, I pull my sundress over my head and toss it on the patio. For a single, humiliating moment, the guard's flashlight illuminates my red bra and underwear for all the world to see. Travis better be halfway home by now.

The guard's voice is calm but laden with warning. "Miss…"

"Last one in the water's a rotten egg!"

Drawing in a breath, I give one good bounce on the diving board, leap into the air, form the perfect swan position, and plunge into the water.